Kamouraska

Kamouraska

A NOVEL BY

Anne Hébert

TRANSLATED BY

Norman Shapiro

CROWN PUBLISHERS, INC. • NEW YORK

While this novel is based on an actual event that took place many years ago, it is still very much a work of fiction. The real participants in the drama have lent it only their outermost, "official" gestures, as it were. From that point on, they have gradually developed within my mind, and have come to be imagined creatures all my own. (A.H.)

Original French edition © 1970 by Éditions du Seuil
English translation © 1973 by Crown Publishers, Inc.

Library of Congress Catalog Card Number: 72-96657
ISBN: 0-517-503514
Printed in the United States of America
Published simultaneously in Canada by Musson Book Company
Second Printing before Publication, May, 1973

Kamouraska

THE summer went by from beginning to end. Unlike other years, Madame Rolland didn't leave her home on Rue du Parloir. It was very fair, very warm. But neither Madame Rolland nor the children went to the country that summer.

Her husband was going to die, and she felt a great calm. He was just slipping away, ever so gently, hardly suffering at all, and with such admirable good taste. And Madame Rolland· waited, dutiful and above reproach. If she felt a pang in her heart from time to time, it was only that now and again this waiting seemed about to assume distressing proportions. That peaceful sense of being free, ready for anything—that feeling that surged through her, down to her very fingertips—couldn't bode any good. Everything seemed bent on taking place as if it would soon be clear, past all the waiting, just what her real expectation meant. Somewhere beyond the death of that man who had been her husband for almost eighteen years. But even now grief was working its protective defenses. She clutched at it, hanging onto it like a railing. Anything was better than that awful calm.

I should have left Quebec. Gone away from here. All alone in this barren, empty July. There's no one I know left in town. I go out, and people stare at me like some strange beast. This morning, back from market. Those two young hoodlums, looking me up and down. Watching me every step of the way. I shouldn't go out alone. The city's not safe anymore. No doubt about it now. People are watching. Spying. Following me. They keep coming closer and closer all the time. They're right behind me. That woman, yesterday, almost on top of me. I could feel her there, with that steady, deliberate step. Right at my heels. And when I turned around, she jumped into a doorway and hid. Yes, I saw her disappear inside. Nimbler, quicker than anyone, except . . . Oh, yes, that's what tugs at my heart. So nimble, so quick . . .

I could have shaken her off, silly thing. No trouble at all. Could have taken a cab. Crossed the street. Gone into a shop. Could have sent for my driver to hitch up the horses and come pick me up. But I just kept walking, never looked back. Sure I was dragging her right behind me, there all the time . . . Walking, always walking. People turn and stare as I go by. That's what my life has been. Feeling humanity split in two to watch me pass between the rows. The Red Sea parting to let the holy army cross. That's what this world is like. Life in this world, this life of mine. And one fine day I had to face this miserable world. Stand up to it. With two policemen by my side, no less. Me, Elisabeth d'Aulnières. Widow of Antoine Tassy, wife of Jérôme Rolland. And I felt like laughing in the whole world's face. Oh, what a ride, what a lovely sleigh ride! From Lavaltrie to Montreal. The warrant for my arrest, the two policemen stinking of beer, the ride through Montreal. And in such style! The warden tells me how sorry he is, and he bows and scrapes right down to the floor. The black door shuts behind me. Four moldy walls. The smell of the toilet. The cold. The indictment . . . Court of King's Bench. Session of September 1840. The Queen against Elisabeth d'Aulnières-Tassy . . . My wild youth. Interrogations. Witnesses. And each time I had to spruce up my innocence. Like beauty between two dances, like virginity between two affairs. Two months locked up, then home.

[2]

Reasons of health. Family reasons. Good-bye, prison. And good-bye to you, dear warden. You poor bewildered man. Well, you have my maid to console you. Justice can hold her as long as it likes. Two years behind bars. Poor Aurélie Caron. But time wipes the slate. And now you're free, as free as your mistress. A new life, a new start . . . They'll never extradite my lover. Charges withdrawn. Two years. Just have to accept things the way they are. Get married again. No veil this time, no orange blossoms. Jérôme Rolland, my second husband, and honor is restored. Honor. What an ideal to set yourself when love is what you've lost. Honor. A fine obsession to dangle before your nose. The donkey and his carrot. Daily dole at the end of a stick. And the hungry little ass goes trotting all day long. All his life. Until he can't go on anymore. What a farce! But it keeps you going, a whole life through. Oh, how I love to walk through the streets, with the image of my virtue just a few steps ahead! Never out of my sight. Eyes peeled, like a prison guard. Always on that image. The Sacred Host in the holy procession. And me, right behind, like a silly little goose. Yes, that's all a virtuous woman is. A gaping fool that struts along, staring at the image of her honor . . . To dream, to escape, get rid of the obsession. To lift the mourning veil. To look at every man in the street. All of them. One after another. And have them all look back. To run away from Rue du Parloir. Find my love, at the end of the earth. In Burlington. Burlington. The United States. *In a while you'll leave Canada, won't you? That's all I ask. Please, tell me how I can write you.*

Oh, how the poor thing suffered! How cold he was that winter, all alone, all the way to Kamouraska. Four hundred miles, to Kamouraska and back. Oh, love, love. You've hurt me so! Why pity you? You ran, ran off like a coward. Left me behind, by myself, to face that pack of judges. That horde. My love, my love. Let me bite you, beat you, kill you . . . Never to see that face again, that lovely face. And age bearing down on me, coming to get me. It

[3]

hasn't touched me yet. At least not much. Two fine little lines from my nose to the corners of my mouth. The constant strain to be virtuous, I suppose. But still, I know my good days are numbered. Disaster can't be far away. Crow's-feet—more like claws—all around my eyes. Starting to lose my shape. But still in one piece. Yes, I'm all in one piece. And after the hell they put me through. My trial by horror. My ordeal of the flesh. But flesh that simply wouldn't be destroyed. See for yourself. Like the salamander. My body is so far ahead of my soul. All my teeth, good breasts, my buttocks firm. A filly. A two-year-old. And standing tall besides. Proud look of virgins that won't give in. A husband, two husbands. And the love that left me one February night, left me on the shelf to gather dust. There in Sorel. After the tragedy at Kamouraska. When my love came back from Kamouraska. I'd never come so close to being happy. And he ran away. The one and only man. He ran away, blood dripping from his hands. Burlington. Burlington. I seem to hear that name, ringing in my ears, shrill as a bell. To taunt me. Make me die by inches. Ding, dong, ding . . . No need to play the martyr's role. It hasn't been so hard to lead a virtuous life these eighteen years. Model wife of Jérôme Rolland. Mild little man who insists on his rights before he'll go to sleep. Every night, or so it seems. Until his heart can't stand it anymore. And me, always the dutiful wife. Period or not. Pregnant or not. Nursing or not. And sometimes even a galling little pleasure from it all. Oh, the shame of that pleasure stolen from my love. Why mince words, why pretend? I was nothing but a faithful belly, a womb for making babies in. Eight children by him. And three with the one before. With Antoine Tassy, the squire of Kamouraska! See the third? Who could his father be, do you suppose? This child . . . The source. The real beginning of my woman's life. Dear little Nicolas, whom do you look like? Your eyes? My lost love's eyes. I know it for sure. The image of my love, this third son of mine. So dark, so slender. This little man. My little devil off at school.

[4]

Soon I'll be free. A widow again. Oh, to be decked out already in fine, sheer crape and the best black veils. The cheap ones turn green before you know it. Wiping my eyes, my tearless eyes. Breezing along in some unknown city, huge and endless, filled with men. My sails unfurled. Roaming the seas . . . The city is like the ocean, haughty and wild . . . Leaving, to find the only tenderness my heart ever knew. Lost love. And this squalling brood of mine. Carrying them, giving birth to them, nursing them, weaning them. Days, nights, my every minute. The death of me and my reason for living, both at once. No time for anything else. Eleven babies in twenty-two years. This dull, blind land. And all the blood, the milk, the chunks of crusty afterbirth. So much, so much. Poor Elisabeth, unstinting Elisabeth. Dear little Nicolas, one and only child of my love. The holy sacrifice I offered up, there in the snow. In the cove at Kamouraska, frozen over, smooth as a dry, dusty field. Murderous love. Treacherous love. Deadly love. Love. Love. The only living thing in this world. The madness of love. *Please tell me how you are and how the poor child is doing.* His last letter, stopped by the judges.

ADAME Rolland stands erect, hardly breathing, hands poised on her crinoline skirt. Bends her head toward the shutters and takes a sharp look between the slats. Pricks up her ears, hidden by her hair pulled tightly back. The street below exhales its warm, wet breath. Along the eaves the gutter clatters, overflowing. In the bedroom thick with velvet, filled with furniture from England, a man's voice rasps in an inaudible mumble, something about the gutter.

Off in the distance, the sound of a horse's heavy gait, dragging a wagon behind him. It's two in the morning. What can a wagon be doing out now, in this empty, deserted night? There's been so much prowling about in the streets . . . Now it's closer. Rue Saint-Louis, Rue des Jardins, Rue Donacona . . . Quiet . . . Good God! It's turning the corner. Closer and closer, the iron-rimmed wheels, the plodding, lumbering hooves . . .

Any minute now, the horse and carriage will be pulling up under my window. It's me they're after. It's me, I'm sure. One day, a carriage . . . No, a sleigh, it was a sleigh. It's winter. I can hear the runners behind me, scraping along the hardened snow. They're after us, tracking us down, Aunt Adélaïde and me. The team of horses, galloping hard. Trying to catch me. Oh, those tremendous

[6]

horses, the sleigh dashing after me. And me, nestled against Aunt Adélaïde, screaming I think. Faster! The American border, and I'll be safe. If only I can convince her. My frightened accomplice. Faster, faster! My love, somewhere behind that imaginary line. The border, in the middle of the forest, and freedom. No use, that trip to Montreal. Talk to a lawyer about the tragedy at Kamouraska? Too late now, it's no longer up to me. Off to find my love. Faster, faster. Just enough time. And my poor aunt, weeping: "I'll do anything you say. We'll both be damned together, darling. Oh, God help us! We're done for! I told you to be careful, didn't I? Oh, Elisabeth! What madness! But it's his fault too, that monster's fault, Antoine Tassy. Oh, what's to become of us! It's a sin, Elisabeth, a terrible, terrible sin . . ." Too late to go on living now. We only get as far as Lavaltrie . . . The police. My arrest. My poor aunt wipes her eyes. Did I want to die? Did I really want to, deep in my bones? Live, live. I want to go on living, no matter what.

Madame Rolland closes the window. She turns toward her husband. Back against the glass, hand still on the bolt, she gauges the narrow space between the rain-soaked street, an old, creaking wagon, and that man—that small, round, ever so fragile man whose every thought is of impending death.

"Haven't you had the gutter fixed yet? How can I get my sleep with all that noise? Even a minute's rest?"

Madame Rolland hears only the sound of a wagon in the night.

"Do you hear that wagon?"

"What wagon?"

"In the street. That wagon, creaking . . . The horse . . ."

Monsieur Rolland listens for a moment, ear cocked, like a bored confessor. The rain, the wind, the torrents of water gushing from the gutter. That's all he hears. No other sound.

"You must be dreaming, Elisabeth, poor dear. It's only the rain . . ."

A sudden splash of silence. The rain must have stopped. By

now the wagon must be in front of the door. Madame Rolland looks round the room for some place to hide. In the full-length mirror she sees the little table by the bed. Cluttered, covered with glasses, bottles, medicines. Newspapers and religious books strewn here and there. And propped up on a stack of pillows, the harried face of Jérôme Rolland, ghastly white, watching.

Madame Rolland draws herself up, straightens the pleats in her skirt, smooths back her hair. Over to the mirror, to find her own reflection, her best defense. My soul—my musty, mildewed soul—off somewhere. Held prisoner, far, far away. And yet I'm pretty. Still pretty. Let everything else come falling down around my head, why should I care? One thing is clear. One thing that keeps me going, through all the nagging fears, all the horror of my days. A man . . . One man . . . Lost. To stay pretty forever, for him. Just for him. Day by day love cleanses me. It washes away my every sin, my every fear, my every shame.

Monsieur Rolland sees a triumphant figure approaching in the mirror. His wife looms up like that very image of transfigured death that haunts his visions through the long, tortured nights. He cringes, smaller and smaller. Crouches, buries his head between his shoulders. So smooth, so open to attack, his whole being limp and unprotected. An oyster caught without his shell. Nothing but his eyes alert, his sharp-pointed eyes, with something in them very much like hate.

He asks for a lump of sugar so he can take his drops. Not yet, she tells him, it's not time. He calls for Florida. He pouts. His lower lip trembles, like a child about to cry. He's afraid. Florida, send for Florida, he pleads. Madame Rolland's calm voice assures him that it's half-past two in the morning. Florida must certainly be asleep. Her words, clear and irrefutable, ring through the night. Like a sentence of death. Florida is asleep, the children are asleep, the whole world is out of reach. Only this woman. Monsieur Rolland is all alone, offered up to his wife's malevolent power, a wife

[8]

who already once before . . . He begs her to go wake Florida.

"Don't be absurd. The poor girl has to begin again at six. She needs her sleep. Now there's nothing to worry about. I'll get you the sugar myself. It's not time for your medicine yet."

Monsieur Rolland looks at the clock on the mantel. Four more hours to wait before Florida appears in the doorway, gaunt and efficient, a smug little smile on her homely face.

"Did Monsieur have a good night's sleep? Here, let me freshen you up a little. And let's not forget to do our little business if we have to."

With Florida it's all right to be yourself. Sick and disgusting, frightened and resigned, complaining and demanding. But with Elisabeth . . .

"Would you like something to drink? Isn't there anything I can get you?"

Don't take a single swallow while she's here. No, nothing while she's here. She wants to kill me. Don't let her give me my drops! Watching them fall on the sugar, seeing the color slowly change while she squeezes them out one by one. No, no, that's more than I could bear. I'd rather die right now.

What an admirable woman your wife is, Monsieur Rolland. Eight children, and still everything so neat and tidy. And now, the whole time you've been ill, the poor thing hardly ever leaves the house. Always by your side. What devotion, what attention! A saint, Monsieur Rolland, that's what she is, a saint. And so pretty too, pretty as a picture. Age, tragedy, crime . . . Nothing seems to touch her. Like water on a duck's back. Yes, an admirable woman.

"Please, go get Florida."

Madame Rolland knows better than to tell a sick man no. Try to interest him in something else, like a child.

"Would you like me to read to you?"

She pokes among the books piled high on the bed table. He points to one.

[9]

"That one, *Poems from the Liturgy*. Where the bookmark is."

Jérôme watches his wife's expression. She opens the book, finds the page. "Day of Wrath, that day . . ." A passage underlined in pencil. "Whatsoever is hidden shall be manifest, and naught shall remain unavenged."

Pretend you don't see through the game he's playing, little man propped up on his pile of feather pillows. "Whatsoever is hidden shall be manifest." Speak for yourself. What's hidden inside of you. Inside of you. Deep in your heart, uncovered, turned inside out like an old, worn-out glove. So, you never believed I was innocent after all. You really never did. Afraid of me, weren't you? Always frightened to death. And now, to let me know it now, after eighteen years . . . To call down everlasting vengeance on my head, and hide behind the words of the Holy Book . . . He's watching out of the corner of his eye. He wants to see if his little barbs hit their mark . . . I'm your wife! Your devoted wife! For eighteen years . . . I'm innocent! Innocent! . . . Suspicious? You? Always so good, so kind? . . . No, my head is reeling. But I won't give myself away. Mustn't let you know. You have no hold on me, no hold at all. Give nothing of yourself, take nothing in return. Strangers, that's what husbands and wives should be. Strangers to one another. Now and forevermore. Amen.

"Why are you smiling?"

"No reason. Maybe my nerves. I must be tired . . ."

Monsieur Rolland, your wife is tired. It's three in the morning. Really now, you don't expect the poor thing to stay up till dawn just because you can't sleep?

"I asked you to go get Florida. Then you can sleep to your heart's content."

Sugar. You need sugar, Monsieur Rolland. It's time to take your drops. Mustn't forget to take them right on time. Not a minute later. It's a serious matter, that flurry of pain that rattles your chest. Better stop it before it starts. Or else you're done for, Monsieur

Rolland. Disaster is ready, waiting. Just one breath late, the slightest bit late, and your heart will gasp its last. Go thrashing about like a fish out of water. No blood will get to your heart. No blood at all. Thrashing about for air. For life. You're choking, choking, Monsieur Rolland. Sugar, sugar, sugar! Your drops!

"I'll get the sugar."

That calm, unruffled voice. Monsieur Rolland tugs at his collar, rips it open. Beads of sweat are streaming down his face. Madame Rolland is bending over him now, her tight-drawn bodice full of her buxom breasts. She wipes his face. Unwavering, her voice assures him:

"It's nothing. Don't be afraid. I'll run and get the sugar."

What good to call for Florida now? Just one word more and that cage around your heart will use up all the little air it has. That clump of underbrush inside your chest, that mass of branches, giddy little tree where the air has to struggle now to get around. Don't try to pump more air from that dried-up bush. Or to call for Florida. Nothing to do but beg, plead with your eyes. The drops, the drops, the drops . . .

Elisabeth already has gone running out of the room.

THE doctor's orders must be followed to the letter: five drops on a lump of sugar, every four hours. Exactly fourteen minutes from now, and it will be time.

Madame Rolland tucks up her skirt and petticoats. Hurries down the stairs. She has to act quickly to keep another tragedy from descending on her house.

There are moments that burst with such a flash of light that truth comes rushing on full tilt. Reveals its deepest, innermost sense, its sharpest anguish. Quick! Quick! Ward off the danger. Must stop at nothing to keep the order of the world from being shaken again. Fail for a second and anything might happen. Madness will rise again, reborn from its ashes. And once again I'll be its victim, bound hand and foot, like so much kindling for the eternal flames.

Madame Rolland runs down the steps as fast as her legs and her skirts will let her. The sugar! The sugar! Must find the sugar! The carpet-rods on the steps flash by, bright yellow copper. Fill her heart with a kind of extravagant joy. Like finding, one by one, the reassuring signs that her house is still in order.

No sugar in the pantry. Where on earth did Florida put it? Madame Rolland looks everywhere. No use. Rummages behind the empty sugar bowl, the saltcellars, the mustard pot. Still nothing.

But the sugar has to be there, it's supposed to be there, somewhere. An endless supply, replenished there in the darkness by hands whose duty is to keep providing sugar. That's how it works. It always has. Since the day she became the wife of Jérôme Rolland. And it's that way, too, with all the other things: the salt, the flour, the oil, the eggs . . . All provided without fail, one after the other, according to the time of year, like the phases of the moon. Perfect order. But who on earth could have moved the sugar? Or even worse, let it run out? Go wake Florida. Five drops on a lump of sugar, every four hours. I'm partly to blame. I must be. How could I let the sugar disappear like that? . . . My God, the children! Why didn't I think of that before? It must have been the children . . . Maybe Anne-Marie. Or little Eugène. He's always filling his pockets with sugar . . . Of course, the children! Suddenly Madame Rolland has the urge to wake them up, then and there, to call them all down from that sleepy top-floor room of theirs that looks so much like a dormitory. She would like to gather her children around her, hug them close to her skirts. Ask them to help her, to save her. Stand with them there, defiant, in a single, solid, indestructible mass. Even go off, perhaps, and find the eldest two, at Oxford. High silk hats, blond whiskers and all. Handsome young strangers now, seeds that another husband planted one day, brutishly, in her womb.

Yes, go wake the children. Let them be a bulwark. Let them run through the house. Station them at the windows, post them behind the door. Let them go clambering up the stairs, all of them, all at once, kicking and singing, shouting and knocking one another about. All those fine little dears with their plump, beribboned nannies. All those sweet little dears to be nursed, and weaned, and stuffed full of food again. Pissing and slobbering in cashmere and lace. Gorged and bathed, swathed and starched, shown off all shining and well behaved. Rosaries, dominoes, jump ropes, scarlet fever, First Communion, whooping cough, earaches, roast beef,

[13]

plum cakes, sweet corn, fancy puddings, rabbit-fur coats, fur-lined mittens. Lacrosse and toboggans. Convent school, then classes with the priests. "No more to the woods we go, Tra-la-la-la-la-la." Clementi sonatinas. Sweet, sweet childhood, growing up and stretching tall on tiptoes. Eight little imps, eight boys and girls to take the stand in behalf of Elisabeth d'Aulnières. Seven sacraments, plus one. Seven capital sins, plus one. Seven holy terrors, plus one. All suddenly waking up, shouting their war cry. Seven little lambs, plus one. And that one in a sailor's blouse, singing so sweetly with downcast eyes: "Someday in Heav'n, the Virgin fair I'll see." Just let them loose and hear what a fuss they'll raise! The call of the blood in their spontaneous cries. Just watch the angel choir sprout horns if anyone points a finger at their mother. Have we ever run out of sugar before, children? Or jam? Come, come, children. Have we? Answer me, all of you. All of you. Even the one and only child of my love, dark and slender. My little Nicolas. And the eldest two, my two young lords who went to have their minds improved in haughty England. And you, Eugène and Sophie. And you, Anne-Marie, so prim and proper, forever fussing the way you do with the frills on your elegant pantalets, peeping from under your crinoline skirt. And you, Jean-Baptiste, stammering a little and dreaming that you'll preach retreat in the Basilica, with a mouth full of pebbles. And you, baby Eléonore, with your little embroidered bib, still in the nursery. All of you. Who could contradict your testimony? You can speak your piece and go right back to bed. Monsieur Rolland, your father, never loves you quite so much as when you're lying fast asleep, way up there, under the eaves. With hand-picked nannies watching over you. Safe from your parents. Sheltered against parental crimes by the coarse caresses of peasant women in their fluted bonnets.

The sugar! Ring for Florida! Give her a proper talking-to for being so careless. The peal of the bell rips through the silence of the night, echoes into every corner of the sleeping house. Madame

Rolland stands startled by the noise. Still holding the cord. Vibrations rippling through her hand in little waves, diminishing. Let go of the cord before it's too late, before a deafening clamor rings out and wakes the town. A ghostly carillon, pulling at all the strident, clangorous chimes, drawing them in. This time it happens by itself. All through her arm, an explosion, bursting through her arm. Fingers to shoulder, like an electric shock. Silence for a moment, then a timid reply, ever so slight. The front doorbell. Struck once. One single peal, left hanging. Incomplete.

Madame Rolland jumps. There, hidden behind the breadbasket: the sugar. She tucks up her skirts with one hand, throws a few lumps into the hollow. Picks up the lamp, still burning. Goes scurrying up the stairs, out of breath. Stands before her husband. Heaven be praised, he's still alive. He smiles at her, dimly.

It's only the pain . . .

MADAME Rolland begins to count the drops. Her hand is trembling. He must trust her, reassure her, do anything to stop that trembling in her hand. He has no choice, he must make peace with this woman who stands there trembling. His life depends on it. Again Jérôme forces a feeble smile. He feels his dry lips tighten against his teeth.

"Please, Elisabeth, control yourself."

Madame Rolland draws close to her husband's side. She measures out the drops before his eyes.

"Count them with me, will you . . ."

Have her husband count the drops, share in his distrust. Let him watch her to be sure. Accept an insult, an indignity like that. Allow his loathsome supervision, after a lifetime as a model wife. Anything, anything is better than to be a party to another death.

Monsieur and Madame Rolland are safe again, joined to each other like the fingers on a hand. Wholly united in one being, reduced to their simplest terms. One single mind, frenetically intent. One single, concentrated life. One single fear, one single wish, one single prayer: to measure out the drops. Above all, to stop trembling. To let them fall, flawless, spaced out one by one, round as tears.

The husband, thankful, crunches his sugar, swallows it down. He closes his eyes in gratitude and fatigue. To go on living. Living. Such an unusual woman, this wife of his. But why is Elisabeth still so shaken, so disturbed? Won't she ever collect herself? Won't she ever let me rest? Oh, to sleep. To force my wife to come away with me, off into a deep, eternal slumber. No thoughts of the past, no fears for the future. Only a present. A peaceful, slumbering present. My wife by my side. To sleep. "Whatsoever is hidden shall be manifest." To sleep together. *In pace.*

Elisabeth is still trembling.

"Jérôme, did you hear the bell?"

Monsieur Rolland opens a doleful eye.

"The bell? When you rang for Florida?"

"No, no. I mean the doorbell."

"The doorbell? At this hour of the morning? Are you out of your mind?"

Yes, no doubt I am. That's what it means to be out of your mind. To let yourself be carried away by a dream. To give it room, let it grow wild and thick, until it overruns you. To invent a ghastly fear about some wagon wandering through the town. To imagine the driver ringing your doorbell in the middle of the night. To go on dreaming at the risk of life and limb, as if you were acting out your own death. Just to see if you can. Well, don't delude yourself. Someday reality and its imagined double are going to be one and the same. No difference at all between them. Every premonition, true. Every alibi, gone flat. Every escape, blocked off. Doom will lie clinging to my bones. They'll find me guilty, guilty before the world. It's time to break free, break out of this stagnation, now. To stifle the dream before it's too late. Quick, into the sunshine. Shake it off. Throw off the specters. Only one hope: to step out into the daylight. Not to miss the chance. To keep from being crushed by the dream. To strike that regal pose again, all haughtiness and injured innocence. Like all those days before, those days

[17]

of endless questioning: "But how can anyone suspect me of such an awful thing?" To state your name. To be forever named Elisabeth d'Aulnières. To live to the fullest in your flesh, intact, like blood coursing happy and free.

Madame Rolland goes over to the window. With a sweep of her arm she opens the shutter, throws it back against the wall. May as well clear things up right now. We'll see if there really is a blasted wagon . . .

There in the street, in front of their door, an old horse, head hung low, seems to be sleeping. Hitched up behind him, a cart spread over with a canvas. Small and frail, the driver, perched on his scanty load—vegetables more than likely—sits curled up in the rain, elbows on knees and head in hands. He looks like a stubborn little child, locked tight in his sodden wretchedness.

Madame Rolland holds back a scream. Runs to her husband's side. Kneels by his bed.

"Jérôme . . . In the street . . . A wagon, in front of our door!"

Just then the wagon begins to move. Goes slowly off, into the distance.

Monsieur and Madame Rolland keep still. Not a word between them. For a long time they follow the sound of the rig as it disappears into the night. The cool, damp air comes wafting into the room. Madame Rolland can't seem to budge. Monsieur Rolland begins to shiver.

"Please, Elisabeth. Close the window."

"I'm afraid . . . I'm so afraid . . ."

She buries her head in the blanket, nestles her cheek against her husband's hand.

This man can only protect me just so far. When the fright becomes too real, when it fills the night with the noise of a rattling old wagon, Jérôme is caught up in it just like me. Caught in the trap, the two of us. That's what marriage is. One fear shared by two, one need to be consoled, one empty caress in the darkness.

"Close the window, Elisabeth, I'm cold."

ELISABETH closes the shutter and the window. She's almost tempted to draw the curtains too. To barricade herself inside, to stave off any attack. It's beginning to get light already. Dawn, that ominous time. That dim, uncertain moment between day and night, when body and mind suddenly give way and hand us over to our nerves and their mysterious powers. Awake all night. This sleeplessness has worn us down.

No, Monsieur Rolland, it isn't death quite yet. Still, you can feel yourself going under, about to drown. Weariness washes over you, in one long wave, heavy and dense. Rolls over you in its broad, heavy sweep. Throws you onto the sand, weak, exhausted, tasting the salt and slime, a body fairly ringing out with pain. And getting worse all over. There, the pain, easy to recognize. You can hear its echo under the fingernail, just beneath the skin. And at your bedside, your wife, far off in her solitude again.

Better hurry, call her back. Make her return to this slender brink of life, Monsieur Rolland, here where you're spinning out the last few threads of your sickly days. You mustn't be left alone like this. Unthinkable. This agony, this narrow little plank. Just enough space to force one living creature up here with you, someone to keep you company a little while along the way. Quick. Better call her back.

"Elisabeth!"

Madame Rolland is miles and miles away, lost in contemplation of her right sleeve, fringed with lace. Absorbed, engrossed, assiduous. Scrutinizing and obsessed.

Oh, to be well enough to rape that woman. To force her back with us onto the marriage bed. Lay her out on our deathbed, here beside us. Force her to think about us, to suffer with us, to share our agony, to die with us. What a riddle she is, this wife of ours. This guilty woman who went unpunished, our wife, our tainted beauty. Oh, to convict her of her sin, to catch her mind red-handed in its wanderings. To break the pact of silence. To rattle the past under her pretty little nose, as casual as can be.

"Elisabeth! That girl . . . What was her name?"

"What girl? What are you talking about?"

Her voice is flat, vacant. She seems to be staring in rapt attention at the lace frills on her left sleeve now, no different at all from the right. She looks at both sleeves under the lamp, compares them carefully.

"You know, the one who used to smoke a pipe? . . . Aurélie Caron . . . Wasn't that her name? . . . Yes, I remember now . . ."

Jérôme Rolland has pronounced each syllable carefully, distinctly. Now he lies in fear of what Elisabeth might do. As if, for revenge, she might stone him to death.

Elisabeth grows pale. A shudder shakes her from head to toe. "Why bring that up? . . . What's come over you? . . ."

Silence. Then a kind of scar forming fresh over the silence. Jérôme Rolland's insidious little question slithers its way in. Silence, wound closed. Silence, sewn up again with great needlefuls.

Madame Rolland picks up the pitcher. Try to change the subject, pretend you've forgotten the question, put on your compassionate Sister of Charity face. She pours out a glass of water. Walks over to her husband.

"Would you like some water?"

[20]

Monsieur Rolland shuts his eyes. Nothing to drink, certainly not. He's waiting for Florida. Time doesn't matter anymore. Why spare Elisabeth's feelings now? Why not come right out with it, show her how much we distrust her? Show her we've never been duped by her innocence.

"No, nothing to drink. I'd rather wait for Florida."

Madame Rolland puts down the glass and pitcher. The shameless arrogance of the dying. Jérôme Rolland has nothing to lose anymore. How he must despise me, my young fiancé of days gone by, beside himself with gratitude: "Elisabeth . . . Marrying me! . . . How could I ever dare to hope for a gift like that!"

Elisabeth is sitting now, far from the bed. She rests her head against the back of the chair. Strands of hair fall loose from her chignon. Her eyes are ringed deep with circles and her full lips throb with blood. Me too, awake the livelong night. I'm mad, but my mind is clear. Oh, if you only knew, Jérôme, if you only knew, dear husband, how I share your feverish sleepless nights . . . Both of us, together in the same delirium, yoked up together for the selfsame chore. Dragging the waters, together. Our huge nets scraping the ocean floor for its meager treasures. Infallible, a madman's memory drags up details like mussel shells. The first time you came to my bed, Jérôme, so round and plump, so small in that enormous dressing gown of yours, with its checks and its fancy buttons. I wanted to laugh out loud. I couldn't stop humming to myself: "Papa has found a man for me, Good God, he's small as small can be!" You caught my glance. That look of wistful disbelief in your colorless eye, that mute reproach. The failure of our wedding night . . . My God, can it be that nothing inside of us ever gets washed away? We go on living as if nothing at all had happened, then suddenly the poison deep in our hearts comes rising up to the surface. It's clear, he never forgave me, not really . . . Aurélie Caron . . . That name he dredges up from the stagnant water, like a rusty weapon to kill me with.

Twice more Monsieur Rolland whispers distinctly: "Aurélie

Caron . . . Aurélie Caron . . ." Elisabeth doesn't flinch. She feels her forehead covered with sweat. He must be delirious. If not, he wouldn't dare . . .

Monsieur Rolland is breathing hard. How he would like to fling away that wretched girl's name, throw it back, back into the shadows. It's a two-edged sword, and now it's falling on me. Tearing at my breast. Aurélie Caron . . . With every fiber of her being she clings to the guilty heart of Elisabeth d'Aulnières, my wife in the eyes of God and man. I don't want to know about it. I swore I would never know a thing about it. Just close my eyes and go on living. Oh, God, the sordid memories, filling my veins, smothering me . . .

Elisabeth comes over to his bed. Looks at her husband's haggard face.

"Try to relax and get some sleep. Florida shouldn't be much longer now."

Monsieur Rolland closes his eyes. What a good wife you have, Monsieur Rolland, so attentive to the slightest sign of death on your sallow face.

Elisabeth pulls herself together. Fixes her hair, spreads a large shawl about her shoulders. Why not take her stand here and now? Stop caring for this man, once and for all. Too bad. Isn't that what he wants? Let it all be just between Florida and him, between him and death itself. Doesn't he always call for Florida? Well, she can take care of him now, I wash my hands of it. I'm turning him over to Florida, for good. Time now to rest. To stretch out on the bed. Lengthwise, crosswise, all to myself. To live . . . And what's the harm? The only time Florida ever came to life, the only time her eyes lit up, was when she caught the scent of death. Then all at once a spark in the clumsy hulk. Transformed by the intuition that her master is about to die. A simpleton stepping out of her stupidity. A cataleptic learning how to use her life. A lost soul finding her way and her reason for being . . . Good God, is it

[22]

possible? This gawking, good-for-nothing maid of ours! Letting the milk boil over on the fire, breaking the glasses and the plates. Can't even put the children's shoes on right. Never knows which foot they go on. What are we going to do with her? Useless, absolutely useless. Shouldn't we send her home, back to the town she came from? . . . Then there she was, watching, while Jérôme was having his last attack. All she needed to make her emerge from the depths of darkness. Become a new person. Discover her deathly calling. The transformation is complete. Now the new Florida: eyes sharp, movements precise. Strange, agile creature, ready to officiate at the final moments of Jérôme Rolland, with all the sacred rites. Leeches and poultices, hot-water bottle and eggnog, compresses and Extreme Unction, tears and shroud. Nothing has been forgotten and nothing will be. You can count on Florida. Madame can go off and cry in peace. I'll see to everything.

There she is now, standing in the doorway. Impossible to hear her coming, with those slippers she always wears. The heavy, muffled step, those big feet and their giant strides. That long, curved, equine neck of hers, with its little head of braided hair bobbing about. Just like an undertaker's horse, tossing her little gray braids, ribboned with black. She's smiling now, a mouthful of long, white teeth.

"It's market day. Some of the wagons are coming by already. Madame can go to sleep now. No need to worry about Monsieur. I'll be here."

Florida lifts up Jérôme Rolland in her powerful arms, turns him over like an empty box. Takes off his nightshirt, soaked with sweat, washes him all around, puts on a clean one. Elisabeth feels she's in the way, stands aside. Leans out the window. Sees in the reflection of the room behind her—now suddenly Florida's room— all the early-morning bustle of a hospital.

Madame Rolland surrenders her husband to those soothing hands that take possession of him. And as she steals out of the room, Monsieur Rolland—washed, shaved, and much relieved—falls off to sleep between fresh sheets, exhausted. Florida keeps watch, motionless in her chair beside the bed. Monsieur Rolland is dreaming that he will lie forever, nestled in Florida's lap.

THROWN out! Out of the room we shared to-
gether. Out of my bed. Eighteen years with that mild little man,
lying together in a fine, big bed, all carved by hand. Feather
mattress, linen sheets . . . And now, alone. In this tiny bed, this
ludicrous little bed the governess sleeps in. The children's governess, Léontine Mélançon. And Léontine, upstairs in Anne-
Marie's room, sleeping on a sofa. Since yesterday. Now that
Jérôme is so sick . . . That smell. Like ink. A musty, old-maid
smell . . . I have to fall asleep. Sleep. Quick, before the children all start waking up. Have to get used to sleeping by myself.
To put up with my horrible dreams. Alone. No man to run to,
no man to protect me. Knowing that someone is there, under the
covers. The heat of a body to keep you warm. An embrace to
comfort you. Cleanse you of every ill: short-lived eternity, at peace
again with the whole wide world. Today I can admit it, dear little
Jérôme. If not for you, I'd be dead by now, frightened to death.
Devoured by my nightmares, ripped to shreds. A storm of terror
rages around us. There, in the snow, I see a man all covered with
blood. I see him there, stretched out forever, his stiff arm, frozen,
pointing up to heaven . . . Oh, Jérôme! Dear, dear Jérôme! I'm

so afraid! Take me in your arms just one more time. Help me find my lost salvation. A little peace. A little sleep at last!

Madame Rolland gets up with a start, surprised to be lying on Léontine's bed in all her clothes. I must have dozed . . .

Twice she tries before she can pull down the covers, tucked in so smooth and tight. She loosens her bodice, unbuckles her belt. Thinks about calling someone to come unbutton her shoes and help her out of them. But no, she doesn't dare. It might wake the children. A mouthful of hairpins between her lips, she bends over to unbutton the shoes herself. Almost chokes on one of the pins, almost swallows it. Bursts out sobbing. Locks of reddish hair, disheveled, falling in her eyes. A breast bulging out of her corset.

At last she lies down. On top of the covers. That sour, slovenly old-maid smell! Too much, I can't stand it! . . . Elisabeth closes her eyes.

Guilty! Guilty! You're guilty, Madame Rolland! She jumps up, listens. On the floor below, Florida's solemn step is bustling about, here and there, by her husband's bed. Has Jérôme taken a turn for the worse? No, Florida would let me know, I'm sure. I have to sleep. Besides, it's all her fault, that dismal creature. I never should have left Jérôme alone with her. He's sick. Who knows what devilish plots they may be hatching between them? My poor husband, in league with Florida, for his everlasting perdition . . . And now my husband is dying once again. Peacefully, in his bed this time. The first time was nothing but violence, blood, and snow. Not two separate husbands, one by one, following each other in the marriage registers. But one man, one and the same, rising again from his ashes. One long snake, always the same, coiling himself about in endless rings. The eternal man, who takes me, then lets me go. Over and over. His first face, cruel. I was sixteen, and I wanted so to be happy. Swine! The filthy swine! Antoine Tassy, squire of Kamouraska. Next, love in all its somber radiance. Eyes, beard, lashes, brows. All black. Black love . . .

[26]

I'm sick, Doctor Nelson, and I'll never see you again . . . My, what a lovely triptych! The third face, so gentle, so dull. Jérôme. Jérôme, now you're in Florida's hands. And all I want to do is sleep. Sleep.

Is Florida moving the furniture? Is that what I hear? What is she doing? Right now the house is hers, all hers. She's busy arranging the rooms, getting things ready for the ceremony. She's opening the carriage entrance wide. I hear the gates slamming. And the door to the street, I'm sure that's open too. What on earth is she doing? Am I dreaming? Dreaming? Florida, perched on her spindly legs. Standing at attention on the sidewalk. I can see her now. See her and hear her. A real Swiss guard, with a halberd on her shoulder. And that little starched apron she put on just this morning, flapping about on her dried-up body. She's shouting terrible things to the people passing by on their way to mass at seven: Oyez! Good people, oyez! Monsieur is dying. It's Madame who's doing him in. Come one, come all. We're going to put Madame on trial. We're going to grill Madame like a rabbit sliced up the middle. Zip! Her miserable belly full of her miserable guts. Oyez! Good people, oyez! The indictment, writ in the Queen's own English, by the masters of this land:

At Her Majesty's Court of King's Bench the jurors for our Lady the Queen upon their oath present that Elisabeth Eléonore d'Aulnières, late of the parish of Kamouraska, in the county of Kamouraska, in the district of Quebec, wife of one Antoine Tassy, on the fourth day of January in the second year of the reign of our sovereign Lady Victoria, by the grace of God Queen of the United Kingdom of Great Britain and Ireland, defender of the faith, with force and arms at the parish aforesaid, in the county aforesaid, wilfully, maliciously, and unlawfully, did mix deadly poison, to wit one ounce of white arsenic with brandy, and the same poison mixed with brandy as aforesaid, to wit on the same day and year above mentioned, with force and arms, at the parish aforesaid, in the county aforesaid, feloniously, wilfully, maliciously, and unlawfully did administer to, and cause the same to be taken by, the said Antoine Tassy, then and there being a subject of our said Lady the Queen, with intent in so doing feloniously, wilfully and of her malice aforethought to poison, kill, and murder the said Antoine Tassy, against the peace of our said Lady the Queen, her crown, and dignity. Oyez!

The court is now in session!

A cry, sharp and guttural, both at once, piercing my skull. Florida is the devil. I've taken the devil himself into my house. This is the second time, Madame Rolland. The second infernal creature you've hired. The first one's name was Aurélie Caron. Aurélie Caron, you remember? No, that's not true. I don't know whom you mean . . .

Elisabeth takes her head in her hands. Every cry becomes a blow. I'm dying, dying . . . She sits up. Sunlight is pouring into Léontine's little bedroom now. It's the middle of the morning. Upstairs the children are raising a terrible row, seeing who can stamp and squeal the loudest. Suddenly, two piercing cries come ripping through the air, above the clatter. The child isn't screaming with anger or pain. Just for the sheer joy of making himself heard, at the top of his lungs, over the troop of brothers and sisters.

Madame Rolland pulls on her dressing gown, dashes upstairs. There she is now in the nursery, wild-eyed, breathless, giving a healthy slap to little Eugène, so startled he forgets to whimper.

"What's got into you, screaming like that? And with your father so sick!"

The chaos of the room defies description. Chunks of bread scattered about the rug, a cup of milk spilled over. A big rocking horse, lying on its side, as if craning its neck to reach the puddle. Piles of dirty underwear. Baby Eléonore, half naked, displaying her bottom and its chafed little cheeks. Madame Rolland seizes the children's nursemaid by the shoulders, gives her a shaking. Hair-

[28]

pins fall to the floor in a shower as the poor girl is jostled back and forth by a steady hand.

"Agathe, you stupid child!"

"But . . . Florida said she'd help me. I can't do it all by myself."

In no time at all Madame Rolland has powdered little Eléonore's bottom, dressed her up in pretty embroidered drawers. The rocking horse is put in its place. Agathe takes out the dirty underwear, wipes up the milk, picks up the bread, sweeps up the crumbs. Everything is back to normal. The children—dressed, combed, calmed down—strike a delightful pose around their mother. Agathe, hands joined in admiration, stands before the touching tableau.

"Just like the Queen with her little princes by her side!"

Out of the mouths of fools. How true. The Queen, against Elisabeth d'Aulnières? Absurd. Who would dare accuse me of offending the Queen? When it's obvious that I look just like her, enough to be her sister, with all my brood around me. I look like the Queen of England. I act like the Queen of England. I'm fascinated by the image of Victoria and her children. Perfect imitation. Who could find me guilty of doing anything wrong?

Suddenly little Anne-Marie's sweet voice pipes up:

"But Mamma is wearing her robe! And her hair isn't combed. And besides, her face is all red!"

What a nuisance, this bright, clever child. Too clever. In a flash the charm is broken, the sham unmasked. In her state of disarray, Madame Rolland rings a clashing note. And in such a lovely picture of the children, cleaned up all spick-and-span. Agathe seems a little ashamed to have let herself be taken in by such a sorry sight.

"Oh, Mamma, let me fix your hair!"

Anne-Marie pleads with her shining eyes. For a while Elisabeth lets her pull and tug. Again and again, without success, comb and brush attack the thick, tangled growth.

All right, what's the shame? Let's show the children the backside

[29]

of Victoria's image. Let it amaze them. Let them be good and bewildered. It will teach them something. Here's your mother, unkempt and disheveled. See what she looks like fresh from a couple of hours of haunted sleep. So, Anne-Marie, my dear, you think my face is red? You'll never know how it hurts me to hear you say that. You'll never know the pain . . . Your childish voice, dredging up another voice buried deep in the darkness of time. A long root, torn thundering from the soil of memory, still covered with earth. Justine Latour, before the magistrate, testifying in her peasant's twang, shaking with fright.

"The whole time Doctor Nelson was on his way to Kamouraska, Madame was all excited and red in the face, even more than she usually is."

Send the children off for the day. Anne-Marie and Eugène to Aunt Eglantine's. She asked them over. They can go with Léontine. The rest of them Agathe will take to the park near the fort. Let them play to their hearts' content until dark. That's that. Amen. And I'll have nothing to do but put on my clothes and wait for the doctor. He won't be long.

Redressed, refurbished, standing at attention, Madame Rolland returns to her post at her husband's bedside. The doctor has made it very clear:

"Your husband could go at any minute."

And now, not even to take your eyes off Jérôme Rolland. To watch over him like the mystery of life and death itself. To be there, waiting, when the hand of God seizes its prey. To reassure this pitiful prey in human form. To be vigilant to the utmost limits of your attention. To bow to this man's merest shadow of a wish. To be there. To give him a drink, to tell him hello, to tell him goodbye. To tell him it's summer. To convince him that God is merciful. To show him a face full of peace, our face, the very image of peace and harmony. Innocence, spread out like skin over bones. Jérôme, are you there? He's tossing in his sleep. Muttering Florida's name. He's asking for Florida. And again. He doesn't seem to see me. He passes me by and calls for that woman who's hand in glove with death.

"Florida's out shopping. She'll be back soon."

Madame Rolland stands up. The color is leaving her face. She feels cold all over. No, I won't let things go on this way. He's going too far. He's insulting me. No, it simply isn't right. I'm his wife, and no one else is going to look after him. When Florida comes back I'll send her to the kitchen.

Jérôme's voice, soft and slow.

"Tell me, Elisabeth. You were lucky to marry me, weren't you?"

Elisabeth's voice, flat and unwavering.

"If not for you, Jérôme, I would have been free. I'd have made my life over, like a worn-out coat you turn inside out."

Not even a heated exchange. Two perfect thrusts, right to the point. Straight to the heart of the truth. Hitting the mark in an intimate whisper. In the face of impending death.

THE morning drags on, and still Florida isn't back. Monsieur Rolland is beside himself. What can that fool be doing? Elisabeth has done all she can to quiet him down. She runs back and forth between the door and the window. Runs upstairs, downstairs. Calls out to Florida. Even steps outside, out on the wood-planked sidewalk, watching for her. Then back to Jérôme.

"It's only eleven. She's not really so late after all . . ."

"But she should be back by now. She knows I'm waiting. She's doing it on purpose . . ."

Florida appears, coming down Rue Donacona, taking her time. Loaded with vegetables and fruit, waddling along like a pack mule calmly making its way through the summer morning. How slowly she's walking. Madame Rolland lets go of the curtain, runs to meet her. She pokes about in the baskets of food. Discovers all kinds of wonderful things.

"Green peas! . . . And raspberries! . . ."

To taste the raspberries, to bite into the green peas, raw like firm little beads. Once more Madame Rolland feels safe, standing there, lost in a kind of rapturous joy. But not for long. In a moment she's running around again. Dashing up the stairs, picking up her skirts, trailing them along the floor. She opens the window, straightens the pillow, smooths out the sheet. Madame Rolland is a machine now, a machine that mustn't stop moving. Don't give in. Do anything, but don't let yourself doze off . . . Look, Jérôme's fingernails. They're all blue. No, my God, I mustn't fall asleep. Maybe I should get the children. Drink a big cup of black coffee. Whatever I do, don't rest my head against the chair, or I'm finished . . . Look at Florida. Just look at her shuffling around his bed! That foolish apron! So much starch you could break it in two! . . . The doctor's voice, dull and flat, and that sermon of his, like something he learned by heart.

"Really, Madame, you're asleep on your feet. You should go lie down. You haven't slept for days. You can't go on this way. You should go lie down . . ."

The doctor and Florida are in this together, trying to get rid of me. Resist. Don't lie down. Send Florida away, and the doctor too. Stay here, alone, by Jérôme Rolland's side. His wife . . . I'm his wife. Send for the children. Give him something to drink. Sponge his face. Close his eyes. Only me, no one else. Take him in my arms. Down from the cross, his fat little body, cradled in my arms. And me, a kind of backwoods weeping Virgin, statue defaced with tears. To save us both . . . Oh, God, he's looking at me!

"Elisabeth, you should go get some sleep!"

He wants to get rid of me . . . The priest is on the way. Extreme Unction. I have to be here. Let the children know. And Jérôme's sister Eglantine, whimpering since the day she was born. All this to add to her fountain of tears! They're going to fill the house, drown us all in a flood of dirty water, full of face powder. I have to be here. Jérôme has only one thing in mind, one dying man's obsession. To send me off to sleep, catch me shirking my duty, plain as day. And that creature in there, all stiff and starched, plotting with him to rob me of his last, dying breath. I'm the only one who should be here. The only one, me, Madame Jérôme

[33]

Rolland, for better or for worse. Worse? What could be worse than this? My husband, sending me away, trying to get rid of me . . . Mustn't give in. Mustn't let go . . . That hysterical crying. Who is it? The tears well up, they're filling my throat. Heaving, sobbing. Racking my chest . . . And again the doctor's dull, obsequious voice.

"Madame, you have to get some sleep. You're feverish. Here, take this powder with a little water . . . Really, you can't go on this way. Believe me, you're exhausted . . ."

Léontine, with that clipped step of hers, takes Madame Rolland to her musty little room.

"Come, Madame. Lie down. I'll take off your shoes."

She tugs at Elisabeth's shoes as hard as she can. Her pince-nez goes bouncing madly all over her meager bosom.

THE room is so absurdly small. A kind of square hat-box with flowered paper. The red linen drapes are pulled tight. Someone forgot to close the shutters. Sunlight is coming through the curtains. It casts a curious glow over the bed, the color of raspberry juice. My hands in the light, like a pool of red water. The doctor's powder, a tall glass to wash it down. Oh! My head stuck tight in a vise, like an iron crown pressing against my fore-head. My temples are throbbing. They should have closed the shutters, locked the door. Blocked all the exits. Alone, to be all alone. No company but this aching head of mine. Let nothing in, no other torture but my pounding head. Keep everyone out. Every-one and everything. Just rest. Appease the evil spirit of sounds and visions, give in to him on a minor point or two. Trick him into giving up. Choose my own mad fantasies. Listen to the wonderful words of the doctor and Léontine Mélançon. Be comforted. Have my praises sung all over town. Give out halberds and cocked hats. Give Léontine and the doctor great armloads of them. The uniform of my heralds, going through the streets exalting my name.

"Monsieur is dying! And so is Madame! Madame has cared for Monsieur so long, she's dead on her feet. Oyez! Madame's devotion to Monsieur. Madame's fidelity to Monsieur. Oyez! Madame and

Monsieur, and their model life together! What God has joined together only He will put asunder. Oyez!"

A rosary hanging from the filigree frame of the little iron bed. On the dresser, a weather-beaten missal, a statue of the Virgin, a cheap brooch, a cake of camphor. Léontine Mélançon is well protected. The arsenal of every poor old maid.

My eyes are heavy. Sprinkled with sand, with stones. My face, eyes closed, turned to the wall. Tiny women in white aprons and bonnets filter through my lids. Like rays of light, sparkling with glints of fire. Why didn't they close the shutters? All kinds of little creatures dancing between my lashes. Blurring my vision . . . Justine Latour, Sophie Langlade . . . Those two I recognize, so timid, so frightened . . . The third one, wearing a paper mask. A pipe, dangling by a ribbon from her belt. A clay pipe, well seasoned. Yes, I know. Of course I know. The third one's name is Aurélie Caron. Aurélie Caron! . . . I'll call Léontine and Agathe. Tell them to close the shutters, get rid of these creatures. It's the light. It's playing tricks. They came in on those rays of light. Those sharp rays of light, tearing at my eyes. Those hideous visions, like needles, pricking my eyes. Trying to get inside my head . . . Turn aside, open my eyes. Mustn't let them take hold. Pluck them out, whisk them out like a speck of dust . . . Can't move. My eyes, so heavy . . . Like lead . . . The doctor's powder, that's what it is . . . But I've got to turn around, I must be able to . . . There. I've done it. Not easy, but I've done it . . . Oh, just what I was afraid of. The women, the three women . . . They're bigger now, big as life. And here they are, bursting into Léontine's little room. They're cleaning house . . . No, they're putting things out on the dresser. Evidence for the judges, evidence to convict me.

Strange, even Léontine's things are changing. So very slowly, but they're changing, I'm sure. Little by little, they're being transformed. Now, on her dresser, everything a rich old maid might own. Silver Virgins, gilt-edged missals, emerald brooch, rosaries strung with pearls. Treasures spread out on the marble top, black, with streaks of white. All the treasures of my spinster aunts, the three little Lanouette sisters.

Justine Latour, Sophie Langlade, Aurélie Caron . . . Now they're bustling about the room, moving the furniture without the slightest effort. Hardly a touch. Their bodies are light as air, there's nothing to them. You could poke your arm right through, like a cloud . . . Look, that upright piano. They're rolling it over to my bed . . . No, I won't look at it. I won't hear the rustling of the music as they spread it out on the stand. The name of a single song, out in the open, and I'm done for . . . Whatever else, don't let them touch my needlework! That piece of petit point, stitch by stitch . . . I couldn't bear to see it. The yellow background. The rose, bright red, left unfinished. No, no, that's more than I could bear! Suddenly, coming to life . . . The long needlefuls of scarlet thread, the patient outline of the flower. The blood-red flower. The plan . . . Conceiving it, working it out stitch by stitch, evenings on end, by the light of the lamp. Plotting the murder, setting the wheels in motion, gradually, all in our own good time . . . Pull on the thread. Little silver scissors hanging from my belt. Moistening the thread, slipping it through the eye of the needle. The crime, crossing the threshold of my willing heart. Antoine Tassy's death, hungered after like a piece of fruit. Silent accomplice by my side. His dark, handsome face close to mine . . . I'm spellbound, Doctor Nelson . . . And my ear, listening hard, picking up the murmur of his blood. At the slightest move his knee grazes mine. On the surface, everything correct. My mother, leaning on the table, playing with the cards, trying to read the future. In vain. The cards are silent. She begins to lose interest. Ace of hearts . . . A love letter . . . Lies, lies. Mother doesn't believe in the cards. Or in love either. Besides, the deck is fixed. And so are our hearts . . . Queen of diamonds . . . Elisabeth, my only child. Her blond hair, with flashes of red in the light . . .

[37]

Two of clubs . . . The evening is peaceful and calm, like a tub of fresh-drawn milk. My aunts, busy with their embroidery. Beneath their dry little fingers, dull, lifeless flowers take shape, slavishly copied from the pages of the *Boston Ladies' Needlework Magazine.*

"Look, Adélaïde. You see how much red the child is using on hers? Really, it's outrageous. Why can't she follow the model? Nice subdued colors . . ."

A typical winter night in Sorel. In the cottage, a single lamp burning. The child is well protected. Her brute of a husband can go gallivanting to his lordship's heart's content in his domain of Kamouraska . . . Here, all these women, quietly embroidering. And one male, only one, allowed in this room, with its low wooden ceiling, all white and shining like porcelain, covered with flickering shadows. Every evening Doctor Nelson comes to visit with us and pass the time. He's so pleasant, such a gentleman, this Doctor Nelson. And he took such good care of the child when she was sick. A trifle nervous, perhaps. A little too pensive. It would take a clever one to find out what it is that's preying on his mind, what secret makes that look of anger flash across his face from time to time.

"I'll call Aurélie and tell her to bring us some lemonade."

"You would do better to get rid of that girl. With her reputation . . ."

"Now you mustn't do anything to upset Elisabeth. The child is so miserable with that husband of hers . . ."

My mother and my aunts are speaking in a whisper. Doctor Nelson and I don't say a word. He hands me the lengths of thread as I need them. Together we sit looking at the canvas, watching a flower take shape, a flower that's much too red.

Footsteps in the hall, brisk and confident. Aurélie with the lemonade. A jumble of other footsteps. Sophie Langlade and Justine Latour are with her. Frenetic, these two, always caught up in a flurry of activity. Forever opening doors, as if they feel they have to open every room in the house, connect them all together. Mysterious, these rooms one after another. They beckon to me. With their sly little looks they urge me to hurry and live in this house again, here in Sorel. To live in it all, and not leave out a single room.

"Madame would always go and lock herself in one of the bedrooms with Doctor Nelson."

Who said that? Who dared say such a thing? It's written down on paper, with an official stamp. Aurélie Caron's sworn deposition. That lying child. And innocent little Justine Latour, testifying later.

"Madame was never alone with Doctor Nelson. Her mother followed them everywhere they went."

Good-hearted child, Justine. But the consolation of your simple little soul doesn't last too long. Listen to the clerk, reading the last words of the indictment.

With intent in so doing feloniously, wilfully, and of her malice aforethought to poison, kill, and murder the said Antoine Tassy, against the peace of our said Lady the Queen, her crown, and dignity.

The Queen! Always the Queen! Couldn't you just die laughing! As if it makes the slightest difference to our dear Victoria-beyond-the-sea! What does she care if there's a little adultery, a little murder, way out there on a few acres of snowy waste that England once took away from France?

Elisabeth d'Aulnières, widow Tassy. You hear that? You're being charged in a foreign tongue. The language of my love. Nothing matters now but the shape of the words on his lips. Elisabeth d'Aulnières, widow Tassy. Remember Saint Denis and Saint Eustache! Let the Queen have every patriot hanged if that's her pleasure. But not my love. Let him live, him alone. And let me belong to him forever.

The servant girls from Sorel have finished arranging things on the dresser. Now they're bringing in hats, and coats, and gloves for the Lanouette sisters, off to testify before the magistrate. My three aunts . . . Husbandless, hopeless . . . Dressed as women of respectable years and good family should be. Some brown, a little lace, very little . . . Some gray, a good deal of gray . . . Some beige, but not too much beige . . . Black, the choicest, finest black . . . And a tight-lipped, straight-laced look to rival any lady of the Congregation.

"Place your right hand on the Bible and repeat: 'I do solemnly swear.' Go ahead, I'm listening."

The feather quill scratches over the paper. The clerk bows his head and writes. Everything you say will be put down.

Mademoiselle Angélique Lanouette, being of legal age and in exercise of her legal rights, residing in the town of Sorel, being duly sworn, does testify and affirm:

"I am the aunt of Madame Elisabeth d'Aulnières, her mother's sister. And I don't know how anyone can think my niece is guilty of such a terrible thing. A lady of her breeding, a child that I helped raise myself to lead a good, religious life? No, she could never be a party to her husband's murder. She loved Monsieur Tassy. She was a devoted wife. And as for Aurélie Caron, everyone knows what a reputation she has. Elisabeth's worst mistake, the only thing she can be blamed for, was keeping that girl on. That shameless, unprincipled liar . . . That drunken beast . . . That . . . That slut . . ."

Aunt Angélique bursts out sobbing. Tears roll down her sunken cheeks, stop at the corners of her lips, pressed tight. Her left hand, gloved in kid, wipes them away. The smell of the fine leather grazing her nose only adds to her distress. So much refinement, so much good taste . . . Kid, lace, first Communion, Walter Scott . . . Such elegance, such dignity . . . That it should all come to this. This disgrace. All of us, dragged through the mud with our haughty little darling. Pride and joy of our barren existence. Impudent idol of our miserable spinster life.

Mademoiselle Luce-Gertrude Lanouette, being of legal age and in exercise of her legal rights, does testify and affirm:

"I declare for all to hear that my niece, Madame Elisabeth d'Aulnières, widow of Antoine Tassy, is a young lady of flawless reputation. Raised in a manner befitting her fine background, and according to the best religious principles, she is utterly blameless and above reproach."

Aunt Luce-Gertrude doesn't cry. Her voice is curt and precise. She has taken off her gloves. Her hands are moist and cold. She feels her pulse throbbing, racing along her arm, with sudden spasmodic twitches. Feels it reaching her shoulder, her back, her other arm. Feels it shaking every inch of her body. An apple tree in the wind.

Mademoiselle Adélaïde Lanouette, being of legal age and in exercise of her legal rights, being duly sworn, affirms and testifies:

"Madame Elisabeth d'Aulnières, the wife of the late Antoine Tassy, is a lady through and through. A fine, upstanding Christian lady. And so young, so pretty. Simply an adorable child. And now, maligned, slandered before the whole wide world! Why, the love and affection she lavished on her husband . . . Her late husband . . . The attention she showed him! And their three little ones . . . Why, the baby is scarcely four months old. An angel . . . No, I wouldn't believe a word, not a single word that Aurélie Caron says against her!"

Aunt Adélaïde, till then so self-controlled, so pleased with her bit of storybook fiction, trilled out with just a touch of affectation, suddenly breaks down at the mention of Aurélie Caron, begins to sputter disconnected phrases, while a flood of tears furrows her contorted little face:

"Aurélie Caron . . . Nothing but a liar . . . A slut, a drunkard

[41]

. . . Little Elisabeth . . . Her father died before she was born . . . And we raised her, the three of us, because her mother couldn't . . . Marie-Louise, poor dear . . . How could she bring her up? . . . So young to be a widow, so soon, only six months married . . . And her husband, dead at twenty-two, from the pox . . . A terrible, terrible shock for her, poor dear . . . Such grief . . . Never got over it . . ."

Is that how pious women live? Up bright and early, off to perjure themselves, with only one thought in mind, one order to carry out. Risk your immortal soul, but save the family name. Bring the child back home, snatched from disgrace and prison. Save the child. She's so pretty, after all. Who wouldn't trust her with the keys to heaven! . . . No, the trial must not take place. We'll teach this worthless rabble that some of us are above the law. Besides, the child will do the rest. Just let her appear, she'll silence her accusers. Just let her stand there, straight and tall, with her haughty, cunning air. That dazzling flesh, that stance, those well-cut clothes of hers. That arrogant little smirk, and her cold, unbearable statue gaze. She could walk through fire and never be burned, wallow in the depths of vice and never change her expression. Tragic, implacable beauty, sufficient unto itself, bowing to no laws but its own. You wouldn't understand. She's above the ordinary laws of men. Try not to wither under her gaze, sharp, the color of grass and tart green grapes . . . We'll take her home, we'll comfort her. We'll wash her body from head to toe, and her long hair too. In great red copper tubs. With perfumed soap. Big white towels. We'll wrap her up like a newborn infant. Tiny newborn babe, this niece of ours, fresh from her mother's womb. Her little wrinkled face, with slits for eyes. Her very first squeals . . . Yes, we'll restore her honor, build it up again, impregnable. And her good name, invulnerable . . . Invulnerable. Impregnable. Adorable . . . What an adorable child. Three little fairy godmothers, all pointy and shrill, bending over her cradle . . . We'll raise this child. We'll teach her to read. We'll have her make her First Communion. We'll take her to the governor's ball. We'll make a fine match for her, give her an enormous wedding. Antoine Tassy, the squire of Kamouraska . . . The squire . . . Antoine . . . Of Kamouraska . . . Dear me, indeed! What an enormous wedding . . . Oh, what an enormous crime, Elisabeth! Your poor dear husband, dead in the snow! Who could have killed him? In the cove at Kamouraska? The snow . . . And so much blood . . . Your pretty face, all stained! . . . Snow . . . Snow . . Kamouraska . . . It's our fault, all our fault. We didn't raise you right. We spoiled you, Elisabeth. Our little idol, the little golden statue in the desert of our lives. Three old maid sisters from Sorel. Good God! We're damning our very souls to protect her!

Eccentric aunts of mine. Black furs, black veils. Strings of jet beads tangled about their scrawny chicken necks. Silly old maids. Look, there you are in the midst of a circus, a huge circus, black with humanity on all sides. Adélaïde, Luce-Gertrude, Angélique . . . Tiny, hemmed in, hooted down . . . Shaking their tight-clenched fists up in the air. Their rosaries, jingling around their wrists like so many little bells. They're shouting, struggling in vain to be heard over an endless roll on the drum. In the front row, three immense judges. White wigs and all. The biggest one waves his hand, gestures for the drummer to stop. Silence. So abrupt that Aunt Adélaïde can't hold her tongue. She keeps on shouting, as if the drum were still rolling. Shouting, all by herself: "The child is damning her soul! And we're damning ours to protect her!"

Suddenly, the crowd, struck by her confession, bursts out laughing. Row by row, the crackle of laughter spreads like fire, leaping from branch to branch. The three little sisters, caught in the thundering laughter, rush headlong from the arena. Shaking, trembling, leaving a drunkard's zigzag tracks in the sand.

The judge orders the clerk to take note: "The child is damning her soul! And we're damning ours to protect her!" Over and over

[43]

the clerk rewrites the sentence. Ad infinitum. Fills up pages and pages. Fast and furious, taking special care with the capitals.

"The child is damning her soul! And we're damning ours to protect her! . . ."

Big thick peals of lusty laughter. Filth showered on our heads. Madame Rolland tosses and turns on Léontine's little bed, dreaming she can't escape from the arena. She has to stay and watch the next scene. A woman, breasts bare, is standing with her back against a board. Her hands are tied behind her. The crowd stops laughing, holds its breath. The three judges, in their white wigs, bend over to watch. Gazing in rapt attention, as if the fate of the world were suddenly at stake. An invisible hand is throwing daggers at the woman, held fast to the board. Aiming at her heart.

Madame Rolland, on Léontine's bed, struggles to shake herself free of the nightmare. Sees the metallic flash of the knife, flying, striking the doomed woman square in the chest. Manages to close her eyes. Gropes through the blackness, feverishly looking for some hidden escape from the circus. Comes to a straircase in the darkness, climbs her way up. Thinks she's waking at last. Makes out the flowered paper in Léontine's room and clutches her breast. Feels a biting pain.

WHY this calm? Why this soft, gentle light spreading over a little deserted town? Sorel. Its streets with their handful of houses. Wooden houses. Brick houses. Square Royal. Rue Charlotte. Rue Georges. The corner of Rue Augusta and Rue Philippe. Close by, the river flows between its level banks. The long green islands, property of the parish, where cows and horses, sheep and goats are grazing.

Life here is calm, radiant. Not a soul to be seen. I feel I'm going to be happy in all this light. The river, unruffled. The pasturelands, down to the water's edge. This frieze of peaceful creatures, grazing as far as the eye can see. I stretch. I heave a deep, deep sigh. Is it for my early innocence, suddenly mine again in this childhood setting?

But something seems to be happening. Something over by the light. A kind of glow, rising, getting brighter and brighter. Getting stronger, too strong, almost unbearable. I want to raise my arm and shield my eyes from the dazzling glare.

Now, all at once, it comes to a stop, singles out a red brick house on the corner of Rue Philippe and Rue Augusta. Set off from its neighbors, bathed in light, the house begins to shine. So clearly. As if magnified under a glass. Gleaming. All glazed and bright. In back, the little garden pales beneath so powerful a sun. The blue hydrangeas seem to be all powdered white. Two floors of brick. Green wooden shutters, scrupulously shut. A wooden balcony, narrow columns. The façade, cut into the surface of the wood, fine fretwork, whitewashed. So very white, so elegant, so absurd. I could reach out and touch it. Each notch, each figure in the molding, alive in a blaze of awesome brilliance. Hard, sharp, yellow . . . A sun, stock-still above the house, off a little to the left.

Try as I may, I can't move away from this circle of light. The whole town seems to be plunged in darkness. All except my house on Rue Augusta, corner of Rue Philippe, standing out, glittering like a chunk of broken glass. Oh, how I'd like to leave it behind me. Go back to Rue Georges and the house where I was born. Escape from the clutches of this frightful place on Rue Augusta. My life! My whole life, with all its turmoil, all its passion, waiting for me there behind the shuttered windows on Rue Augusta. A wild beast, caged, lurking in the shadows, watching for a chance to pounce. Can't I run away from that part of my life? Back to where I was born? Back to the gentle, peaceful time before I was born? My mother, deep in mourning, carrying me in her womb. Like the stone inside a fruit . . . Poor little child, growing in a black crape cocoon . . . Could I glimpse the world outside through the red, weeping eyes of this young widowed mother of mine? . . . They're taking my father's coffin out of the house. My mother is fainting dead away. And here I am, shut in tight, kicking her in the belly. Trying to wake her up. Jumping and bouncing about. Why, such a long, frightening faint could kill us both!

"What a naughty little girl!"

Is that the first voice in the world to reach my ears?

No sooner do you get used to one nursemaid's face than a new one appears. Madame d'Aulnières changes nannies with every breath. On account of the child. It's the servants who take charge of the child, body and soul.

[46]

"Simply can't keep her. No two ways about it. Believe me, she's just too smart for her own good. You'll never change her!"

White bonnet perched on a dingy chignon. This one has lice. Get rid of her at once. Cook can't stand for it. It's too disgusting. Mother grumbles:

"What a nuisance . . . Oh, my poor head! . . . Really, cook is just too fussy . . . Oh, well, if I must, I must. All right then, find me another one as soon as you can!"

The nanny is gone! Long live the nanny! This one is clean and uncompromising.

"The child is full of lice!"

A fine-tooth comb, that's what we need. Ayyy! Like needles, raking my poor skull back and forth.

"Sit still or the lice are going to eat up your brains!"

The child's hair is so thick, it would really be better to cut it. Only way to take care of these vermin. Snip, snip. Curl after curl. Down to the scalp. The kitchen floor is strewn with golden fluff. Just look at that shorn head! Like a convict! The child goes rummaging through the sweepings, looking for her blond curls. The red copper pots shine in a row along the wall. Cook says if you slice a raw onion and put it in a saucer it will keep the mosquitoes away. I swear, I can hear her mumbling it now, leaning against her hot black stove.

Once her daughter is born, Madame d'Aulnières puts aside her widow's weeds of deepest mourning for that somber garb that will mark her sorrow for the rest of her days. Just like a grandmother, though she's only seventeen. With her black dress, white bonnet, collar and cuffs of fine linen, she sets about growing old and disconsolate. Day and night. Never leaves her room. Quite satisfied merely to sit there, feeling her pulse at regular intervals. No other care but the feeble beating of a heart wrapped in swaddling.

My dear little aunts begin to prod her. Use their authority as older sisters.

"You can't stay here. Think of your daughter. Why not come back home and live with us? The way it was before?"

Madame d'Aulnières, my mother, shakes her head sadly.

Go back to the family home? That trap! Let people confuse me with my spinster sisters? Risk an insult like that? No, I've paid too much for the honor of being Madame to give it up so easily.

"Listen to me, all of you. Nothing will ever be the way it was before. I'm Madame d'Aulnières. And that's how I'm going to stay until my dying breath. Until then, I have a right to my own way of life, to my daughter, my servants, my household, even my mourning. This is my husband's house. This is where I'm going to die. My mind is made up."

"But what about the child? She's growing like a wild little weed. Someone's going to have to look after her education. See that she learns English, and catechism . . . Teach her good manners . . ."

"Please, my headache . . . No, for goodness' sake, don't open the curtains . . . I'm tired of thinking about the child. And I'm tired of our good father from Sorel, who keeps coming to console me with Our Lord and Saviour. And if you must know, Our Lord and Saviour himself is beginning to get on my nerves. That's what kills me. This terrible boredom. Eating me up by inches. I can't stand it much longer . . ."

My dear little aunts shower me with hugs and kisses. They smell of naphthalene and gingerbread. Are they really here with me now, at this very moment? Pathetic and perfumed, just as they were when I was a baby? My three aunts, with their little birdlike frames, and their skin, still almost fresh. Their jet-black eyes, round and shining, staring at me. All the adoration in the world.

Again and again they renew their attack. My mother keeps managing to elude them.

"But something has to be done. It's absolutely dreadful. Why, the child is up every morning before daylight, sneaking out the window, with that tomboy haircut of hers, and running off with a gang of urchins to go fishing for catfish. Over by the islands . . ."

One day, my mother, just to keep peace . . . No, too soon! I haven't had time yet to remember a single room on Rue Georges. Oh, my first house, gone for good! A kind of white fog, like milk, spreads over the town. Only one house is left lit up. Standing out. The least little speck of dust, as clear to the eye as a moth fluttering around a lamp. The air itself is like the light, bright and resounding. You could hear a mouse breathing. Whatever happens here will be decisive. Exact. Sharp as the clink of crystal. Pure and uncompromising. Like a judge's verdict.

Rue Augusta. You can see the space between the bricks, as if you were right on top of them. The mortar sticks out a little, here and there, dotting the red ochre with bits of gray. A foul cloud of soot hangs over the garden. A withered vine clings to the little courtyard wall, like hair on an old woman's head. You can see every detail in the shutters. The knots in the wood. The green paint fading in patches. To the left of the front door, the right shutter, pulled off its hinges, slamming against the wall at the slightest hint of a breeze.

I'd swear that it's even brighter now than before. A young widow is climbing the well-worn steps. There's something both childish and stilted in the way she walks. For just a moment she turns a crestfallen face in my direction. My own young mother! Holding a little girl awkwardly by the hand. A little girl, bareheaded, hair cropped short.

Tired, I suppose, of changing nursemaids every other day, Madame d'Aulnières resigns herself to going back where she came from. The family cloister. Celibate seraglio, all in red brick, in the shadow of the tall, trembling poplar. Mother surrenders. Turns herself over, lock, stock, and barrel, to the comforting guidance of her elder sisters.

I must be seven or eight. And my education begins.

"Elisabeth, sit up straight!"

"Elisabeth, don't speak while you're eating!"

"Elisabeth, make that curtsy again, this very moment!"

"Elisabeth, how many persons are there in God?"

"Repeat after me, *the cat, the bird* . . . Don't forget, you make the *th* in English with your tongue on your teeth."

Adélaïde, Luce-Gertrude, Angélique. All beaming with delight. Stop reading their favorite novels. Fill up the emptiness of their existence. Intensely, by a kind of osmosis, they share the lot of the weeping widow and live through a whole rebellious childhood.

Elisabeth's hair grows back in dizzying abundance. The three little sisters vie for the joy of combing her tawny fleece. Their own sparse locks light up and shine with vicarious pride. My first period. Their chaste excitement.

"Are you sure, Aunt Angélique, that it's going to happen like that every month?"

"Yes, darling. It's something we all go through. It's the way of the world."

Aunt Angélique is ill at ease, embarrassed. But still delighted. "The way of the world." A deep, mysterious communion with all of womankind seems to hold a fabled, romantic fate in store for her. Is each and every wasted ovule of her sterile life about to be made fertile? Gallantly? By tender husbands? Tender lovers? Is mad passion and all its magic, somehow, old as she is, about to make her pregnant at last, with a hundred happy, blue-eyed babes?

ABOVE the house, the sun has gone out. Sud-
denly, like a lamp. All at once it's very dark. My dear little aunts
are getting excited, running about in every direction. Up and
down the balcony stairs. Rushing to pick up three pots of geraniums. Disappearing inside the house. Each one clutching her pot
of flowers, red or pink, tight to her bosom. The front door slams
shut. Behind the closed door, an extraordinary echo. The sound
of the door slamming lingers for a time, as if in a great empty
space. An immense space, with no furniture, no drapes. Huge.
Like a railroad station. A vault, high and bare. A moment later,
a sharp voice pipes up, caught in an endless echo.

"I assure you, it's going to freeze tonight. It would be a shame to
leave the geraniums out on the balcony . . . Ge-ra-ni-ums . . .
bal-co-ny . . . co-ny . . . ny . . . y-y . . ."

The words well up in waves. Roll and subside. The voice was
coming from the drawing room. Aunt Luce-Gertrude? Yes, that's
who it is, I'm sure. It's night now, altogether dark. My house, shut
tight, fills all of Rue Augusta with its somber silhouette. It seems
to be rising up from the middle of the street. Massive, unavoidable,
provoking. Like a barricade.

I want to run. To keep from going inside the house. Not risk

[51]

the certain chance of seeing my bygone days spring back to life, shake off their ashes in powdery little flakes. Each burnt-out log rekindled. Each rose-red ember blazing, bursting into flame. No, no! I won't! I'll never cross the threshold of my house again. There must be some mistake. You're confusing me with someone else. I have a perfect alibi. My pass is in order. Let me go. I'm Madame Rolland. My husband is Jérôme Rolland, notary in the city of Quebec. None of this is any of my affair. All these mysterious happenings of dubious taste, long dead, here in this brick house on the corner of Rue Augusta and Rue Philippe, in the town of Sorel. You've got the wrong person, I tell you. Let me go. I'm supposed to be somewhere else. My duty calls me. I've got to get back to Quebec, to Rue du Parloir. This very moment my husband is dying. My place is by his side. I have no business on Rue Augusta, here in Sorel. I'm Madame Rolland. I swear I am! Madame Jérôme Rolland!

I don't dare turn aside. I keep staring straight ahead. And yet, to my right and left there's something happening, something I can't see. Coming closer, from both sides at once. Now it's grazing my body. Pressing against me. Right beside me. Someone rumpling my skirt. Touching my knee. I'm being lifted off the ground. Under my arms, two powerful arms seizing me. Will I have to put up with this outrage again? Must I cross that threshold, in front of me there, with two policemen by my side? And the witnesses! All of them, packed into the vast drawing room, safely behind closed shutters. I can hear them whispering. No, I won't be brought to trial before the likes of them! Servants, innkeepers, boatmen, peasants! Good-for-nothing witnesses, every one! None of them can stand up against me. And as for Aurélie Caron . . .

There! My fear has called her back, conjured her up. Aurélie has hold of my arm. I steal a glance her way. See her profile with that jutting jaw of hers. Her bosom heaving with each labored breath. She seems consumed with indignation. Somehow I manage to turn my head and look the other way, painfully, like a sick man lying prostrate on his pillow. Now it's Justine Latour, gazing at me, bewildered. Half smiling, half in tears.

"Good God a'mighty, but Madame has really got us in a stew!"

Aurélie's wild laughter. Exploding in my face. My two body-guards hold me tight. Hurry me up the steps, four at a time. Someone I can't see, inside, opens the front door. Now I'm standing in the hall. The door to the drawing room is closed. Behind it the witnesses stop talking. I can hear their muffled breathing, hear them clearing their throats, snorting, crumpling bits of paper or cloth between their fingers. The muted sound of restless footsteps fills the room.

The silence that follows is so sudden, so complete, it almost takes my breath away. There's no one in the drawing room now. The door opens, slowly, onto the empty space. There's no one standing beside me either, no one making me move along. Aurélie Caron and Justine Latour have disappeared. I'm alone in the hall. That strong, stale smell of houses shut up tight spreads over me. Goes up my nose, stings my eyes. Sticks to my skin.

You can see where the plaster has peeled off the walls in great flakes. The chips have been swept into little piles against the baseboard. There's a fine dust falling, effortless as snow. Am I going to die in this utter void? Here, under glass, smothered in this dry, endless dust?

In this minute space, this gray and thinning air, suddenly a little girl appears, dressed for Communion. All in white, from head to toe. Her long veil reaches to the ground. A crown of white roses on her head. I'm powerless to move. In her heavy hand, in my own arm turned to stone, expires a feeble, half-attempted sign of the cross. My childhood self smiles soberly and looks me in the eye. Makes me listen to that solemn little voice I thought was gone for good.

"I renounce Satan and all his works and all his pomps, and I take Jesus Christ unto myself forever."

And so, the vows of baptism are solemnly renewed. Now the

rest can proceed apace. The door is open. The clear, brisk air fills my lungs. I find I can move again, while here in the hall the child before me is taking off her Communion clothes. My three little aunts go bustling about her. Removing her veil, her crown. She drops her white dress gaily to the floor in a snowy ring around her feet. Hops over it quick as a wink.

But let's not linger. Her childhood is past. Now the rearing of a rich young miss can all unfold in order. Quickly the tulle of her First Communion dress gives way to silk and sheer batiste, to muslin, velvet, satin and furs, to fine cashmere. The fashion books, the bundles of cloth, still fragrant with the smell of distant oceans crossed, deep in the hold, wash up ashore here in this shabby hall. This scene of the reenactment.

"The child is growing up before our very eyes!"

"Elisabeth, sit up nice and straight. Don't stoop. And don't lean against the back of the chair, for goodness' sake!"

"We'll have to find another seamstress. This one can't even stitch a straight line."

"Don't forget your Easter duty. Just keep your eyes on your embroidery. Your good looks and good manners will do the rest."

Adélaïde, Luce-Gertrude, Angélique go whirling about the child, dancing attendance on her. Keeping an eye on her weight, her figure.

Aurélie is fifteen years old. She's forever walking back and forth in front of the house. Dawdling along the sidewalk in her little print dress. Gesticulating at me. She and that band of good-for-nothings with her, hustling her about. She taunts me, this child, and makes me green with envy. At fifteen she knows as much about life as the dead themselves.

Aunt Luce-Gertrude shuts the door.

"That child is ruined already. What a disgrace at her age!"

"I wish I could go out like that. Go fishing for catfish, the way I did when I was small! With boys!"

Aunt Luce-Gertrude doesn't try to reply. Aunt Luce-Gertrude can only gasp. Aunt Adélaïde too. It's clear, the child has become a woman.

Here she comes, dressed for her very first ball, all rustling and shimmering, shoulders uncovered and flowers in her hair. Lucky for us, in this wilderness, that we have the governor's ball!

The three little sisters let themselves plunge into a mad, yet agonizing, dream. As if they themselves were about to take part in some carnal, wild, erotic mutation.

My mother comes quietly into the hall. Looks at me in blank amazement. Feels a surge of melancholy. Finally makes up her mind to speak.

"We'll have to find a husband for the child."

HAVE just enough time to run along the towpath after Aurélie. We may as well meet right now, the two of us, in the tart freshness of our fifteen years.

We stand eyeing each other. At a distance. Wary as a couple of cats.

Her tight skirt clings to her legs. Her bare feet are caked with mud. Two long woolly braids flap against her back, like two black straps, haloed about with little bristles reddened in the sun. Her face, her neck, her bare arms all have the ashen pallor of mushrooms, freshly picked.

"My, but you look pale, Aurélie."

"Oh, Madame knows . . . I always had this prison look. A taste of what was coming . . ."

And that's that. From the very first, we get right to the heart of the matter. She mentions prison. She calls me "Madame." Now she'll begin growing older before my eyes. Heavier. Under the weight of her every passing day. Take me to task, perhaps? . . . I'd give my soul if only I could keep all that from happening again! My very life, just to recapture, as it used to be, that time when both of us were innocent!

"But I never was innocent. And neither was Madame . . ."

It's as if we're rehearsing a play. Groping for words and gestures already used before, already worked out at leisure, but reluctant now to appear in a certain light.

Her voice grows more piercing as she speaks. More like a grown-up, more unpleasant.

"And me, in prison, those two years and a half. All on account of you. 'Held at the court's discretion.' Isn't that how they say it? While Madame gets out on bail . . ."

"Are you forgetting the two long months I spent in prison, Aurélie?"

Her voice, shrill, as she jumps aside. Crouching. About to pounce.

"I don't forget a thing. Not a thing."

I have to act fast. Protect myself from Aurélie's rage. Have to save us both. See that we make our peace once and for all. Rid ourselves of one whole part of our lives. Go back to when we both were growing up. Long, long before . . . I seem to be tugging, trying to pull a certain phrase out into the light. Just one, heavy, from far away. Such an important one, like a weight, sunk in the earth. A rusty anchor. Buried underground, at the end of a long rope. A kind of root, embedded deep . . . Down deep . . .

"Charges withdrawn! Charges withdrawn! . . . You must have heard, they've dropped the charges, Aurélie!"

Over and over Aurélie repeats: "Charges withdrawn!" Hardly seems to believe it. Not too sure. Like someone learning a new language. "Charges withdrawn!" Then suddenly the meaning of the words shines clear. Makes her burst out laughing.

" 'Charges withdrawn!' And the judges scratch their heads . . . And the witnesses all go home . . . And the reporters have to shut their traps! . . . Oh, yes, Madame is saved, and so am I! We're free! Free! Both of us, free!"

She laughs until she's out of breath. Lets herself collapse in a heap on the ground. Her shoulders, heaving, as if she were crying. I kneel down beside her on the towpath grass, worn thin.

"Remember, Aurélie. You're fifteen, aren't you?"

She looks up at me with that little Mongol face of hers, still laughing. Two narrow slits for eyes. Trying to hold back something burning, something poisonous in her look.

"Back then they called you 'Mademoiselle,' if you please! 'Mademoiselle'! . . ."

Another burst of laughter. She fingers my clothes. Gingerly, as if they were made of fire or snow.

"What nice things you wear! So fancy! But you don't know a thing about boys, I'll bet."

I purse my lips, very prim and proper. Turn aside, give the pleats in my skirt a few smug little pats.

"Oh, this is nothing. You should see my party dress. Low neck, all made of silk . . . For the governor's ball."

The word "governor" makes her more daring. She feels my skirt with both her hands.

"It's so soft and pretty . . . Anyway, who cares about the governor! . . . I live with my uncle!"

"Some people say he's not your uncle either!"

Again she screws up her eyes. All at once, a little viper darts out from between her lids and disappears.

"Who cares what they say! He takes good care of me, and I hardly have to work at all. And besides, I have a nice lace collar to wear to mass on Sundays."

"People say you're a witch. You know that, Aurélie?"

Suddenly very calm, very poised, Aurélie shrugs her shoulders. She takes the pipe hanging by a ribbon from her belt. Taps it empty against her bare heel. Reaches into her pocket for a pouch . . .

Now she's filling the pipe. Holding a match to it. Making little sucking noises with that big mouth of hers. Like a baby, nursing.

[58]

On her pallid face, a look of absolute contentment. She's talking in a cloud of smoke. Her voice, distant. Indifferent.

"Oh, there's one thing I can tell, all right. I always know if babies are going to live or die. But that's easy. Right when they're born, as soon as the midwife washes them clean, I give them a lick from head to toe. And if they taste real salty, that means they're going to die. I've never been wrong. Not even once. Mothers are always sending for me, just so I can tell them . . ."

"And what about boys, Aurélie? Tell me about boys."

I seem to be shouting now. Cupping my hands and shouting to her. She's getting away from me. All of a sudden I'm out of the blinding sunlight, into a kind of shadow. Humid, enveloping. One single thought boring its way into my head. Go home, I have to go home. If not, they'll never let me go to the governor's ball. If my aunts ever hear I've been talking to Aurélie, they'll be sure to punish me. And the thought bores deeper, embeds itself sharp and clear. And as it does, I find that I'm leaving Aurélie behind. Moving with dizzying speed, but without so much as taking a step. It's as if I'm skimming over the river, standing still on a kind of raft. The river, smooth and quiet. No resistance from the water. No sound of waves or oars. I'm going to the governor's ball. I have to go to the governor's ball. Good-bye, Aurélie. If I ever see you again, I'll make believe we're strangers. I'm sorry I know you, sorry we met . . . My mother promised me a string of pearls to wear to the governor's ball. I'd give my soul for a string of pearls . . . And what about boys, Aurélie? What about . . .

Her profile, sharp, the color of ivory. Her jutting jaw. Her pipe. A cloud of smoke. Then nothing. Aurélie has disappeared.

The ball is superb. I even dance with the governor himself, feel his breath on my neck. Aunt Adélaïde taps me on the arm with her fan. The chandeliers are splendid. Glints of pink, fluttering along the ceiling. I'd love to dance all night. Not that the boys are very special, all dressed up in their Sunday best. And the girls? So many nasty little snobs, laughing like a pack of cackling geese. There's really no one besides the governor . . . All red. With his rust-colored whiskers. I think I catch him staring . . . I've pulled my neckline down as low as I can . . . The music, my legs. My waist, the music. The music. Going to my head. One . . . Two . . . Ah, the polka. I'm mad about the polka. Supple as a melting candle. Nimble as a flame. I think the governor . . . (Dancing . . . dancing . . . all out of breath . . .) I think he dips me over his arm. Like a wilting flower. Or did I imagine it? And my mother says we have to find me a husband . . . Then the quadrille again. And the boys huff and puff, and snort like little piglets, awkward and clumsy. They cast sly looks my way. Again my mother says we have to find me a husband. Of course, the governor is a man of forty. The interesting age. And all the rest? Just what I said, a lot of little piglets, all dressed up . . . I really must have a talk with you, Aurélie. What do I do? I want to know . . . All about boys . . . About boys . . .

I T'S out on a hunt that I first meet Antoine Tassy.
The islands. The flat-bottom boat. The sound of the oars in the
early morning silence. The drops of water, thick and round, falling
from the oars. The narrow, winding inlets, green with weeds.
The long hours waiting, hidden in the rushes. The rain, the mud.
The shotgun hitting its mark. The smell of the powder. The
bird, plummeting like a feathered stone. The dogs lying in wait.
Their raucous barking. The taste of the mist against my face.

"God, but I love this life! Oh, how I love it!"

My male companions. Their cheeks black with a growth of
beard. Their deep voices. Their brash looks at "the huntress," as
they call me. Their bare hands on my shoulder sometimes. And
Antoine Tassy's large, pale blue eyes, dimming with tears as he
stares at me. Autumn. The ground carpeted with leaves. Blue
smoke from the shotguns.

"It's not a nice way for a young lady to be spending her time!"

"But my dear aunties, you simply don't understand! I love to
go hunting, and I'm going to go hunting!"

My three chaperones in the gamekeeper's cabin, chilled to the
bone. Surrounded by doleful, discreet young wives, all bundled up
against the cold, waiting for their husbands. And our black dog,

[61]

on a leash, suckling her brood and dreaming of game. Whining softly at every shot, her snout between her paws. Her sad-eyed stare, fixed on the cabin door.

"What a beautiful shot! I'd say you're in trim, Mademoiselle d'Aulnières!"

I smile. Yes, in fine trim, Antoine. You're on my trail now, stalking me, like a good hunting dog. And I'm getting your scent too, and tracking you down. Squire of Kamouraska. Worthless game. Easy prey, hip-deep in the mud, lurking in wait for goose and duck, finger on the trigger.

"After you, Mademoiselle."

I fire. Hit my mark. A bundle of feathers, white and gray, spinning against the gray sky, falling into the rushes.

"Congratulations, Mademoiselle."

The handsome red setter retrieves the quivering bird, a red star on its breast. Antoine Tassy weighs it in his hand with gluttonous admiration.

"You know how to aim. That's rare for a woman."

His full face, plump and pink. That lower lip of his, protruding, like a pouting child. That sensual glimmer lighting his cheeks in bright little waves. He'd like to lay me down then and there, in the mud and the rushes. And I wouldn't mind it at all, feeling his body on top of me, struggling a little as he covers my face with great moist kisses.

He's not from these parts. He's from farther down the river. I don't know a thing about him. But he's a scoundrel, I'm sure. Good family and all, but a scoundrel just the same. I'll make him show me the respect a marriageable young lady deserves.

Antoine Tassy puts the huge bird into my game bag. He puts the bag on his shoulder. Then he holds out his gloveless hand, all warm and soft. Smooth.

"Come . . . Shall we take a little walk?"

[62]

The path cuts through the pine grove. The ground is covered with red-brown needles.

"Oh, no, Monsieur. I have to go back. My aunts are waiting for me in the cabin."

His hand presses mine. For just a moment my hand submits. Like a wounded bird. Then pulls away, with a show of chaste reserve.

Angélique, Adélaïde, Luce-Gertrude . . . Gazing in wide-eyed rapture.

"Pinch me! Am I dreaming? Or is that the child I see? Coming from the marshes, covered with mud . . . With her cheeks all red from the cold, and her curls in a tangle . . . Holding hands with a big, tall, handsome lad . . ."

"No, my dear, you're not dreaming. That's Antoine Tassy, the young squire of Kamouraska!"

Antoine Tassy doesn't give my aunts much time to revel in the romantic bliss of a first encounter. The very next day he asks for my hand. Through Madame Cazeau, who comes and pays my mother a lengthy visit.

"Excellent match. Fine old family. Two hundred and fifty acres of land and woods. And the islands opposite the estate. And a salt marsh. A bakehouse. A wharf. A fine stone manor built out on the cape. The father, dead last year. Lives alone with his mother. Married sisters in Quebec . . ."

Madame d'Aulnières bursts into tears. Dreads having to explain to her daughter the mysteries of marriage and death. For her, one and the same.

"What a life! Good God, what a life! A widow at seventeen, with a baby on the way . . . No, I'll never get over it. Never . . ."

I'M going to be married. My mother has said yes. And so have I, deep in the darkness of my flesh. Will you help me? Tell me, Mother, will you? What's your advice? And you, dear aunts? Tell me, is it love? Is it really love that's troubling me so? Making me feel as if I'm about to drown . . .

Is this how little girls grow up? I preen you and primp you, fix your hair. I send you off to mass and catechism. I shield you from life and death, hide them behind big, high embroidered screens, covered with roses and exotic birds . . . We get babies from the Indians. They come by and drop them into women's beds. You know, those tiny, teeny infants with their puckered little faces, that you find one morning all wrapped and swaddled in a white woollen bundle? Next to a new young mother, exhausted and smiling . . . Oh, the fables we tell. The ones about God, the ones about men. "The Wedding-feast at Cana," "The Bride of Lammermoor," "Down by the crystal fountain, e'er shall I remember thee . . ." Love. Beautiful love of song and story.

Swine! Lord of the manor. Foul swine! I saw you in the street. And that whore, Mary Fletcher. Lord! Her red coat. Her flaming red hair. And you, Milord the Fool, tagging along like a dirty little lamb. To her great big bed with its filthy sheets. Oh, yes,

I guessed the kind of shameless games you two were playing. And what a blow it was! Innocent little me. Elisabeth d'Aulnières. Marriageable young lady.

The Cazeaus' ball. Strange how a man so big can whirl and twirl with so much grace. I keep looking down, refuse to lift my eyes. He squeezes my arm. His soft, liquid voice.

"Please, Elisabeth. Look at me!"

"You've humiliated me! I saw you with that . . . that person. Yesterday, in the street."

"I didn't realize . . . Please . . . I'm sorry."

His lip quivers as if he's about to cry.

My pride! I call my pride to come to my defense. Like my God. While the flame-red image of Mary Fletcher makes me burn with curiosity, with jealousy and desire.

For a long moment we look at each other. Without a word. His embarrassment. His helplessness. Mine too. And my pride, giving way little by little. We turn our heads, the two of us, worn out, like a pair of wrestlers.

"Eléonore-Elisabeth d'Aulnières, do you take this man, Jacques-Antoine Tassy, for your lawfully wedded husband?"

You have to say "yes," say it nice and loud. Your bridal veil. Your crown of orange blossoms. Your gown with its long train. The wedding cake, three layers high, covered with icing and thick whipped cream. Behind you the guests are sniffling in their handkerchiefs. All of Sorel is waiting to watch you go by, hanging on your young husband's arm . . . Good God, I'm doomed! Married to a man I don't even love . . .

This fair-haired giant. Eyes so blue, like flax, filled with tears. A little too plump, perhaps. And always ready with a tear or two . . . They say he drinks and chases the ladies, this squire of Kamouraska. Barely twenty-one years old. And I'm sixteen, Elisabeth d'Aulnières. And I've vowed I'll be happy . . .

No, don't let Madame Rolland settle down just yet. Don't let

[65]

her wake up all of a sudden in Léontine Mélançon's little room. To sort out the recollections of her marriage and hang them on the wall, so she can look them over at her leisure. Nothing is less innocuous than the story of Elisabeth d'Aulnières' first marriage.

It's not the unrelenting light. No, it's this terrible stillness. This distance that ought to be comforting me, this sense of detachment. It's worse than all the rest. Seeing yourself as someone else. Pretending to be objective. Not feeling that you and that young bride dressed in blue velvet are one and the same. Her traveling costume. Fashion plate for Louis-Philippe of France. The groom looks like a dummy made of wax. Long frock coat, tall silk hat.

And now the bride begins to move. Little mechanical doll, clinging to her husband's arm, climbing into the carriage. Her white silk stocking, her elegant shoe. Sitting back, she reassumes the pose. The wedding guests crowd around, joking and laughing at the top of their lungs. Again the bride gives her mother a kiss. And her aunts, and all the guests. The groom takes the reins, can't wait to start out on the long trip all the way to Kamouraska. Stopping at inns. Changing the horses. Aunt Adélaïde shouts something, swallowed up in the wind. Repeats the question, as the groom struggles to hold back the team of two black horses.

Again and again the groom kisses the bride. The groom is made of painted wood. So is the bride, colored all blue.

And me, I'm Madame Rolland, and I'm off again on my first wedding trip. The way you tell a story. Not taking it too seriously, with an amused little smile. Even if happiness turns to vinegar, to bitter gall . . .

The road is lined with trees. I count the grains of rice strewn everywhere in the carriage. I close my eyes. The warm, dry wind passes over my face, my hands. Between my lashes I can see the cloud of dust stirred up by the carriage along the road.

We should have taken the steamboat to Quebec. But my husband insists that he'll drive his young wife by himself, over his favorite route, all the way to his home down the river.

The smell of cut hay. The fragrance of clover. The chirping of crickets. Great armfuls heaped over me, now burning hot, now fresh and cool. Out of the sunlight, into the deep, dark shade of the forest. So sensitive again to the slightest touch. This one desire, the very center of my being . . . No, no! I won't admit how willingly I let myself be bound to this fair-haired man beside me. The carriage, madly flying over these treacherous roads, in the blazing summer heat.

In front of the inn the sign is swaying in the wind. *Auberge des Trembles.* The Gothic letters blend with the white wooden frills that trim the narrow columns and the balcony.

The innkeeper seems to know the groom. The groom's clothes have thrown off their nice little fashion-book air. The tall silk hat, pushed back on his head. A childish lock of fine blond hair falling over his forehead. The vest—unbuttoned, rebuttoned askew —all full of wrinkles.

The groom gives the inkeeper a couple of healthy slaps on the shoulder. His booming voice fills the low-ceilinged room.

"Hello, old man! I'm here to eat. And to spend the night. The lady here is my wife. So give her your nicest, deepest bow and call her 'Madame.' Then go round up some fiddlers and dancers. Fast as you can. This is my wedding night. And we're going to have ourselves a time!"

I like the polka better. Good God, the governor's ball! Help me! Save me! The young men are wearing white gloves and such pious expressions. And the governor . . . With his whiskers, reddish gold, like cat's fur. And his oh-so-British air . . . I speak such elegant English. The governor told me so . . . Then why am I here? Tell me, what am I doing here? My husband gets such strange ideas . . . All these ignorant, backwoods boors! Reeking of sweat and dirt. Doing their noisy dances, shrieking like so many beasts off to be slaughtered . . . My husband likes his women unwashed, heavy with the smell of musk. He told me so. He mixes whiskey in his wine. He eats his shortbread hot off the fire . . .

"What a wonderful life!"

The groom, shouting as he twirls the bride about.

I'm sick. Sick to my stomach. That swallow of shortbread that won't go down . . . It's stifling in here . . . The Irish jig . . . The devil's own dance! And that jarring sound of the fiddles, scraping, piercing my skull . . . I must have had too much to drink. Tin cups full of liquid fire. Good God, I'm dying! . . . At the governor's ball little round slices of lime float in a pink punch, nice and sweet . . . Mustn't forget my position . . . I feel so weak, the way I do before my period . . . This country inn is so far beneath me . . . Now he's playing with the lace on my petticoat. Under the table. Slipping his fingers between my stocking and my shoe. Ever so gently. Behind the long linen cloth, hanging down.

"I'm a happy man!"

The groom, proclaiming his joy. Everyone watching, a little embarrassed, cooing with delight. Then they all laugh and laugh. Cast sly little looks at the bride. Knowing glances . . .

In the wee, small hours, the bride is still awake, nestling head to toe against the groom, who lies submerged in an exhausted, alcoholic sleep. With that fresh-cut gash between her thighs, the bride looks round the room. Dismayed to see her clothing strewn about in a tangled clutter of velvet, linen, and lace.

TWO-WEEK journey. Long, deserted roads. Through forests. Little village inns. The fatback and molasses make me sick. Sometimes there are bugs crawling out of the bedsteads. And the sheets are always so rough. The heat is unbearable. The rain comes through the hood into the carriage.

Louiseville, Saint-Hyacinthe, Saint-Nicolas, Pointe-Lévis, Saint-Michel, Montmagny, Berthier, L'Islet, Saint-Roch-des-Aulnaies, Saint-Jean-Port-Joli . . .

The air of the river, downstream, filling my lungs. The evenings, growing cooler. Stronger and stronger, the smell of the sandy banks.

Riding along, Antoine Tassy points to an invisible line where the river becomes as salty as the ocean. Elisabeth d'Aulnières lets her thoughts run back home to the sweet, fresh waters of the Richelieu.

Sainte-Anne, Rivière-Ouelle, Kamouraska!

The hills loom up, rise out of the underbrush. Sudden whiteness, speckled with black. Layers of marbled rock, larded here and there with stunted trees. And close by, the forest . . . The flat banks, stretching along the river. Reeds and rushes. And sea grasses, long-stemmed eelgrass, swaying in the wind. Like ripples along the water's edge.

The groom waves his whip against the July sky. Points out the islands. Names each one, slowly, as if they were human beings. Introduces his domain to his young bride.

"Ile aux Corneilles, Ile Providence, Ile aux Patins, Grosse Ile . . ."

Summer landscape, warm and misty blue. The long expanse of muddy banks. The smell of low tide fills the air. The water blends with the sky. You can't see over to the other shore.

I have plenty of time to live here with my young husband . . . A few years of violence and despair . . . See how I cling to him, like a pussycat! Nestling against him as he introduces me to his mother, standing at the manor door to greet the newlyweds.

The manor . . . Someone is asking where the manor is. A man's voice, with a hint of an American accent. It's winter. Freezing cold. A slow, deliberate gesture, peasant-fashion, points toward the other end of the village. A cape jutting out, alone, into the river.

At the Dionnes' inn, a girl with kinky hair, a stranger in the village. Asking for the manor. She puts her hand against the frozen windowpane and scratches with her nails to melt the frost. She stands for a long time looking out into the darkness, toward where the manor must be.

The manor . . . You don't risk much going back there, Madame Rolland. You know there's nothing left of it. All burned down in 18—. Burned to the ground, not a trace left standing. Who else can boast of wiping out a past like that, all at once? A few flames, a lot of smoke. Then nothing . . . Memory has to be tilled like a plot of land. You have to fire it from time to time. Burn the weeds down to the roots. Plant a field of imaginary roses in their place.

It's no great feat to have a double life, Madame Rolland. But to have four secret lives, or five, with no one any the wiser. Yes, that would be harder. Like all those pious ladies, mumbling their endless rosaries, with viper's venom flowing through their veins. Good day, Madame Rolland. Good evening, Madame Rolland. And how is Monsieur Rolland? And the children? Quite a brood you have! But all strong and healthy, thank heaven! . . . Really, Madame Rolland, what can you be thinking, to give you such a sullen look? To give you such a wrinkled brow? . . . Above reproach. You're above reproach. Oh, but you're a daydreamer. That's what you are, Madame Rolland. No use denying it. Your husband is dying on the second floor, and here you are, on the governess's bed, pretending to be asleep. Hearing voices, Madame Rolland. You make believe you're hearing voices. Having hallucinations. Come now. Are you so desperate for amusement that you have to go digging, deep in the shadows, to find the phantoms of your youth?

In the autumn the birds take over all of Kamouraska. Canada geese and ducks, brant and teal, wild geese of every kind. Thousands of birds from miles and miles away. All along the shore. Aren't you simply delighted? You who love to hunt so much . . . The wind. There's too much wind. I'll never get used to it. At night it whistles around the house. Rattles the shutters. The wind will be the death of me . . .

On stormy nights they say the dead are moaning in the wind. But nobody here is dead. I'm alive, and so is my husband. In Kamouraska, here in the manor. Living out our bitter youth, day after day. Alive! Both of us, alive! Married to each other . . . Two people, confronting each other. Hurting each other. Insulting each other as much as they please. And under the prying eye of the dowager Madame Tassy! . . . It can't go on this way. It has to come to a head. One of them will have to pick a spot, the right spot in the heart, and plant it with death. Quietly, calmly . . . And the one who does it first will be saved.

[71]

AGAIN, nothing moving. It's evening. Everything, stiff and still. Lifeless. I'm all alone. And yet, there's something watching me, here in the petrified landscape of Kamouraska. Something motionless, agape . . . I never should have come back. The charred ruins of the manor, all black against a sky of stone. The front still seems to be intact. The door, wide open. Through the doorway you can see the wild weeds growing madly in massive clumps behind the house. The drawing room window has a few little panes in place, smoked black . . . Upstairs, a lamp is burning in the couple's bedroom, glowing orange, dead. Somewhere in the wall, one motionless speck of life, stony but alive, aims itself in my direction. Holding its fire. Stuck in the stone . . . All at once, it moves. A lizard, I suppose, hidden among the stones, now suddenly scurrying down the wall. In nimble zigzags. Falling at my feet. Good Lord! Now all the ruins seem to be coming to life. This living speck decides to budge, and bit by bit it wakes up all the walls left standing. The stones licked black by the fire. Just as if all the ruins . . .

That little black eye, riveted on me. Those fleshy, puckered lids, never blinking . . . My mother-in-law is alive. She looms up out of the fire-charred stone. Standing there, the color of dust, her scraggy, scrawny, fidgety little form.

"Hello, Elisabeth dear. Welcome to the manor."

She steps aside on her short, crooked legs. She's leaning on a cane, gazing with rapt attention at her two club feet in their new high-button shoes.

Frugal in every other way, living like a peasant, Madame Tassy allows herself the luxury of having her shoes made in New York. Sometimes it takes them a year to get to Kamouraska. And all that time she delights in the knowledge that a bootmaker in the big American city is carefully preserving the mold of her misshapen feet.

Her long mourning veils reach to the ground. I turn aside. If only I can keep from crying and trembling in front of her. Tears are foreign to her way of life. For her, tears and hysterics are part of that unseemly world of bad taste and excesses. A world which, for want of a better term, she calls the theatre.

And that's my world. The theatre. Emotions, passions, great shouts and gnashing of teeth. I'm not afraid of anything. Only of being bored. I'll play out my madness to the very end. It's something I have to do. I'm on my way. Afterwards I'll settle down. Become Madame Rolland again . . . There, I've settled down already. I am Madame Rolland. As for your son, Antoine Tassy, he's part of the theatre world too, with his flailing arms and passionate outbursts. And so much the worse for him, because . . .

Madame Tassy looks at me so sternly I'm sure she can read my thoughts. Another flash of her little eye, and for a moment I'm afraid she's going to bring down her heavy cane across my back. Now she's speaking. Calmly. In a flat, dull voice. Slyly repeating the little speech she made on my first day at the manor, when, clinging to Antoine, I . . .

"My dear, there's something I should tell you. My son is a good boy. But he will go off on his little flings once in a while. Now then, I'm not going to say you should try to get used to it . . . I've never been able to. Or his father either. My poor husband,

God rest his soul! . . . You'll just have to turn your back, my dear, if you ever find him coarse or shocking. Simply ignore it. Like all those folks who tell us how beautiful life can be! Don't forget that, and you're sure to be happy. No matter how my son mistreats you . . ."

My mother-in-law knits for the poor people in the village. All night long. With that homespun wool, rough and prickly, the color of porridge. Early one morning she sends for me. My hair disheveled, my eyes puffed up from crying and lack of sleep, my huge belly bulging. I feel like a toy tumbler, rolling from side to side, up and down. I can't see my feet. I'm a tower. Keeping watch, like the tower in the song. My husband has run off to Quebec with a silly little village girl. On my mother-in-law's face, that tough look of wise good sense. A face whose tears are dry as dust. A letter from Antoine lies open on her lap.

"The child is dead. She died on the way. Her heart . . ."

"Good enough. Let that be a lesson . . ."

"But you don't understand. She's only fifteen. My son is responsible to her parents. Who would ever dream . . . A child like that, to up and die in the middle of a trip . . . You'd think at her age she would be strong and healthy, wouldn't you? Well, at any rate . . . The messenger is waiting in the kitchen. What answer shall we send Antoine? The poor boy certainly needs advice . . . Of course, what he really needs is a good fright, once and for all. Don't you think?"

Her reply is already written. A few words scratched out in pencil:

You've damned her soul. Manage as best you can with her body. Caroline des Rivières Tassy.

Just as she never cries, so too she never laughs. The slightest quiver at the corner of the mouth, nothing more. An almost invisible pucker of her shriveled cheek.

With the message sent and received by her son, Madame Tassy sets about at once to hush up the whole affair.

[74]

ONCE again, Léontine Mélançon's little room. I don't have the strength now to move my head on the pillow. Flat on my back, my eyes fixed on the ceiling. The elaborate plaster moldings. That blinding whiteness. That sun, still there, still . . . The moldings. Staring at them, scrutinizing them, putting them together, taking them apart. To my heart's content. Impossible to move. Not even my little finger. My body is weighted down with hundreds of leaden pellets, like the ones they sew into the hems of cloaks and skirts to keep them hanging straight. Wrapped up like a corpse being buried at sea. Dropped overboard into a briny dream. My memory still in perfect order. Like a clock. Tick-tock, tick-tock . . . Who's going to lift me up? Gently . . . Take me out of this room, with its silly flowers? Who's going to lead me to the stairs? Help me down. One by one, like a child. And leave me, safe and sound, by Jérôme Rolland's bedside . . .

Two bullets in his head. His brains, coming out his ears. They've bandaged his hideous wound. Laid him to rest in the church, beneath his lordship's family pew. On stormy nights I can hear him moaning . . . The wind plays such havoc with us here . . . Then stealthily he gets to his feet. Walks through passages deep in the earth. Dark pathways flowing with underground streams. Comes to the ruins of the manor. Sits in his armchair, fragile as

[75]

charcoal. The velvet, withered. Next to the fireplace, still intact. Gaping black hole. Complains how cold the earth is. How many masses he has to listen to, day after day. The squealing chants sweep over him in gusty blasts. Down in his hole, under the floorboards of the church. Great puffs of incense . . . There he sits now, dreaming of giving orders. Calls all his servants. Asks them to bring him food and drink. Says he has all the time in the world to live. Tells them he's waiting for his wife to join him. Groans again. Says that his nasty temper is dead, along with his blood. Begs them to send him his wife, right away. Thinks he's just barked a decisive command. All the time, whispering behind his hand, gloved in black. Announces that everything is ready now for the reenactment of the crime.

"This way. If Madame will be good enough to follow me . . ."

That high-pitched voice. It's Aurélie Caron. Just as she was, that December, 1839. All dressed in new clothes, from head to toe. Ready for the long, hard journey to Kamouraska. Ready to perform her awful mission. Her hair curled over her forehead like so many little commas. Her teeth stained with tobacco. She bundles up in her coat of homespun wool. Collar, cape, kerchief, and scarf.

I walk up the path to the manor, hard on the heels of this girl with the swinging hips. Can't keep from following her. I have no choice.

Aurélie leaves me at the foot of the stairs.

"This is as far as I can go. You know that. I never worked in the manor house at Kamouraska. Not me. I only came up here once. And then, never inside. Something about a certain errand . . ."

Look, there's Rose Morin and little Robert. Marie Voisine, Alma Ouelette, Charles Deguire, Desjardins, Dionne . . . All of them, standing in a double row. With their lamps held over their heads. As if to greet me. Escort me to the staircase. Then let me go up all alone, into the darkness . . . The steps are gutted by the fire. Every other one, eaten away. The sixth . . . Yes, it still creaks.

There's life here after all. And that man, waiting for me at the top of the stairs. Good God, please, let him be alive!

Why does he have his head all bandaged? Haven't we only been married a couple of months? No one has tried to murder my husband for me yet! Not yet, I'm sure! . . . I'm standing at the threshold. I don't want to go in. Our bedroom door is gone . . . I can't stop looking at that head all wrapped in white. Inside the room, such utter chaos, nothing in its place.

"Well, come in! What are you waiting for? Close the door."

I don't know that voice. I can scarcely hear it. A kind of dull crackle, breaking with every word. Now he's standing up. Almost on top of me. Suddenly he has his booming voice again, the one he used to have. His pale eye, bulging from its socket, tries to catch my glance. I hide my face in my hands.

"Damn you, woman! Damn you! See what you've done!"

Good God! He's going to take off the bandage! Show me the wound! . . . He pulls my hands away from my face. Seizes my wrists, holds both of them tight in one big hand. Makes me look at him, right in the face . . . Again I feel the oily smoothness of his heavy hand, the strength of the bones. Wide-eyed, I recognize his features. A little child's plump and puffy cheeks. No bandage now to hide his fine, blond hair. If only I could thank him somehow. Thank him for that unscathed image of himself. Hug him and kiss him for it. Most of all, make him forget the attack, the murder. In the cove at Kamouraska . . . My young husband. Six months married. God be praised! Nothing has happened. Not yet . . . He looks at me and laughs.

He waves his arms. Points to the bed, covered with clothes and linens and toilet things, all strewn about. And the big pine cupboard, both doors open wide, shelves empty.

"Your chemises, dearest? You're looking for your chemises? Well, find them if you can! Look for them. Keep looking. And your fancy pantalets? You'd like to find them too? To show off a little? To tempt the devil, and your poor husband too?"

I go about picking things up. Sorting them, putting them back in the cupboard. It's easy to see that most of my bridal linen has disappeared.

"No more. Gone. Disappeared. My wife's chemises and pantalets. Now you'll have to go naked under your gowns of cashmere and silk! A fine joke, don't you think? I'm really a clown!"

Antoine Tassy is choking with laughter. He downs a healthy swallow of brandy. Hangs his head, sheepishly, like a naughty child, caught and punished. Again, his strange voice, barely audible, brittle.

"Don't look at me like that. Go away, please. Go away. I'm a swine, I know . . ."

A swine! His words, my husband's very words. Yes, that's what he is. A swine. That's just what he is. And he admits it. It's all his fault, not mine. He's to blame. I'm innocent. Innocent . . . Disgraced, humiliated. Six months pregnant. And he insults me. Makes fun of me. I look so foolish with my belly sticking out. It's Sunday, high mass, and I'm walking along. Heavy, hanging on my husband's arm, my cape pulled round me, all askew . . . Oh, no! My blue muslin dress. The one that disappeared. Look, there it is. On that filthy Aglaé Dionne! His latest conquest. See? She's smirking at me. Clasping her hands, making faces behind them as I go by. Laughing at me. Oh, to have her stripped bare, here and now! To have her whipped on the spot, that slut!

He's snoring now and stinking of alcohol. I have to undress him. Take off his boots.

Today he begged me to forgive him. Took me tenderly in his arms. Kissing, caressing my belly and the little one inside. He's crying, taking great pleasure filling my navel with his tears. He calls it his holy font. And he tells me that I'm so pretty, so kind. And that one fine day he's going to kill me.

My mother-in-law keeps repeating:

"Just ignore him. Turn your back. Let it all go in one ear and out the other . . ."

[78]

MY first son is born. Endless ordeal, a day and a half. They had to use forceps. And Antoine, nowhere to be seen. They found him four days later, dead drunk. All huddled up, feverish, shivering with the cold. Lying on the wet sand. In the rushes. By the river.

He swears on his son's life never to drink again. We toast the baptism with champagne just off the boat from France. Antoine goes drinking all through the house. Down in the kitchen, up in the attic. Looking for a green and yellow pumpkin, to mix up a special punch of his own.

"A party for my wife and son! Like none you've ever seen before! Ring the bells! Bang the glasses! Ding, dong! Ding, dong! You see? I've gone mad! . . ."

My mother-in-law goes scurrying here and there, filling the cups. Tells everyone that her grandson is quite a bawler, and that her son is twice as bad!

All's right with the world. The dead below. The living above. Little baptismal scenes. The manor, lit up, shines in the night. Like a ship out of water. Perched on a promontory. Up for repairs. All lights ablaze. And inside, swarming with life. All the towns-folk, drinking and eating their fill. In the kitchen, bursting with

[79]

eels and every kind of bird. Flowing with their wine and whiskey brew.

"It's a boy! Monsieur has a son!"

The scene is such a happy one, so full of promise. Why not hold on to it, cling to it?

On the walls in the couple's room, a piece of mirror is still in place above the chest of drawers. The soot falls away in a velvety powder. Uncovers a clear, round, silver space . . . Look through the little porthole. See the pretty scene reflected in the stagnant water. Family portrait. Father and mother, all aflutter, bending over a newborn baby, red as can be. Mother-in-law brings over a homespun shawl, one she knitted herself. Mother says it's too rough for her baby. Mother-in-law, offended, raps on the floor with her cane. Three good raps, loud and clear. Announcing the drama we're destined to play. Leaves in a huff.

"Theatre, that's all it is!"

Now we're on our own. For better or worse. Antoine Tassy and I, Elisabeth d'Aulnières, his wife.

Again my husband is wearing a band of white, wrapped round his forehead. Raising his arm above my head, waving his fist. To curse me. I'm holding my son in my arms. I close my eyes. Now my mother-in-law comes back. Tells us we're just a couple of puppets . . . Oh! The piece of mirror is breaking, smashing to bits . . .

One last sliver clings to the wall. Tiny triangle, all jagged around the edges. But so clear. Limpid. No, I refuse to move. I'll stand like this as long as I have to, clutching my son to my breast. I'll keep my eyes shut tight, no matter what. They'll have to pry them open to make me look. That mirror, too flawless. Its flash is sure to pierce my heart. Better to face his anger. Awful, like a wounded beast's. Antoine and his revenge. Anything, rather than see that clear, blue, childlike look of his again. That look of sad bewilderment.

[80]

"You? Elisabeth? My wife? How could you . . ."

His tortured voice, too soft and gentle. God, what have I done? What's the crime . . .

My skirts are covered with mud. My bodice, ripped apart. We're running, the two of us. So fast. Can't catch our breath. Over the wet bank. Falling in the rushes. The little puddles of greenish water splashing under our weight. The slimy seaweed, red and yellow. The sea fern, outlined on our skin . . . Antoine Tassy, my husband . . . Good heavens, if ever the servants or the folks in town . . . We're two wild children. Let's hold each other's hands. Kiss each other on the lips. So hard we almost smother. Let's take off all our clothes again. Run quick and hide in the little house at Paincourt that my husband uses for his own affairs . . .

He's throwing a kitchen knife at me. Straight for my head. I barely have time to move. The knife is stuck in the woodwork, right on a level with my throat.

He's mad. Look at him, sitting in his chair, so quiet and motionless. Or on his feet. Stiff as a heavy stump. At the window, against the light. As if the burden of immobility builds up inside him, bit by bit. Bears down on him with all its ponderous weight. And all its silence. Like an earthen jar filled up with iron pellets, one by one, right to the brim . . . Everyone away! Locks and seals on all that excess weight. On his petrified gaze. No other thought in mind but following the secret workings of that awesome something, forgotten, left behind almost unthinkingly to gather dust. Though everyone knows what kind of beast it is, there in the sack. What mischievous little mouse, what devilish sprite triumphant. Antoine seems so far away. But he's listening to that deadly voice within him. The underside of his noisy, brawling joy. The bitter, all-commanding voice of his despair.

I throw myself at his feet. I beg him to come to his senses. If only I could rid him of that one idea, that obsession. He looks at

[81]

me but doesn't see me. Speaks in a voice calm and controlled.

"I'm going to kill myself. Kill myself. I have to kill myself. You know I have to. There's no other way. I'm going to kill myself, Elisabeth. Kill myself."

His mother says he's been like this five years now. Says to make him drink black coffee. Talk to him about other things. Keep an eye on him all the time . . .

At night he raves, delirious. He goes to confession. Calls the priest a dead tree. Beats his breast.

"I'm living in filth, Father. Stuck in the mire. I say the foulest things, Father. Debauched, depraved . . . Doing my tricks, cutting my capers. My somersaults. Squealing like the swine I am . . . A clown, Father. That's it, I'm a clown. Full of brandy and beer. A clown who laces his wine with whiskey. Plenty of it . . . Ugh! I'm falling, Father. Into a black hole. Going blind . . . You're a big dead tree, Father. With lots of dead branches."—"The better to hang you with, my child."—"Look, Father, I'm putting my damn fool head through the noose. Right now. Amen!"

Antoine, down on his knees, drags himself along the floor. Tries to get up. Wants to confess again, in front of the piece of mirror stuck in the wall above the chest of drawers.

"I want to see my damn fool face!"

He stares in the mirror, wide-eyed. Opens his mouth, sticks out a coated tongue. Shoots a bullet at the glass. Misses. Hole in the wall. While the one last sliver still intact, stuck on a nail, quivers. Dizzily . . .

I'm pregnant again. I like being pregnant. It makes me so awfully important in the house. Surprised, Antoine goes slinking about, almost unnoticed. My mother-in-law attacks her knitting with a vengeance . . .

Antoine is calling to me from a shed in the courtyard. He's sitting on a white wooden box. Behind him, tied to one of the beams, a thick rope, ending in a noose, swings back and forth. He struggles to his feet, mumbling.

"Are you coming, Elisabeth? I'll make the noose bigger and you can come too. Swinging from a rope. Husband and wife, hanging together, two heads in one noose. Isn't that nice? And the baby will split your belly, all by himself. No midwife to help him. He'll fall on the straw like a rock. And his very first screams will ring in our ears. Just before we get to hell, the two of us. Come on along. The rope is big enough for two, Elisabeth. You see? The bonds of marriage. A thick rope, nice and solid. A noose to strangle in together. You promised, for better or worse. Come on, come on . . ."

He's screaming with laughter, trying to slip the noose around my neck. I push him away and make believe I'm laughing too. A moment later he loses his balance and falls on the straw. With a great, dull thud.

ALL ropes and straps and halters out of sight. Strictest orders to the help. To keep this man from hanging himself. And destroying me along with him . . . Go on living. Another child. Ten months after the first one. A second boy. More of a bawler than the first . . . The wind. The sound of the waves dashing against the rocks. The great autumn tides. The manor, jutting out above the rising waters, lost in a fog as thick as milk. The wooden shutters creak and come unhinged. The storm rages for two whole days. No sleep. Watching the branches breaking. The cataracts gushing. A man staggering through the darkness. Helping him out of his sopping clothes.

I think it's fear alone that keeps me here. I'm spellbound. Held fast to a madman's bed. His crazy wife, still bewitched by love. Once in a while. In great, sudden flashes. Fewer and fewer . . . Go on living. My new baby screams and screeches all night long. My milk is almost all dried up. My mother-in-law says I should get some sleep and find him a wet nurse instead. Yes, I'll look for one. An ugly one, not too young. Neat and clean, with plenty of milk.

My mother-in-law has no objections.

"My son is such a terrible spendthrift. It's up to you, my dear, to see that my grandchildren never want for a thing."

Madame Tassy leans on her cane. Screws up her little hook nose and goes digging in her numerous pockets. Rummages through her woollen skirts, here and there, inside and out. Finally produces a handful of coins and thrusts them into my hand. Scratching my palm with her little nails. As if she were clawing the earth to bury a treasure. Keeps telling me that she's the mistress of Kamouraska.

Antoine could puke at his mother's feet, all over the rug, and she'd never call him down. Never say a word. Instead, she delights in making our meals an act of strictest penance. Boiled potatoes, pickled eels, buckwheat cakes . . . Day after day.

My aunts come running to the baptism of my second child. Look at me, aghast. Decide to take me back to Sorel for a while, me and the children. I give myself over, body and soul, to these three little creatures, appearing all at once from the ends of the earth to save me. Antoine swears that he won't allow it. Then suddenly changes his mind and decides that we'll all go back to Sorel together.

My last mass in the church at Kamouraska. My aunts, gazing with pity at the hapless wife.

"How thin she is!"

"And so pale . . ."

The people of Kamouraska whisper as I go by.

"Wonderful woman . . . Wonderful wife . . . Such a pleasant disposition . . . Such Christian resignation . . ."

My head bowed low over my missal. I take a certain curious pleasure in my role as martyred wife and outraged princess. Over and over I repeat to myself the tender praises of the parishioners gathered in the little stone church. Mechanically I begin to spit out the words of the Our Father . . . A savage frenzy seems to seize me. Wakes me up, all at once, like someone walking in his

[85]

sleep. Makes me sink my teeth into four words of the prayer, wrenching them out of the text, explaining them, devouring them. As if to make them my very own, forever. Giving them one supreme and ultimate meaning. "Deliver us from evil." While the evil I must be delivered from, at any cost, takes shape beside me in the family pew. Takes on the flushed face and the trembling hands of the man who is my husband.

What a pretty sight when the high mass is over. All the townsfolk leaving the church. Row after row, crowding behind his lordship and his lady. Arm in arm, just for the occasion. The young wife, smiling sweetly, still so pale from her confinement. Inside, her hidden heart. The underside of all that sweetness. Violent counterpart. Your delicate face, Elisabeth d'Aulnières. Film of angel skin laid over your loathing. Thin as can be.

YOU have just enough time to say good-bye to Kamouraska. Take a good look at the gigantic man coming toward you, covered with snow. Rising up out of some deep hole, dug in a snowbank out on the ice. To bury him forever. The long, flat, broad, bare, powdery stretch of snow. The lovely cove between Saint-Denis and Kamouraska. This man, lost. Standing out against the blurred horizon. His head is wrapped in white. He's growing, growing before your very eyes. Still coming toward you. Intent on making it perfectly clear that your love didn't fool him one bit.

I cry out. I'm sure I cry out. This vision of Antoine, murdered, is about to pounce. Knock me down. But all of a sudden . . . My shoulder, made of stone. And the giant smashes against it. Breaks into bits. Penetrates my very being. Thousands of splinters stuck in my flesh. I'm possessed, down to the roots of my hair, the tips of my nails. Antoine, multiplied beyond all measure. As if he were crushed in a mortar, pounded into a mass of tiny fragments. Each minuscule grain still bearing all the burden of crime and death. His blood, shed. His skull, smashed. His heart, stopped. About nine o'clock at night. January 31, 1839. In the cove at Kamouraska.

His blood, his head, his heart. It's all beginning again. Dancing around in my bones. A swarm of Antoines, murdered, milling around in my bones. Black ants with huge eyes. Blue ones. Good God! I'm dying! I'm dying, I tell you . . .

I sit up on the bed with a start. All those morning glories on the paper, twining around me, holding me prisoner. The four walls grip me and weigh me down, like a fist clenched tight against my throat.

"Anne-Marie! . . . It's you, darling! . . ."

Madame Rolland is sitting there, her head, Medusa-like, poking out of her crumpled robe. Anne-Marie stares at her mother, a look of fright in her wistful eyes.

"Was that you that screamed, Mamma? . . . Are you sick? . . ."

"Me? Sick? . . . Don't be silly! . . . Now be a dear and get me a glass of water."

Madame Rolland gulps it down. Passes the moist glass over her brow, her cheeks. Still under the dark and piercing gaze of Anne-Marie.

Madame Rolland begins to get up. The child runs to the bed, smooths out the covers. Speaks in a commanding tone. Repeats the doctor's orders in a solemn voice.

"No, no. You mustn't get up yet. The doctor said you have to rest . . . All the care you give Papa, all your worry . . . You're all worn out. You have to sleep a little longer."

Madame Rolland savors her daughter's words. With gluttonous relish. "Care," "worry" . . . She'll find her peace someday, hidden inside a compliment, hard as an almond.

Madame Rolland, grateful to her daughter, gives her a hug and a kiss. Then, dutiful, and in her dolefullest of voices, asks how Monsieur Rolland is doing.

"He's asleep. Florida is staying up with him. You don't have to worry."

What a good little girl your daughter is. And Florida, what a

[88]

devoted maid. Nothing to worry about. But be sure not to fall asleep again. Stay up and keep watch.

Keep watch over my husband. Follow him every step of the way, as far as I can. Over this narrow plank that leads to death. Until I can't take one more step without dying myself. Just at the very moment prescribed by law, leaving him alone to take the last step over . . . Hanging from a thread, thinner and thinner. Watching him disappear. Standing here, still living. At the edge of the cliff. And the thread, broken, hanging. Cut . . . Waving a handkerchief good-bye, over the void. A widow again . . . No, you can look all you want. This time my hands are clean. I'm innocent. My husband's name is Jérôme Rolland, and now I'm going to see him off. Walk with him. To the brink of death.

THIS dangerous urge to keep falling asleep will be your undoing, Madame Rolland. See, you're drunk with dreaming. You're babbling, Madame Rolland. Turning your heavy, sluggish body toward the wall, as if there were nothing else for you to do. And all this time, in his second-floor room, in your house on Rue du Parloir, Monsieur Rolland . . . Who knows, is he gasping his last? . . .

My legs are like cotton. My eyelids droop in spite of myself . . .

Sorel again. The house on Rue Augusta, open to the lovely October sun. They're expecting me. The russet leaves fill the tree-lined street with their splendor. A gentle breeze wafts its colors on the light.

No neighbor sweeping up the leaves outside his house. No children running, laughing. No woman's voice. No bird singing. They've emptied the town. Like a squash with its insides hollowed out. Only my house left standing. No life but the bare essentials. Just what's needed for my trial.

The dead leaves crinkle along the garden path. The threshold is bathed in light, dappled with the fluttering shadows of the leaves. The hall looks like an old abandoned station, just as it always did. No time to pride myself on how I can avoid the drawing room—

the black piano, the needlework left unfinished. Already I feel myself being pushed toward the stairs by an overpowering force. There's someone waiting for me at the top. Someone in petticoats, her tiny feet planted squarely on the floor.

Aurélie Caron is there to welcome me. I don't like that sly little grin of hers. She knows the way the story goes. Swears my intentions are anything but pure.

"Madame knows just what's going to happen. No need to act so innocent."

"I'm sick . . . I've come back home to rest. There's nothing wrong with that. It's perfectly natural . . ."

"If Madame would kindly step into her old room, please?"

Aurélie laughs and dashes off. Her sprightly steps on the bare floor echo through the little corridor.

Why have they taken up the carpet? And my old room? No, nothing seems changed. And yet . . . It's all so neat. Everything almost frozen in place. Like a museum. Look, those drapes of pink percale hanging around the bed I slept in growing up. The flowered quilt. The doll, stuffed with bran, sprawled out on the pillow . . . I don't dare step over this wall. Rising, invisible, all about me.

"Go on, Madame! That's all you have to do. Come back to Rue Augusta and begin again. Just after your return from Kamouraska. As if the first time never even happened. That's one thing the judges are adamant about. Ab-so-lute-ly a-da-mant!"

She makes a display of hammering out each syllable. That gaptooth grin. That impudent air. Her scrawny arms gesturing me on. Again and again.

I struggle to put one foot in front of the other. As if I were wading through some strangely thick, resistant water. I collapse on my bed. Flat on my face. My head in the pillow. Sobbing, sobbing my heart out. A moment later, Aurélie tiptoes out of the room.

[91]

The patter of little feet around my bed. Plaintive whispers . . .
My three little aunts! They're here! I let my tears flow free, more
than I really need to do, to feel the flood of pity my aunts will
lavish over me. I'm even afraid to open my eyes, afraid I might
not find them still alive. Adélaïde, Angélique, Luce-Gertrude . . .

A stifling smell of withered roses. A stench of mice, poisoned,
down behind the baseboard in the hall. My dear aunts, broken-
hearted, dead from grief. One after another, a year apart.

"This child will be the death of us. Good God, what a calamity
in Kamouraska!"

Their clothing, black and dull. Their amethyst and silver jewelry.
Three dead birds, stuffed in all their faded feathers.

I clap my hands together. (Where do I get the strength, the
burst of energy?) To chase away the ghosts. Dispel my fears.
Arrange the dream. Maintain a kind of balance. The past, relived,
but sensibly, and only on the surface. Everything just as it happened, in proper order. Without trying to live it over from start
to finish, all at once. Like a mad bird, flying the length, the
depth, the breadth of all that life's eternal desolation . . . To rear
up at the slightest hint of death along the way, like a horse when
it changes direction. To find my aunts alive again. Yes, I have
that power. And I cling to it with all my might. To make the most
of this sudden burst of strength.

Whatever else, to keep from standing trial! Not right away!
Postponed, delayed. Then taking the offensive. Making accusations of your own. Raising your right hand and saying: "I swear."
Saying: "Antoine Tassy is the guilty one!" Under oath. Repeating: "He's the one who . . ."

"The child's not happy. You can see how thin she is. The air
in Kamouraska must be bad for her."

"And her hair! Did you see her hair? So dull, so woolly."

"Yes, we'll have to wash her hair. And give it a rinse with
camomile."

My mother joins her sisters. Four virtuous ladies of excellent background, assembled to condemn Antoine Tassy to death. So much black, so much mourning. And the blinding white of collars, cuffs, and bonnets. Bare hands lying flat on their laps. Rosaries entwined about their feeble wrists.

I'm telling them about my life in Kamouraska. Crying. Sobbing. Dissolving in tears. Twisting my hair. Biting my fingers.

My mother is the first to speak. Breaks the heavy silence that follows my story. Pulls off her rosary. Rubs her wrist, like a prisoner whose handcuffs have just been removed. Says that all this praying is getting on her nerves. Tries to get back to the subject.

"It's no good for a woman to stagnate in the country with her husband."

A cloud comes over her face. Again that faraway look in her eye. Seeking, off in her distant past, a curious dream in which every married woman first gives birth to a daughter, and then becomes a widow as soon as she can.

"Too bad the child didn't have a daughter . . ."

The three little Lanouette sisters echo a sigh. Sorry too that the dynasty of solitary women isn't going to continue forever, here in the house on Rue Augusta.

WE'LL keep the child with us. Her and the children, nice and safe. As for her husband . . ."

"He can go back to his mother's in Kamouraska!"

"Eating and drinking the way he does, he won't last long!"

With this vision of a man not lasting long—an excellent solution—my dear aunts let their thoughts go running wild. Say to themselves: "Dear God, please let him die!" Then panic at having dared bring God into their wicked fancy. Quickly correct themselves. Embark on another prayer, one they can allow. At night, kneeling beside their convent beds: "Dear God, please let him repent and be con-ver-ted."

Rosaries, novenas, stations of the cross, in endless succession. Day after day. A flurry of little aunts, to and fro. Frilly bonnets tied round with ribbon bows. And rosaries clutched tight. Going from the house on Rue Augusta to the church. Casting a kind of pious spell. Thousands of sly Hail Marys, all in vain. So many poisoned darts, bouncing off Antoine Tassy's impervious heart.

"Our little Elisabeth will take her old room back, the one she slept in as a child. You, Monsieur, can sleep in the guest room . . ."

Poor saintly ladies of Rue Augusta. You really don't understand a thing. By day I'm more than willing to weep on your shoulders. To vote for the villain's death. To play the decoy, nothing more, with mournful voice and haggard eye. Set out to bring the hideous husband tumbling down.

"See what you've done . . . Your lovely little wife . . . You ought to be ashamed! . . ."

But by night, again Antoine's accomplice. Though it disgusts me to the core. Drives me mad with fright.

The bed I slept in as a child. So narrow. Made up for the final sacraments, or so it seems. White feather coverlet . . . The door is never locked. Despite my aunts and all their warnings. A man comes fumbling his way into the room. One night in three. Whenever he's not too drunk. The saintly ladies have piled up chairs out in the corridor, against my door. Just so Antoine can go bumping into them. Sometimes, with that drunken sailor's gait of his, flat on his face . . . Then a volley of foul and angry language. And I can't help laughing, frightened as I am. Sure that my dear little aunts are wide awake, crossing themselves and trembling all over. They learn so much at night. Drunkenness, blasphemy, violence, love, disdain . . .

Sometimes, at night, the child will moan and groan. In pain or pleasure. No matter, the crime is all the same. The man is guilty. He stole away the smiling, sunny little one we love. The days and months are going by. Antoine is spending his money on every whore in Sorel. He's drinking and gambling. We're all the talk of the town.

Elisabeth has been bewitched. She's under his spell. The devil must be cast out . . .

That time. That one time. A certain time of my life, moved back to, moved into like an empty shell. Enclosing me again. With the sharp little click of an oyster snapping shut. I'm forcing myself to live within this narrow space. I'm settling into the house on Rue Augusta. I'm breathing its rarefied air, an air I've already breathed before. I'm taking the steps I've already taken. There is no Madame Rolland. Not anymore. I'm Elisabeth d'Aulnières, the wife of Antoine Tassy. I'm pining away. Dying, dying. I'm waiting for someone to come and save me. I'm nineteen years old . . .

In honeyed tones my mother treats her son-in-law with feigned solicitude.

"You'll be more comfortable on the corner of the table, with those long legs of yours . . ."

Antoine gives a foolish smirk. He's just caught sight of the rabbit stew steaming on the table.

"I'll bet there's plenty of white wine in there!"

My gentle voice bounces against the intimate tête-à-tête Antoine is having with his rabbit stew.

"At least it's a change from the eels and buckwheat cakes we have in Kamouraska."

I seem to hear him chewing his every mouthful. He doesn't bother to wipe the gravy dripping down his chin.

I'm sure my mother is trying to sound pathetic now.

"I've gone to Angélique Hus and ordered Elisabeth three dresses. Some shoes too, and some chemises. Really, Monsieur, the child doesn't have a thing to wear. And the babies need new clothes, new underthings . . . And you know, Monsieur, Elisabeth is beginning to cough. She really should see a doctor . . ."

Antoine asks for another helping. Gulps it down. Then struggles to pull his legs out from under the table. With a roar.

"Elisabeth, go pack your bags. And get the children ready. I won't stay here another minute and be insulted!"

Aunt Angélique clears her throat, tries to give a little substance to her voice.

"You'll go back to Kamouraska by yourself, Monsieur. Elisabeth and the children are staying here, where we can take care of them."

"But I'm the squire of Kamouraska! I'm entitled to some respect . . . I'll go back down the river, back home where my word is law. And everyone will bow low . . . And then I'll kill myself, you hear? I'm going to kill myself, Elisabeth. In Kamouraska, on the beach . . ."

Antoine pours himself a drink. Sits there sobbing, crying his eyes out. My mother tries to catch her breath. Buries her face in a lace-trimmed handkerchief, heavy with the smell of camphor.

Antoine pretends he's leaving for Kamouraska. His leather valise, tawny brown, hastily buckled. With a white shirttail sticking out. The initials A. T. shining bright. He goes out, slams the door . . . But look, first thing in the morning, here he is, back again. Valise and all. Just as my aunts are leaving for their five o'clock mass. Antoine stands gazing at this frieze of tiny ladies, all cloaked in black and ruffled in white. He picks one out at random. Throws his arms around her. Lifts her off the ground. Kisses her on the cheeks. For a fraction of a second two little feet kick at the air.

"Well, well, Sister Adélaïde! . . . Have a good day now! Have a good mass! And pray for me, won't you? You know, I'm out of my mind, Sister Adélaïde! . . ."

Scarcely does she touch the ground when Angélique, peeved at being taken for her older sister, protests with a vengeance:

"Angélique . . . I'm Angélique . . . My name is Angélique Lanouette . . ."

Antoine sits down on his valise. Begs pardon in his humblest, most correct of tones.

"Excuse me, Sister Angélique. My mistake. But one little nun looks just like another!"

OOD morning, Madame. You slept well, I hope?"

Quick as a wink, Aurélie has put the pitcher of hot water down on the washstand, next to the flowered blue basin. Pulled the curtains open with a sharp tug. Light comes streaming in, intense, like a tide of rolling waves, breaking against my bed. I hide my face in the covers. The light is unbearable, brighter than the sun. Aurélie is mumbling as she sets my clothes out for the day.

"Can't go on living in the dark. What will be, will be. Your really big scenes are coming up, Madame. You've got to live them over out in the daylight."

The first thing I do, back in Sorel. Hire Aurélie Caron. Despite my mother's and my aunts' entreaties. To play Milady and her maid. Until . . .

"They say you have yourself a merry time, Aurélie! Down by the river, out on the islands. Is it true? Tell me, what do you do? Tell me everything! . . ."

All petticoats and ribbons and fancy shoes, the typical soubrette . . . Aurélie stands at the mirror, looks at herself, enthralled. Turns toward me. So awfully pale. That sudden yellow spark, flashing from between her eyelids. With muttered words and knowing winks. A volley of chatter. Breathless, disjointed, brazen, uncouth . . . Then voices from my solitude. My own. One confidence deserves another, tit for tat. And here I am, whispering in her ear.

"Really, you know, I'm married to a beast."

"Good God a'mighty! You mean you didn't know they're all of them like that? Sooner or later, just give them time . . ."

Aurélie squats down, fixes a fire. It's morning. I'm nineteen now. I'm combing out my long curls, rolled up around strips of white cloth for the night. Life seems so natural, so calm. And yet . . . This silence. This disagreeable feeling that I've lived it all before. Most of all, the strange appearance of the fire. A kind of curious glare, cold and still. The look of fire, but a fire with no warmth, no brilliance . . . The linen bedsheets with their openwork borders. The fine weave of the cloth, so sharp and clear, as if magnified under a glass. The table by the bed, with its marble top. I'm sure I could trace out each one of the little black veins, follow them as they split and splinter their way along, smaller and smaller.

It's not so much the clear precision of things themselves that staggers me now. It's just that I'm forced, with every part of my being, to pay such close attention. Nothing, nothing must escape me. The real life, hidden beneath the past . . . There, tiny pinpricks all over the bedstead. Insect bites in the worm-eaten wood. Everything in the room has been gnawed away. Still standing by some kind of miracle. Already crumbled. Put back together just for this one blinding moment. Everything so precise, so clear . . .

This stillness mustn't last. Or else it will spread its rot to every fragment of life around me. Weigh them all down in one great, final, ponderous silence.

I turn toward the impudent person standing there in front of me, stock-still, watching. A strange smile frozen against her teeth, stained with tobacco.

"Speak to me, Aurélie. Say something. Anything at all. Only speak . . ."

Aurélie raises her voice, forces it a little as if she were playing a part. Pretends to be talking to someone behind the wall.

"Oh, Madame! Good God a'mighty! Look at that mark on your arm, all black and blue!"

"Don't shout like that, Aurélie. Please, not so loud. Someone might hear you! . . ."

"Oh, the things Monsieur does to you, Madame! I'll go tell the cook. I'll go tell the governess. I'll go tell Madame d'Aulnières and her three little sisters. I'll go tell the judges if I have to."

"Stop it, Aurélie! Stop shouting like that! I'm so ashamed! If you only knew . . ."

"No need to be ashamed for a thing like that! Better to get ourselves pinched a little than never to have a man at all, don't you know! And as far as being ashamed . . . Well, you'd better get used to it now. It's just beginning. The worst is yet to come."

NOW no more looking. No more being looked at. I push Aurélie aside. Storm out of my old room in the house on Rue Augusta. Go running down the stairs. Lifting my skirts high up off the floor . . . Now in the hall again. The outside door is shut, locked tight. The kitchen door too. Quick, the backstairs. There's a door in the attic. Must be a ladder down to the courtyard . . . Up on the second floor. Can't find the attic stairs. All the doors are shut. All but one. The one I forgot to close when I went dashing out. The room I slept in as a child. Pretty, all pink and white . . . I plunge inside, almost as if I were pushed in from behind. The bed has been changed, made up with care. (Though I've only been gone for a moment.) And the covers turned down. My mother is standing beside it. Telling me I'm sick and I have to go to bed. I shy away, look toward the door. Aurélie is there, blocking my escape . . . I obey my mother. Take off my clothes. Put on a chemise, trimmed with lace, set out for the occasion. And all the while my mother keeps assuring me that the doctor will be here any minute . . . Aurélie and her rollicking laugh. Rippling . . . She comes in now with a basin of hot water. A big round cake of perfumed soap. And a napkin made of Irish linen. My mother speaks to her.

"Put it down there, Aurélie. It's for the doctor."

Sophie Langlade is here too. And Justine Latour. They're bringing me my slippers and my robe. Then a voice I can't quite recognize.

"Now let's reconstruct the facts the best we can, day by day."

Aurélie Caron, Sophie Langlade, and Justine Latour are standing against the wall. My husband appears in the doorway. I'm sure that's who it is. My mother is still standing by my bed. My aunts are sitting on the couch, pressed close to one another.

It seems to me my bed is higher than it ought to be. Raised up on some kind of platform, or so it seems. With great shafts of light falling from the ceiling, above my head. It's as if I'm lying on an operating table. My mother, clutching my wrist, holding me down . . . Please, not an operation. Not a real one. This sickness inside me, plucked out like a violet. This hidden tumor . . . The silence is unbearable. I close my eyes.

My husband, Antoine Tassy, announcing in his booming voice:

"Doctor George Nelson. Elisabeth, I'd like you to meet an old school friend of mine. Haven't seen him in years, and now suddenly I find him here in Sorel . . ."

I insist that all the servants leave the room at once, even Aurélie. I ask my aunts to do the same. They go out, reluctantly. Beg me, with tears in their voices, to let at least one person stay. Sophie Langlade, whose testimony will be so important for my defense. My mother pulls the covers up around my chin. Now Sophie Langlade steps forward, trembling all over. So violently that she can hardly put one foot in front of the other. She takes her oath on the Bible, then says her piece. So softly the judge has to make her repeat.

"Madame was never alone in her room with Doctor Nelson. Her mother, Madame d'Aulnières, was always with her."

All at once Aurélie's laugh chills me to the bone. It's coming from somewhere inside the house. Piercing the walls. Loud enough to be heard outside. That drill-like voice, higher than any human voice should be. She's speaking now, so painfully slowly. As if the words had to be pulled out one by one. I can hear her in my room.

"I swear, Madame spent a lot of time alone with the doctor. With the doors closed. As soon as her mother went out."

Sophie Langlade has left the room. A moment later, a man's step, coming down the corridor. Steady, self-assured. With something childlike about it. Light-hearted and confident.

I can sense, to my horror, that it's all about to happen. And that nothing on earth can stop it now from happening again, a second time. Once more I close my eyes . . . Antoine Tassy is talking to George Nelson, just outside my room. Now he shuts the door, goes off, strides down the corridor. My husband, deserting me. I'm sure that in his heart of hearts he goes along with everything that's going to happen. I recognize his voice. Deadened, as if through great wads of cotton. (The cotton they use to stuff the mouths of corpses with.) He must have shut himself up in the dining room.

"I'll let him examine her first. Then we'll get something to drink for my dear old classmate from those days with the priests in Quebec . . ."

I wish I could forget that dining room. Forget that it ever existed. That room in Sorel where my husband sits entrenched. His clumsy form sprawled motionless against a table leg. Let them rip that room out of my memory. Hack it to bits, slash it, saw it apart. Like a crate tossed overboard into the water. Let them take Antoine and sew him up inside a sheet. Him and his rabbit stew, his brandy, his schoolboy memories, his lord-and-master air, his big, brutish fists. His fits of anger and his crocodile tears.

[103]

ME, Elisabeth d'Aulnières, here in bed, lying sick. The light still hurts my eyes. I feel it burning, like red-hot needles, under the lids shut tight. The way it feels when you lift your face to the sun in the noonday heat. And the curious height of the bed disturbs me too. I've sworn to close my eyes and keep them closed. To try somehow to escape from my body. My feelings, my heart . . . An emptiness beyond belief. An emptiness hard to bear and still go on living. But I won't give in. By now another woman would be dead and buried . . . All right, they're making me live those days again. Those days when I first met George Nelson. Well and good. But all they'll find is a disembodied spirit. One of those ghostly souls, roaming about with the bats, and haunting the attics of unknown houses.

I do exactly what he tells me. Three times he listens to my chest. Three times I cough. I take a deep breath . . . Deep breaths, there's the rub. They lull me, make me drop my guard. I run the risk of seeing my life come galloping back full tilt. Come looming up, invading my frozen flesh once more. I hold it off, defend myself against it with this emptiness. I do what he tells me, just like an automaton. My every move directed by this doctor, this total stranger. He pokes an infallible finger in my back. Along my ribs.

He listens with care, through a delicate napkin, to hear what's going on inside my body. He hears the beating of an empty heart. His manly head against my breast. His hair, so full. His beard. His whiskers, not too thick . . . No, no! I'm not seeing any of this, not really feeling it at all. None of the substance, the shapes, the colors! None of the pleasure! My life is somewhere else. Secluded, off in some dim, deserted place. A kind of countryside, lying unused, abandoned, where terror casts its shadow-silhouettes.

Above our heads the silence stretches taut, like an impending storm. At last the doctor straightens up. Stops bending over me. A feeling of great relief spreads through the room. My mother goes over, stands by George Nelson's side. She seems almost happy. This first encounter has gone off very well. The judges must be really disappointed. No fault to find with how this man and woman have behaved.

The doctor is talking with my mother. I catch a few words. "Anemic . . . pregnancies too close together . . . weakness in the lungs . . ." People speaking out in the corridor. Whispering, laughing. Heaving great sighs. Pouring them out, the way they do when a terrible danger is over. Then all at once the doctor leaves the room.

I think I'm stretching now, under the covers. A long, delightful stretch, from head to toe. I want to get up . . . Now I'm sitting on the edge of the bed, my feet dangling out of my long chemise, kicking the air. As if to test some imaginary stream and see how cold the water is . . . I'm innocent!

The reprieve doesn't last. The signal! I'm sure there's been a signal. Out I come, slowly, a little at a time. Out of the safety of my dazed confusion. No high, shrill whistle. No nun with her clapper, calling for order. No fire, no smoke. And yet, there's been a signal! It's in the air, filling the very air I breathe. The alarm! No help for it now. The alarm has been given. And it's all beginning again. No place to run to. I have to go on, pick up the thread. Play out the second scene with the doctor. I can't escape it, can't say I'm too tired. The witnesses, already here. All of them, coming in one by one, so stiff and solemn. Striking the pose . . .

My mother puts me to bed. Pulls up the covers and tucks me in. My aunts sit down on the couch. Whimper a little. Sophie Langlade keeps trembling. Justine Latour stands wide-eyed, gaping. Somebody says that it's all so foolish, that reenactments like this have never really done much good. Aurélie picks up her blue basin, her Irish linen napkin, and her big cake of perfumed soap. She squints, as if in the blinding sun. Seems to be getting more and more excited.

"We're all here now. Except for Madame's first husband, that is. And he's so full of brandy he can't get up out of his chair. Too bad. What will be, will be . . ."

I tell Aurélie to leave. Her and the pair of slippered acolytes by her side. Suddenly they disappear in a jumble of little white aprons, all crumpled and askew. The three of them. Aurélie Caron, Sophie Langlade, Justine Latour. My aunts don't wait to be told. They leave by themselves, abashed and despairing.

And so I'm alone with my mother again, as she takes her stance at the head of my bed. An arm stretched out along the black wooden frame. The sheer, transparent oversleeve, falling in pleats, flaring about her shoulder like a wing. Stately and solemn, like an angel sculpted on a holy font, she waits for her daughter Elisabeth's second encounter with Doctor Nelson.

An incredible calm seems to pervade the house. Yet every witness has taken his place, here in this mansion in Sorel. And each one seems to be going about his business, doing his daily chores. But better not be taken in. I'm sure they've all been assigned their roles. Spies and informers, all of them. Except for my dear little aunts, of course, sick to death just thinking of all those lies they're going to swear to.

[106]

The first one, Justine Latour. Hanging the wash to dry, behind the house. Wet towels in hand, she shakes them out, flaps them sharply in the breeze to signal the doctor's arrival. Three times, loud and clear. To let His Honor, John Crebessa, know that it's all beginning.

My husband, Antoine Tassy, comes next. He sees Justine Latour and her signal. Comes back from the farthest ends of the earth, from the farthest reaches of death itself. Plays his part. Tries to cup his hands and shout.

"Someone be sure to tell me when the doctor comes. I want to get something to drink for my dear old . . ."

Doctor Nelson doesn't stop in the drawing room. He climbs the stairs. Goes straight to my door. A sharp little rap. He comes in . . . Now he's standing in my room, a small black satchel in his hand. This time I can see him very clearly. I steal a glance when no one is looking. Especially at his neck, when he turns to say something to my mother. That slender neck, with its air of determination, brisk and bold . . . His eyes. Yes, I think it's on the second visit that I look at his eyes. Black. An awesome light, burning. Aimed at me . . . I turn my head. Let it toss on the pillow. From side to side. Again and again. Like a whining, wailing little child. As if I would deny the fire that already consumes me.

Now he's noticing some bruises on my arm. Mutters in outraged tones.

"Good Heavens, you're hurt. But who . . . ?"

The space of a second. No more than a second. And the life I've driven away comes galloping back. Makes up for lost time, in that single moment. My defenses crumble like a house of cards. I throw my arms around his neck. This stranger with his smell of fresh tobacco. I don't seem to care that this is just what the judge is waiting to see. The one thing he wants me to do before he can direct his questions. Nothing can stop me. Nothing and no one.

[107]

Not even my pride. I have to go racing headlong to my doom. It can't be helped. The scandal has to break . . . I'm bursting into tears now, can't hold back the flood. Between two gasps I manage to tell him how miserable I am. Misunderstand his angry look. Think he must be objecting to my behavior. Frightened, I pull my arms away.

My mother complains that this scene is really out of order. She's whispering to the doctor. Careful not to look him in the face.

"My daughter is a very nervous child. You must forgive her. And . . . Oh, yes, about her arm . . . She bumped into a table, or a chair, or something. We're so awfully cluttered here, you know . . ."

The doctor gives her a withering glance. Leaves the room without a word. A moment later Aurélie comes back. Still loaded down with her basin, her napkin, her round cake of soap. She seems beside herself.

"The doctor didn't even wash his hands!"

She drops the soap, watches it roll along the floor. Doesn't think to pick it up. Stands there, transfixed. Filled with a kind of envy. An envy mixed with fear, some vague preoccupation. I see the look come over her face, catch the first glimmers of that curious fascination that's going to be her downfall.

"Say what you want, love really can take your breath away, Madame! And that affair of yours . . . You and Doctor Nelson! . . . Well, I never will get over it, believe you me! . . ."

THE woman who's been nursing my second son has suddenly gone dry. She weeps and whimpers. Swears it's all the doctor's fault. Says that he's put a curse on her.

"He's got the blackest eyes. And he stares at you so. Why, the minute he first came near me to look the baby over, when I had him in my arms . . . Well, I felt like a shock . . ."

Aurélie, in no time, has spread the word all over Sorel that this Doctor Nelson is some kind of American devil who goes about casting spells on women's breasts. The way some witches poison the water.

Aunt Adélaïde claims that on Sundays this Doctor Nelson shows up at mass. Even though everyone knows he used to be a Protestant.

Aunt Luce-Gertrude mutters under her breath that the strangest part of it all is the way this Doctor Nelson lives. Out in the country, in a little backwoods cottage. Lives like a settler. And the whole two years he's been in Sorel, young as he is, he absolutely refuses to meet the proper people, mix in the right society . . .

My husband, on the other hand, speaks of George Nelson in a kind of strangely distant, almost childish voice. A voice I've never heard him use before.

[109]

"In school . . . To have had a real friend . . . He's the one I would have chosen . . ."

A blue eye, clouded over with the mist of childhood memories. I turn my head, say that I'm sick. Call for the doctor. He hasn't come to see me since . . . My husband insists that I'm not sick at all.

My mother goes back to having her headaches and shuts herself up in her widowhood again. As if my fate has been sealed now for good. My aunts take on that cringing, anguished look that pets have when they sense a crisis brewing in the house.

I could still escape. Not force the rest to happen. Make contact again with Rue du Parloir. Just open my eyes. Cup my hands and shout: "I'm Madame Rolland!"

Too late! It's too late. The past, remembered, cuts open its veins. My mad youth wraps itself over my bones. I step in its tracks. The way you fit your feet in your very own footprints, walking along the wet, sandy shore. Again, crossing through murder and death. Touching the bottom, the depths of despair. Well, what's the difference? As long as I find my love once more. And find him well. Bursting with life. Pressing his head against my breast. Worried about how much I must be suffering. Outraged, raising his voice: "Good Heavens, you're hurt. But who . . . ?" I'm fingering the watch chain now that hangs across George Nelson's waist. I'm breathing deep the odor of his vest. Much more than pity, I want to find anger in his heart.

"Theatre, that's all it is!" proclaims my mother-in-law, with clear disdain.

As if I were waiting just for that cue, I make my entrance. I use the word "I," and yet I'm someone else. Off with the venerable garb of Madame Rolland! Trampled underfoot. Off with her sacrosanct whalebone stays! Thrown to the winds. Off to the museum with her plaster mask! I laugh and I cry now, unashamed. I'm wearing a pair of pink openwork stockings, a great

[110]

wide belt just under my breasts. I'm letting myself go. I'm living my life in fever and folly, as if they were my native land. I'm in love with a man who's not my husband. This man I keep calling for. Daytime. Nighttime. Doctor Nelson, Doctor Nelson . . . His absence, more than I can bear. I'm going to die. He hasn't come back since the day I put my arms around his neck. Doctor Nelson, I'm so awfully unhappy. Doctor Nelson, Doctor Nelson . . .

"The doctor is out, Madame. The little boy doesn't know when he'll be in."

"He's doing it on purpose! I'm sure he's doing it on purpose! Go back, Aurélie. Go get him. Tell him I'm sick. Make him come with you. He has to, do you hear? He has to . . ."

Aurélie leaves, goes off against her will. I choke back my tears. I gasp. I toss and turn. I threaten to fling myself out the window . . . Finally, exhausted, sinking down into a heavy sleep, I dream that someone is calling me. Urgently, pathetically. A strange force seems to lift me from my bed. Wakes me with a start. Sends me running to the window. My eyes open wide. My heart pounding fast . . . I listen to the sound of a horse's hooves, trotting off in the distance. Turn around and face the utter chaos of my room. The crumpled bedclothes . . . That feeling, like falling through the vastness of space. My head swimming . . . I struggle back to my bed.

"We'd better send for another doctor. The child is really sick." "The first thing to do is keep that husband of hers away from her . . ." "Yes, he's the one. It's all his fault . . ." "Send him back to Kamouraska . . ." "Or at least make sure he doesn't go near her." "Have the servants guard her door and keep him out . . ." "Stay up all night if we have to . . ." "As long as there's breath in my body, he won't get by that door . . ." "He'll have to kill me first . . ." "Maybe get some legal advice from Maître Lafontaine . . ." "A separation, that's the only way . . ."

My husband goes about, telling anyone he can find to listen

that my aunts are three old hags, and that they ought to be done away with.

Every night he passes by my windows. With his black horse, his black sleigh. I'm sure that's who it is. For hours I lie waiting, in the silence of the night, listening for the horse's hoofbeats, the scraping of the sleigh along the snow. Long before they can be heard by any other mortal ear. I pick up the scent as soon as he leaves the little wooden cottage. Way at the other end of Sorel. (The sleigh bells are already laid away, carefully, under the seat.) I don't dare get up now and run to the window. I just lie curled up in my bed. I wait for him to go by. And I listen, filled with despair. Listen, as long as I can, to the sounds of the horse and sleigh, vanishing into the night.

I can't go on this way. One day I'll go find him. And I'll say to him, with a haughty air: "Well, doctor, is this how you let your patients waste away and die? Don't you even try to save them? . . . Doctor Nelson, I've gone mad. Doctor Nelson . . ."

"Elisabeth! Why don't you answer me? That's the second time I've asked you the same question."

You shouldn't be so insistent, Aunt Adélaïde. My mind is taken up, you know. Day and night. Watching the growth of a giant living plant, spreading within me. Ripping me to shreds, devouring me. Yes, I'm possessed.

I have my one idea. Like those lunatics they put away. The ones whose minds seem gone, completely. Locked up, in chains. Still clinging, in their little world, to the wild, demented specter of their one idea . . . I never leave my bed now. Just lie there, tossing and turning, or sometimes too tired to move. Laying down rules for myself to follow if I want to be happy. Not to try to see Doctor Nelson for a time. To begin by making perfectly sure I'm not pregnant. Keep myself utterly pure. Fight off my husband if he ever tries to come near me. Wash myself clean of Antoine forever. Cleanse my body of every last trace of his tenderness, his violence. Even the very memory of . . . Be born again, into a new life. Untouched and untouchable. For everyone except the one, the only man in this world, coming to get me . . . Passionate, pure, innocent! I'm innocent! Waiting for my love to come and take me, to keep me by his side forever. My one and only joy, this man. The law itself . . .

I'm sleeping in Aunt Luce-Gertrude's room now. Pretending to be like a little child. So utterly well-behaved. Patiently waiting to have my period . . . I hate Antoine when he's had too much to drink. I hate him when he's sober. I laugh, I cry, for no reason at all. I feel so strange, as light as a bubble . . .

"My wife is a bitch!"

Antoine gets furious when I sleep with Aunt Luce-Gertrude. One night he knocks down the servant guarding the door. Tries to come over to my bed. I scream and scream. A kind of rattle, rasping deep in my throat. Some awful mechanism set in motion. Out of control. Nothing human about it now. Choking me. Filling me with horror . . . The flash of a razor blade, just for an instant, right at my throat. Aunt Luce-Gertrude insists that Antoine had it in his pocket. But I'm not sure. I can't be sure of anything. The blade might have been in the room all the time. Hanging by a thread, over my bed, for all eternity.

Disarmed, shown the door, thrown out. Antoine leaves the house on Rue Augusta. Goes running off to Horse Marine, to nestle his head in her stinking Irish lap and weep. Swears to stay with her for good, to forget his wife. That scrawny Horse Marine. So thin that when she lifts her arms you can count her ribs. Like the skeleton of a ship.

One morning I wake up. There, between my thighs, the trickle of blood that will set me free. The sign. Unmistakable. Now never again will a child of Antoine's come to life in my womb. Never take root. Never choose itself a sex, a face, deep in the darkness. I'm free now. Barren. As if no man had ever touched me. A few more days and I'll be pure again. And free . . .

[113]

MUST go see the doctor. Nothing in this world can stop me. Nothing and no one. I've told Aurélie what I plan to do. She glows with a look of grim delight. Pretends to be obeying me against her will. Grumbles a little, then says yes, she'll take me. Says she'll drive the horses herself. Fixes my hair and helps me dress, without a word. Absorbed in a kind of strange, almost religious reverie. Brings me my fur coat, my shawls, those fur-lined mittens of Antoine's. Then goes to dress the children.

Wrapped in my furs, I'm shivering, shaking . . . All at once I rip the mittens off, fling them out into the snow. Feel a tremendous relief at what I've done. Thrust my hands into my muff. Cheerfully. Dream of throwing all of Antoine's things away. Lost forever, strewn about the countryside. His pipes, his bottles, his guns, his jackets, his shirts, his belts, his suspenders . . . How heavy the children feel in my arms. Antoine's blue eyes, twice over. A sudden spasm shakes my body, wakes little Louis, sleeping on my lap. Starts him crying . . .

And right and left it's "Good morning, Madame Tassy!" . . . "And how are you, Madame Tassy? . . ."

The folks in Sorel are out to see you, Madame Tassy. And the ones outside of town. To watch you go riding by, all pale and trembling, with that wild-eyed look of yours. You and your little blond babies, with their rosy-apple cheeks. A perfect alibi. No need to worry.

The long blue shadows on the snow fade into the spreading darkness. We've reached the doctor's house. Ever so gently the children pass from my arms to Aurélie's. Go back to sleep. I step down from the carriage, alone.

A voice, loud and clear, is asking me in . . . Here in the waiting room now. An old horsehair sofa. Plain wooden walls, unfinished, covered with knots. A small cast-iron stove, round and black, standing on giant twisted legs . . . I'm waiting for the doctor to finish with his patient.

Behind the partition, the sounds of people moving here and there, huffing and puffing. A jumble of footsteps. Muffled gasps. As if two men were wrestling with each other . . . I try to fix all my attention on the stove in the middle of the room. Amuse myself trying to read the fancy letters entwined with garlands of flowers embossed on the metal. Make out the name "Warm Morning" . . .

Suddenly, a scream from behind the wooden partition. Then a long groan. And a chilling, seemingly endless silence. A few moments later, barely audible, the rustle of cloth being rolled up carefully and put away . . . At last, the door opens. A young boy steps out, his arm in a sling. Moving so slowly, he seems ready to fall with every step he takes. He turns his pallid face in my direction, streaming with tears. Studies me long and hard. A kind of quizzical, melancholy look. Lost in wonder. He staggers a little. The doctor has to take him by the shoulders and help him to the door.

George Nelson is in his shirt-sleeves. Cuffs rolled up. Hair disheveled, as if he were just getting out of bed. His movements, quick and precise. Energetic. He casts a suspicious glance my way, then strides off into the kitchen. Takes the lamp with him

[115]

. . . I'm alone in the darkness. The doctor is washing his hands and face. Great loud splashes of water under the pump . . . He's coming back now, rolling down his sleeves, face dripping. Mopping his brow with his handkerchief. Looks me in the eye. A strange, insistent stare, not very polite.

"I had to break that youngster's arm so I could set it for him right. Some butcher went and set the bones all wrong. Really, this place is crawling with charlatans! Everywhere. Ignorance, no matter where you look. Quackery, superstition . . . It's a scandal, that's what it is! We should keep those medicine men from going around killing people. Give everyone proper care, whether they want it or not! Keep your girl Aurélie from doing her magic tricks on newborn babies! . . ."

The white of his shirt, flashing. He holds up the lamp to his face, furrowed and gaunt. Never at rest. Seething with rage . . . I look at him, watch for each spark of life flickering across his swarthy face. I listen to his every word. As if I myself were the object of all this angry passion. Waiting for its secret meaning to be revealed. To turn on me, forever. To shower me with the holy wrath he feels . . . My, my, Doctor Nelson. How you're looking at me! No peace in that look, Doctor Nelson. The blade of battle . . . That sudden pallor. That fever in your eyes. It must be the lamp. That dark shadow over your cheeks . . .

"Is there something strange about me, Madame Tassy? Something that makes you look at me that way? Do you think I go around casting spells? Do you really think I can put the curse on a woman's milk?"

He laughs. A dry little laugh that sets me on edge.

"To what do I owe the honor of your visit? I suppose you're here about Antoine?"

I tell him "no." If the answer were yes, I would have said "yes." No word seems short or sharp enough to do away with all the useless chatter between us.

[116]

"You mean to tell me nobody sent you? You've come here on your own?"

I tell him "yes." But this time I'd like to go on, to say more. To explain myself. Defend myself . . . An odd, sardonic little something in George Nelson's smile—or rather in the whiteness of his teeth—staggers me to the very depths of my being. Won't let another word pass my lips.

He raises the lamp over his head. Asks me to follow him. Shows me around the house.

"Now that you've looked me over, take a good look at the house. Everything perfectly normal, you see? Just a nice little country cottage, like any other. Except for the books, that is. But I'm sure you're not one to go thinking that just because I have some books . . ."

Several square, half-furnished little rooms. Looking so painfully like wooden crates. White, rough, full of splinters. Books on shelves, books on the kitchen table, books piled high on the floor, books used to prop up a massive cupboard.

"Did Antoine tell you about me? Did he tell you how we used to play chess at school? I think he used to like to lose. He never could beat me. Never. Not even once, you hear?"

He's raising his voice again. Almost defiantly. Then suddenly, silent. Becomes very sullen. Withdraws within himself. Drifts off without so much as a by-your-leave. Absorbed, I imagine, in a silent, skillful game of chess, with a young blond fellow, beaten before he starts. I have to bring him back. Quickly. Break up this ghostly game . . . I love you wildly, madly, Doctor Nelson. Please, let me go with you. Cross the stream, back to your childhood. Back to the source. Flowing there, to my chagrin, all intermingled with Antoine's . . .

My legs are shaking. A shudder rocks my body from head to toe. I'm clutching the back of the sofa to keep from falling.

[117]

"I've come to see you, Doctor Nelson. Aren't you going to ask me how I am?"

With one bound he's beside me. Makes me sit down on the sofa. Goes to the kitchen. Brings me a glass of water. Paces back and forth. Takes my pulse. Unnerved. Distraught.

"Not ask you how you are? Good God, poor child! Seeing you bruised and tortured the way you were . . . Do you think I've thought of anything else since then? . . . Not ask you how you are, poor thing . . . For goodness' sake, why did you marry Antoine Tassy? Why? Tell me why . . . You're looking better despite the way he . . . I took good care of you, didn't I? I'm a good doctor, don't you think? . . ."

"You know how miserable I am . . ."

His whole face quivers. He speaks in a whisper. Won't look me in the eye. Pushes me away. His words, one by one. Like stones.

"There's nothing I can do for you, Madame Elisabeth. I'm a total stranger . . ."

Our giant shadows on the wall, so far from each other. A kind of emptiness, digging its way between us. Silence. Space . . . George is leaving me behind again. How can I catch him? I'm weighted down. Oppressed. Bound hand and foot. Prisoner of Rue Augusta and the town of Sorel . . . Oh, to break my bonds. Recapture my childhood, strong and free. That little girl within me, with the close-cropped hair, climbing out the window. Running off to join her nasty gang . . . What should I do, Doctor Nelson? Tell me. One word from you and I'll obey. Cut off all my hair again? Is that what I should do? Run away? Leave my house, my children? . . . Out of this world, if that's what you want. That's how far I'll go to meet you. Free, an entity unto myself. A stranger to everyone and everything but you . . .

"And you don't think I'm a total stranger too? . . ."

He turns aside.

"You don't know what you're saying."

"More than you think . . ."

Silence. Again, a wall between us, smooth and hard. His school-days, that flimsy defense, hurriedly dredged up out of the past.

"I never had any friends at all. Not as a student, not later either . . . But I used to like to play chess with Antoine Tassy . . ."

"And I suppose that's why you go riding past my windows every night?"

This time he looks me right in the eye. Furious. Mortified. Like a child caught doing something naughty.

"You shouldn't have said that, Madame Elisabeth. You shouldn't have. Really, there's nothing I hate more than being found out . . ."

$\mathbf{M}$ADAME Elisabeth" . . . He called me by my name. For the first time. I look down at my lap to hide my delight. Bend over my needlework. Careful not to look at my mother or my aunts. A quiet evening at home on Rue Augusta. "Petit point is done in two steps, diagonally across the canvas. First a vertical stitch, one row down, from left to right. Then a horizontal stitch, from right to left, up the next row. With a wool three strands thick, following the mesh . . ."

The green felt covering on the study table, slashed with knife marks here and there. That ever-present odor of sour cabbage. Mass, evensong, vespers, Rogation Days, Lent, Holy Week. (My knees!) The chalk scraping over the blackboard, the teacher's cane coming down on ink-stained hands. The barrack-room smell of the dormitory. The ice that has to be broken every morning in the pitchers. The tearful look on Antoine's face, bending over a basin filled with floating chunks . . . My, my, Master Nelson, the way you're staring at that big, fat, miserable lad! Why are you turning away? Is it out of pity? . . .

"Protestants can't get into Heaven, into Heaven . . ." Fifteen young fellows, chanting with ferocious glee. The gaunt, dark youth they're teasing is wearing a muffler full of holes and an old sealskin cap. Rumor has it he's a foreigner. No family. He's learning French and studying to become a Catholic. But neither one with very much enthusiasm. Père Foucas is fed up with all his arrogance and disrespect. One day he gives him a thrashing with a hockey stick. Beats him within an inch of his life. But George doesn't make a sound. Not even a whimper. There, Master Tassy. That rugged strength, that's what you lack. That strength, so fascinating and yet so offensive. Two young fellows without a thing in common. Except in the deep recesses of their souls. A silent, premature experience with despair.

Which one first challenges the other to a game of chess? And anyway, the games have already been acted out. The winner and loser chosen in advance. Who can presume to change the course of fate? Recess after recess. Year after year. The same stubborn silence. The same complicity. Through endless games of chess.

"Checkmate!"

Flushed with victory, this youngster with the rough and cracking voice . . . Doctor Nelson, is that you? One day that voice of yours will change, grow deep, and win me over, body and soul . . .

With a sweep of his hand, Antoine clears the pieces off the board. They fall to the floor. Nasty loser. Nasty child. No one can match him when it comes to fiendish tricks. Like blowing up little green frogs, from the pond, with smoke from his pipe, and making them burst. And that great, shattering laugh of his.

"Nelson, you're cheating! . . ."

I keep my jealous watch. Beyond all time. No thought here of any conventional reality. I have that power. I'm Madame Rolland and I know it all. From the very beginning, I play my part in the lives of these two ill-starred young men. Presiding over their friendship with great delight. A friendship destined never to exist between George Nelson and Antoine Tassy.

I LIE in wait, listening in vain for a horse's hoofbeat, the sound of a sleigh. Can it be that he won't come back, won't come prowling anymore beneath my windows? One moment he calls me "Madame Elisabeth." And the next, he rejects me. Runs away. I never should have told him about those nights, leaning out the window, when I . . . The look he gave me! That piercing glance. Like a cornered beast.

Now he shuts himself up in his house. Locks and bars the doors, like a criminal. And I venture as close to his solitude as I can. Provoking him, bedeviling him. The way he provokes and bedevils me.

"That man's a foreigner. It's better not to trust him, anymore than he trusts us."

"Quiet, Aurélie . . . Go away. I'm much too busy . . ."

I'm concentrating. Closing my eyes. As if I were trying to conjure up the spirits. And yet, it's life I'm after. Life . . . Over there, at the other end of Sorel. A man, all alone, leaning on a kitchen table. A book lying open in front of him, not a page moving . . . Standing over him, reading over his shoulder. Trying to work my way down into the innermost recesses of his daydreams . . .

[122]

They won't let you out of their sight, Master Nelson. They follow wherever you go. Protestants are all a pack of . . . And your weatherbeaten old sealskin cap.

The man who makes foolish little mistakes in his French gives himself away. The man who speaks of "the Bible" instead of "the Holy Gospels" gives himself away. The man who says "Madame Elisabeth" instead of "Madame Tassy" is sure to compromise himself and her as well.

How wonderfully selfless. To choose medicine as a calling. Compassion, spread open like a wound. You should find that very comforting. Fighting evil and illness and witches the way you do, all with the very same zeal. Why is it, then, when you do so much good, that nobody here really likes you? They're afraid of you, Doctor Nelson. As if, under all that obvious selflessness of yours —too obvious, perhaps—some fearsome identity lies hidden . . . That original flaw, deeper than your Protestant religion, deeper than your English language . . . Look. Look hard. It's not a sin, Doctor Nelson. Only some terrible grief.

Turned out of your father's house. His house with its white columns, its colonial façade. Like thieves. You, your brother, your sister. Three innocent little children. And your father sends you off, like thieves. And your mother, pressing her face against the window, crying. In Montpelier. In Vermont.

This American independence is really too much for good loyalists to bear. Isn't it better to pack the children off to Canada? Send them away before this new spirit pollutes and infects them? Let them even become Catholics. Even learn French if they have to. Anything, just so long as they keep their allegiance to the British crown . . .

"You don't know my brother and sister, do you, Madame Elisabeth? You really should. You'll see how very much alike we are, ever since we all turned Catholic . . ."

One day, my love, you'll call me just "Elisabeth." No more

formalities at all between us. You'll tell me how your sister Cathy went with the Ursulines when she was fifteen. You'll talk about her Roman nose, her cheeks, all covered with freckles. And you'll tell me about your brother Henry, the Jesuit, and those impressive retreats he preaches . . .

You're groping for my body in the darkness. Your words are strange. Time ceases to exist. No one but me to hear them. We're naked, lying together for all eternity. And you murmur something against my shoulder.

"And I swore I'd be a saint, Elisabeth! I swore, do you hear? And never, never in my life did I yearn for anything else so much . . ."

Once again, a studious young man bent over his books, in a wooden house. And the words going round and round in his head, mocking him: "Mustn't get caught! No matter what, but mustn't get caught!" . . . You jump to your feet, put away your books. Put on your coat, your cap, your mittens. Every movement so precise, and yet so quick. Like a doctor hurrying off to see his patients . . . He knows that, this time too, he'll hitch up his horses and go prowling the streets of Sorel, even at the risk of being . . . Back and forth, maybe a good ten times, in front of Madame Tassy's windows . . . In the hope and fear—both at once, so utterly intertwined—of seeing the wicked husband, thrown out of his wife's house, suddenly appear on the corner of the street. Take careful aim at him. Shoot him down like a partridge. The born loser, Antoine Tassy. "Whosoever hath not, from him shall be taken away even that he hath." I'll take his rook. I'll take his queen. I'll take his wife. It has to be. How can I bear the thought of . . . A woman, so lovely, so pathetic. Being tortured, humiliated . . . Lying next to Antoine, beaten by Antoine, caressed by Antoine, opened and shut by Antoine, raped by Antoine, ravished by Antoine . . . I'll bring back justice the way it used to be. The law of the victor and the vanquished . . . In a flash, a sudden glimpse of being in tune, at one with yourself. Something tried over

[124]

and over again, since the mind can remember. Finding yourself, deep in the marrow of your bones, completely yourself. Admitting at last the sickness within you. The frenzied yearning to possess the world.

Possess this woman. Possess the earth.

I call to George Nelson. Yes, I'm the one who calls out to him through the darkness. The voice of passion seeks us out, lords it over us, lays us low. One thing that must be done. Only one. Let ourselves both be damned forever. Each with the other. Each by the other. And me, the malicious and sinister stranger . . .

IS this what sleeping will be like from now on? A couple of hours, at best, racked by horrible dreams?

A wooden cabin, standing in the middle of a flat, deserted landscape. Off on the horizon, the edge of the forest. The cabin is filled with people. All of them worried about some little pet of theirs that's roaming loose. Such frightful things will happen to it unless they find a way to bring it back right now. Everyone turns and looks at me. Everyone, without exception. They beg me to "call" the animal home. And I'm struck with terror. I know what they mean by "call." I know the awesome power I possess, and it makes me shudder . . . From every side they press me, urge me on. Every second could mean the death of the little creature still on the loose out there . . .

A cry escapes my lips. (This power of mine won't let me hold it back.) A cry so harsh, so terrible, that it tears at my chest and leaves me stunned, transfixed. Echoes on and on all through the countryside. I can't make it stop, can't keep it from surging and swelling, out of control . . . Suddenly all the beasts are on the move. The wildest beasts of the forest and plain. Swooping down, attacking the cabin. Every last one of them, stirred by my call. And men and women too. The cruelest, the most vicious. Charmed, drawn out of their hidden lairs of would-be virtue. And Doctor Nelson is with them. His white teeth, sharpened to a point, like fangs. And I'm wearing a black chignon that sits on top of my head and comes unpinned. With great thick locks falling down around my face . . . A witch. I'm a witch. And I'm calling out, summoning up all the evil from men and beasts. Wherever it can be found . . .

In which of my dreams did I call them both back? Not only my love, but the other one too. My husband. As if I couldn't call one without the other. All the beasts of the forest. All of them, summoned . . . This cry, deep in my chest. This call . . .

Now there are two of them at night, riding past my windows. One sleigh, then the other. Antoine chasing George, in a tinkle of sleigh bells and women's laughter. Brandishing his whip up at my window. Bellowing out his drunken joy.

"I want to get something to drink for my dear old classmate."

The neighbors, roused from their slumbers, don't know what to make of this mad, outrageous romp through the night. And by two young men of such excellent breeding.

I fall asleep long after the clash and clatter disappear. Leaving my frenzied mind filled with the hazy vision of men on horseback. Chases, confrontations. Horses pawing and trampling each other, and rearing up for long moments at a time.

The worthy citizens of Sorel, awakened by night, are bored by day. Thanks to us they'll get their taste of life and death, in a dizzying whirl that frightens them off yet lures them on. Blessed are we through whom the scandal cometh . . .

Never before have there been so many parties, one after another. And everyone vying with everyone else to invite that poor dear Madame Tassy, whose husband is sowing his wild oats here in Sorel. Right under her very nose. With a creature named Horse Marine. Why not invite that young American doctor too? The one who speaks such excellent French. We'll make him come out of his shell. Leave his books and his patients behind for a while. He has some kind of special power, no doubt about it. You see Madame Tassy? See how she trembles? Well, watch her come to life the minute he's near her.

"He's such a quiet fellow, and not the least bit friendly. Why, until just recently he'd never accept an invitation. Not from anyone."

"Have you noticed how that dark face of his lights up as soon as he sees Madame Tassy? And would you believe he's only twenty-five? . . ."

Which one of them insists that my husband should be invited too? That he is the squire of Kamouraska, after all, and that it wouldn't be right to ostracize him from society . . .

One evening, when he's had his fill of Horse Marine, Antoine will appear in the Kellys' drawing room. Or the Marchands'. Bursting in, bumping into the guests. His hat cocked behind his ears. And on his pink face, lost in disbelief, I'll watch the realization of the truth slowly, laboriously dawning in his dull-witted brain. He'll kill us, I imagine. That is, unless . . .

George greets me with a little bow. I look down at his hair, so thick and black. He talks without raising his head, in a low, gentle voice. Almost pleading. As if what he was saying had some hidden meaning, some mournful importance.

"Are you going to the ball at Saint-Ours next Sunday? If you'd do me the honor of coming in my sleigh, I'd be the happiest man alive . . ."

"And I'd be the happiest woman . . ."

YOU never hear her coming in. Then suddenly there she is. As if she could walk through walls. Weightless and transparent . . . Look at her there, spreading my brand-new party-dress out on the bed. Stroking the beautiful velvet, cherry-red, with a kind of gluttonous envy mixed with awe.

"Good God a'mighty, what a pretty dress! I'd give my soul to have one just like that!"

Aurélie sighs. Rekindles the fire. Arranges the room. Her every movement seems so strange, so disturbing. And that high-pitched voice of hers, driving me to the very limits of my resistance.

"Aurélie, please, be quiet!"

"But I'm talking so people can hear me, Madame . . ."

My mother's dressing room. No air at all in here. Impossible to breathe. That musty smell. It's making me sick . . . The green cloth on the dressing table, ragged and frayed. The real world is somewhere else. On Rue du Parloir, by my husband's bed. And yet I let myself sit on the stool. So nice and meek. In front of the mirror, all covered with spots.

Aurélie shakes out the ivory comb and brush, yellowed with age. Blows off the dust.

"I'll just give the mirror a wipe . . ."

I draw back with a start.

"No, no! For goodness' sake, don't touch the mirror!"

A kind of sudden break in Aurélie's voice. Blown glass drawn thin, shattering with the last bit of breath. Now she speaks in a whisper, almost too soft to hear.

"Just a touch of the cloth. There. That's all. Madame has to look herself right in the eye . . . See that pretty face. Those lovely shoulders. I'm going to fix Madame's hair for the ball. Madame should be able to see for herself . . ."

The mirror, come to life like a bubbling spring. My youth, smooth and clear. All those curls piled high seem a little absurd . . . Queenly bearing. Viper's soul. Lovesick heart . . . A single thought fixed firmly in my head. A flower in my hair. My left eye quivering madly. My eyelids drooping. The lashes brushing against my cheek.

A man comes rushing in. Stands next to the woman decked out so ornately. His breath, coarse against the woman's bare shoulder.

I don't have time to be amazed. How on earth did Antoine get in here? I thought the house was so well protected. And what about my aunts? And the servants?

A man and a woman, side by side. Husband and wife. Hating each other. Tormenting each other. By gentle candlelight. Two candles aglow, on either side of the mirror.

"You're not going to that ball."

"I said I would go, and I'm going."

"A married woman, a mother . . . It's absolutely indecent!"

"What does it matter to you? My life is none of your business now. I'm not your wife and you're not my husband. Now get out, or I'll call for help!"

A shattered look comes over Antoine's baby face. Not rage, not amazement. But a meek look of utter desolation. Spreading over his features. I gaze unmoved at this man's reflection. Watch him in the mirror as he comes undone. And the strength of my voice surprises me, as fear tightens its grip about my throat.

"Everyone from Sorel is going together. One long line of sleighs from here to Saint-Ours."

I read Antoine's reply on his lips more clearly than I hear it.

"I'll come and get you. You'll go in my sleigh with me."

"I'm going with Doctor Nelson. He asked me to join him. It's all arranged."

Now the mirror is blurred. Someone is blowing out the candles. This scene is more than I can bear. I can't watch anymore . . . And Aurélie's voice, going higher and higher. Shrill, like a squealing child. Spreading through every inch of space. Filling the darkness. Then sinking down to the timid murmur of the confessional.

"Monsieur gave Madame a punch in the ribs. I saw her there, all doubled up with pain. Then Monsieur left the house. Right away, before anyone could stop him. And on his way out the door he was swearing something awful. And he kept saying: "I forbid you to go to that ball. I forbid you to . . .""

But that evening, when the sleighs set out for Saint-Ours, Madame went off in Doctor Nelson's.

ERCHED high on its open-frame runners, that American sleigh can fly like the wind. And that black horse . . . There's not an innkeeper all along the southern bank, from Sorel to Kamouraska, who'll fail to marvel at his great endurance and his matchless beauty.

We try not to look at each other. Both of us sharing the same tender warmth. Wrapped in our furs. Sitting up straight. So unconcerned. No sign of emotion on our faces. Blank stares. Heads erect. Outlined against the winter sky.

We're riding at the end of the long line of sleighs. Our puffs of white breath, mingling and swirling. And the horse, loping gently along . . . So far, not a thing between us. We're innocent . . .

More than his passion, I want to excite his anger. When it's clear just how awful his anger can be. So easy to imagine it, all of a sudden, exploding . . .

Whispering now, my head on his shoulder. My face buried in the collar of his coat. Telling him that my husband came back to the house, that he forbade me to go to Saint-Ours, that he hit me in the stomach with his fist . . . All eyes, I watch the expression on George's face. Watch as his lips turn pale. A cadaverous gray . . . I'd like to soothe him now, calm his temper. Apologize for his frenzy of indignation . . . Yet all the while an unspeakable joy wells up within me. Sets my heart pounding with gratitude and hope. All of my hatred, a part of him now, joining together this man and me. Both of us bound by one single, ferocious passion.

He leaps to his feet. Grabs the whip and brings it smashing down across the horse's back. The beast goes galloping over the bumpy snow. Off in the other direction, away from Saint-Ours. I'm tossed from side to side. I plead with George. I try to hold his arm, make him stop whipping the horse . . .

Over goes the sleigh, upside down in the snow . . . All at once, that frantic ride behind me. And I'm caught up in the silence and the darkness. No sound but the horse, snorting his fright. Snow down my neck. My fur bonnet, lying on the ground . . . George covers the horse with one of the blankets. Then comes toward me. Without a word. Takes me in his arms. And we go rolling, head over heels. Rolling in the snow. Down the embankment. Like little children, all covered with snow. Snow down my neck, in my ears, in my hair. My mouth full of snow. His icy face against my face. His warm, moist lips against my cheek.

Breathless. Tongue-tied with the cold and with our laughter. We sit by the side of the road. Then one of us, very slowly, pronounces some words between two gasps: "Antoine is a very nasty man." I shake the snow from my bonnet, against my knee. A voice, inside me. (It can't be my own, I'm much too happy.) Telling me loud and clear: "We're sure to go to hell now, all three of us." And my love, embracing me. Saying he loves me "more than anything else on earth." And I tell him that he's "my very life."

We're still in the snow. Lying on our backs. Looking up at the sky, dotted with stars. Shivering with the cold . . . For a long time I try to keep my teeth from chattering.

I STRUGGLE out of my fur coat and my woollen mufflers. Then I just stand there, not daring to move. On view in the public square. The wet snow has spotted my velvet dress. Great blotches all over. A bunch of hairpins, fallen between my breasts. My curls, unpinned, are hanging down my back. A man is with me. I think he has me by the arm. Keeps telling me not to be afraid. Clenching his fists . . .

Dancers and chaperones suddenly freeze, holding their breath. What a sight in the doorway! Madame Tassy and Doctor Nelson, their faces red from the cold, standing there shivering. And their eyes fixed straight ahead. Defiant, though there's no escape. That curious pleasure, that bitter victory. Delirious joy, on the brink of despair.

The thing to do is to walk across the room. Probably face Antoine. Perhaps even both get killed . . .

"We took the wrong road . . . Turned over in the snow . . ."

A big black net, thrown over my head and shoulders. They've taken me prisoner. Dragged and pushed and pulled me away. Captured. My three little aunts, atremble, spirit me over by the fire. Protect me, guard me. And here I am, wrapped in Aunt Adélaïde's gigantic shawl, sitting in the middle of the tribe of chaperones. Delivered up to the scathing looks of old maids and widows.

Mustn't cringe and cower. Mustn't even blink. Just look right over those motionless heads, hair parted down the middle, pulled back tight. All those frilly bonnets, those satin ribbons over their shoulders . . . Pretend to be gazing at one certain spot on the wall. Emptiness . . . A prisoner. I'm a prisoner . . . Steal a careful look all round the room. Wait for Antoine to come in. Imagine his insults, his blows. Maybe a knife, hidden in his vest? Or that heavy silver chandelier that . . . No, I'm falling! Have to gaze at the wall, that spot. Cling to it in my mind . . . I'm going down. The floor is slipping out from under me. My life is foundering, sinking . . . Someone is saying that Antoine didn't come. Stayed away from the ball even though he was invited. Can't let that good news make me drop my guard. Keep an eye out. Search the room bit by bit, for fear that my husband might come bursting in . . . They give me a hot drink that smells of cinnamon. Aunt Angélique whispers something in my ear.

"My dear child, what a thoughtless thing to do! To go riding at night all alone with Doctor Nelson! Just think of your reputation. Think of your husband. You mustn't push that man too far . . ."

Little by little, the guests in the manor at Saint-Ours go back to their dancing. To the sound of the untuned piano. Heave a sigh of relief. And discover that, by some miracle, they're once again intact. Filled with excitement, endowed with new life.

I KNOW *I'm a sinner, I don't deny it. But you, my dear little wife, you're damned to hell. I'll never get over the shame of Saint-Ours. Don't wait for me. I'm going to drown my- self. It's easy. Just break a hole in the ice and jump in. Like a well. You'll see who shows up in the river next spring. Kiss the children good-bye for me. Your husband. Antoine."*

Sham drowning. Sham joy. Can't trust Antoine. But I'll play the game. Pretend to be looking for a corpse and to mourn him. To be waiting for a dead man, all dripping and cold, to be laid in my arms. But hardest of all is persuading my mother and my aunts not to call the police. Keep them out of our family problems. The brook and the river can't be dragged until spring. Just wait until the ice gives way. In the meantime, nothing to do but live like a widow.

"Aurélie . . . Quick, Aurélie . . . That note the doctor told you to give me . . . Here, Aurélie, take back my answer. Right away . . ."

"Aurélie . . . Go have them hitch up the auburn horse . . . The doctor's expecting me . . ."

"Aurélie . . . Make sure no one follows us . . . What a handsome coachman you make, Aurélie . . . I think we'd better bring the children with us . . ."

"Madame knows best . . .

"Good God a'mighty, Madame! It's Monsieur! I'm sure he's following right behind us!"

"You're wrong, Aurélie. Don't you know he drowned himself a few weeks ago? . . . In a big hole in the ice. Remember?"

Have to go back. Retrace my steps. Weep tears of rage. My husband is alive, stalking me like a dead man. Two times, three times, kill this corpse that keeps springing back to life . . .

At home in the house on Rue Augusta, I come down with a fever that sets my little aunts atwitter. I beg Aurélie to go for the doctor. She looks at me, eyes huge with fright. Her pupils, dilated like a cat's. But she does as she's told. Aurélie has no choice but to do what I tell her. No matter what.

"And if Monsieur tries to stop you on the way, tell him you absolutely have to get the doctor. I have an awful cough, Aurélie. You understand? You'll tell him I have . . ."

I close my eyes. Trace out his face and his body in the darkness. With my hands, my lips. The way blind people do. So carefully. Each feature exact . . . For just an instant, the perfect likeness. His manly body, stunning in its nakedness . . . All at once, an enormous wave comes swelling, rolling in, and disappears. Sweeps up my love and carries him away. His head cut off! His body torn limb from limb! . . . I scream . . .

"Madame! Madame! You're having a dream! See, I've brought the doctor."

A look of concern on George's face. His head bent close to mine. I fling myself into his open arms. My mother is taking a nap. My dear little aunts are at vespers. And I have just enough time to live. Careful not to undress completely, and not to light the lamp . . .

WHEN a man and a woman have known that passion once in their lives . . . That total desire . . . How can they go on living like everyone else? Eating, sleeping, strolling, working, being so reasonable . . . And yet, you act as if you still believed in the real world of other people. You say "my patients," or "the poor country folk." You beg me to "be careful for the children's sake." But you gnash your teeth at the mention of my husband's name. You swear you'll shoot him down if he ever tries to come near me again. You stand guard outside my house at night . . .

There's a sun in the sky, and it's moving. A reddish glow, I mean, that pretends it's the sun. That copies the regular rhythm of days and nights . . . In another world another life goes on. Capricious, bewildering. Real trees are budding in the town of Sorel and all about the countryside. We hear that it's spring . . . Doctor Nelson's selflessness, turned sour now, starts to plague him. Soon drives him to distraction. A millstone around his neck, or worse . . .

The great, long, flat expanse of land. The county of Richelieu, far as the eye can see. As if there were no more horizon, wherever you look. I'm afraid to walk out in the open. Walk up to that wooden house standing alone in the middle of the field. My husband could appear, swoop down on me at any moment . . .

Memory. Dark lantern dangling at arm's length, swaying. Your house. Your room. Your bed. The red and blue quilt that nobody thinks to pull down. We have so little time to be together. Aurélie and the children will be coming back. And I promised my mother I'd be home before . . . A tangle of crumpled clothing, hard to unfasten.

"At least let me take my coat off first!"

Heavy clothes, brusquely pulled open, over a tender belly lying bare. Like a beast being skinned.

Time runs short. Thinning out around us. Like air in a glass box, and two birds shut up inside. A single word would be too much. Might wrench us out of each other's arms. One instant less of time, and we'll suffocate in our cage. Even one tear, the time it takes for a single tear, a single cry, and it will be too late. The bell will sound all through the house, ring out our separation. Toll like a death knell . . . Aurélie and the children could burst in any minute. Or even Antoine. Or people limping, covered with running sores. Pregnant women with pleading cow eyes. Scabby children holding out their filthy hands: "I'm sick, Doctor Nelson! . . . Please save me, Doctor Nelson! . . . Doctor Nelson, help me! . . ."

The sick and the feeble will all come rushing in. They'll grab us both. Accuse us. Drag us out into the public square. Hand us over to the law, in chains. A judge in a wig will come between us, force us apart. With a single stroke of the sword . . . Oh, no! I'll die without you beside me to keep me warm! . . .

"Elisabeth! You're having a nightmare. It's only a dream. Get hold of yourself . . . You know I want to share your tears, your terror. Now tell me all about it. Tell me everything. What were you dreaming?"

"Nothing. Really. It's your patients. They frighten me . . ."

One day fear is going to destroy us. Drive us apart . . .

"What's to become of us, George?"

No answer but that troubled look. That quiver in your cheek. A tic I suppose. Can it be that you already know what's in store? I turn aside. Refuse to look you in the eye. To let you look at me. Who'll be the first to give himself away? . . .

Now Aurélie, standing beside me, red ribbons in her curly hair. Excited. Telling me something.

"Monsieur went off to Kamouraska! I heard it from Horse Marine! . . . Of course, that slut's as big a liar as she is a bag of bones! . . ."

FOR God's sake, Aurélie, go get the doctor . . . Please, Aurélie, you have to. I'm pregnant . . .

There's a big blond man in Sorel who's tired of running around with every whore in town.

"They pet me, they coddle me! They rob me and rape me! They cost me a fortune. I'm riddled with debts. I'll go back to my mother's. I'm the squire of Kamouraska. I'll sell some of my woodlands . . . But first I want to make peace with my wife."

Eluding every watchful eye, Antoine shuts himself up in a bedroom on Rue Augusta. While wife and children are spirited through a side door out of the house.

Antoine sleeps for three days. Wakes up at the end of the third and, in a booming voice, demands his dinner in bed. He eats in his room, all alone, like a prisoner. Seems to take great delight in his seclusion. Looks at himself in the mirror, amazed to see a shaggy beard overrunning his face. Orders the beard to be shaved off at once. Calls for hot water and soap. Soaks a good hour in the tub. Tells his servant that all the remains of Horse Marine are washed away forever.

"There, Ignace, I'm nice and clean. Like after confession. Now go tell Madame."

Ignace stares blankly at Antoine. Recites his lesson, carefully learned. Transfixed, trembling from head to toe.

"Madame is gone, and all the ladies and the children too. There's no one here. No one except the lawyer, Maître Lafontaine, and his son. And they're going to Kamouraska. They're waiting for Monsieur downstairs, in the drawing room . . ."

Then, all of a sudden, the one nobody expected. The angry wife. Sparks flying, like a gun. Striding into the house with firm, quick step. And close on her heels, a procession of weeping women.

"Let's make our peace with my husband, once and for all, and let that be the end of it."

Once it's clear what "making peace" means to Antoine, the sooner his urges are satisfied the better. As violently as possible . . . The real world is back in order. Honor is restored. And the blameless wife can announce that she's pregnant again by her husband.

We make our peace in the big guest room where Antoine has taken refuge. The bed, draped with chintz. The sheets, a little rough. A red tulip sits in a pot on the windowsill. And deep inside me my baby suffers the frenzied attacks of an alien passion. My baby, assailed, defiled . . .

But now, suddenly, Antoine throws his arms around me, tries to kiss me. No, that's one thing I won't let him do. I scream. Everyone in the house comes running. Sees me clutching the sheets to my chin. Hears me claim that my husband has tried to choke me . . .

It's three in the afternoon. The drawing room on Rue Augusta, cluttered with knickknacks. My mother has had the bizarre idea of inviting Antoine to tea before he leaves. I'm shaking so badly I can't hold my cup. Maître Lafontaine's rocking chair creaks through the silence.

It seems that Antoine no longer sees or hears a thing. Oblivious to the absurdity of his position. Somehow withdrawn from the world. Consumed in the fruitless search within himself for that

[142]

unbearable, debasing, degrading something down at the very roots of his being.

The sun is too bright here in this house too. Antoine makes no effort to move back from the window, out of the blinding light. His red eyes don't even blink. It's almost as if he were glad to submit to the torturous sun without the slightest struggle.

A long ray cuts through the room, hits me head-on. My turn to be caught in its snares. I look away.

Someone is telling them they'd better hurry. The steamboat leaves Sorel at four.

All at once Antoine is in front of me, face to face. That expression of utter obtuseness. His last look. Too much sun. I don't dare show my loathing, turn away again . . . He's speaking in a whisper, across my sightless gaze. Slowly, faintly. And yet, with a menace in his voice that seems to come from out in space. Its murmur echoing in my ear.

"Elisabeth, my dear . . . You're not getting rid of me so easily. I'll be back, you'll see . . ."

He asks to see his sons. They're brought in. He kisses each one voraciously on the cheeks.

AS soon as Antoine has gone, things are calm and peaceful for a time. And we keep pretending, George and I, that a life of peace and calm can really exist. Keep playing the game. Discreetly. Keep making plans for the future. Chatting about how we're going to be married. About wiping Antoine off the face of the earth. As simply and nicely as can be.

From time to time we meet near the little church. Take leisurely walks. Play at Monsieur-and-Madame-out-strolling. Toss offhand nods at the few passersby. And before we know it, we find ourselves heading out toward the country.

There's not much chance that my husband will challenge my lover to a duel. All the same, we carefully pick out a proper meadow just on the edge of the forest. Let our imagination picture that morning at the crack of dawn. The dew shimmering in the sunlight. The white shirts. The seconds with their hangdog looks. The surgeon's little black box. The choice of weapons. The heavy pistols, gleaming bright. The fifteen paces, according to the rules. The piercing shot echoing through the air. The terse ritual of death . . . Then the smoke lifts. The victor stands revealed, head bare. In the middle of the meadow. Still holding his smoking weapon. Looks aghast at his rival, lying on the ground. Justice has been done . . . But now the wife, weeping bitter tears. Running breathless through the dew-soaked grass. Her shoes are wet. She lifts her skirts to run still faster. Screams in that voice that only a widow can utter: "My husband! You've killed my husband!" Poor Antoine. It's over, finished. Your brawny chest, ripped open by a bullet. Your heart, torn out like a baby's tooth. Your blood, spilled out on the ground. Under your arm, tufts of blond hair matted with sweat . . . It's all well and good to say that the drunkard's hand can't aim. To say that it shakes. But what if, by some awful mistake, that were your heart, my love, ripped open by a bullet? I know I would die . . .

One day won't we have to make up our minds to put an end to chance? To stop dreaming. If we want to go on living . . . My, but you like to lag behind! . . . What are you thinking, here beside me? Sitting on the ground, under the pines. With your body against a tree. As if nailed to a cross.

One of us has to die. Just one . . .

The young man sits motionless. A young woman sits beside him. Her white muslin skirt is spread out around her. She looks up at the man. A calm resolve takes shape on her face. Her hair, severely parted, pulled back tight, outlines her narrow brow.

"My, my, Elisabeth. See how you're staring!"

The young woman carefully writes a message on a pad of paper. Short and concise. Hands it to the man.

"Antoine must be killed!"

The young man writes an answer on the pad.

"That's just between Antoine and me."

For a moment a strange expression comes over your face. A vague little smile. A brief look of bliss. Is it the thought of death that fascinates you so? Transfigures you? I read the words on your lips more clearly than I hear them.

"Antoine must be killed."

Just you and Antoine now, closed off from the rest of the world.

You're speaking, but I'm sure you neither see nor hear me. You seem a little sad. You're saying that pity has rotted away, that it's dead beyond recall. You even remind me that once upon a time, at school, no youngster was more miserable than . . .

That one word, "school." And I'm swept up in a flood of anger. Torn by jealous rage. I wish I could erase forever that part of your being where I don't exist. That schoolboy's world. A private world, with its masses, its Latin . . . But hard as I try to plunge within myself, I can't hold off your childhood memories. Listen. Little by little, with every word you utter, a bell begins to ring, louder and louder, echoing through my ears. Grows sharp as a blade. Forces me to listen. Wakes up a dormitory, fast asleep. In the middle of winter. Cries out the news that it's five in the morning . . . Thank God it's so dark that I can't make out a soul. That smell, like an animal's den. Beginning to choke me . . . The boys are trying to wrench themselves awake. Somebody lights a candle. Dubious shapes come out of the darkness. Move about in the candle's glimmer. Cast giant, languid shadows on the wall. Shiver. Sink back into the darkness. Blend with their shadows on the wall . . . The shadow of a hand makes the sign of the cross, vaguely, off in space. The huge, bare wall, with bits of saltpeter clustered about the cracks, swallows up the shadow of this holy hand. *"In nomine Patris"* . . . Begun in deep, sepulchral tones, and ending high and shrill. Another voice, a little softer, and just a bit younger. Your voice, George, with your thick American accent.

"The hardest thing is to duck in the icy water while your face is still fast asleep!"

I can hear ice now being broken in a pitcher. Someone whimpering, asking for a pick to break the ice. Someone using my oldest son's voice to cry with. (Antoine's voice as a child, I'm sure.) I want it all to be over. All of it, now, this very minute . . .

I'm looking up at the cloudless sky. Up through the dark leaves

[146]

over my head. My gaze, rising past you, up along the pine tree where you're leaning. As far as the great blue burst of sky. On the ground, red-brown needles, prickly and perfumed. Once more you tell me that pity is dead, that it's rotted away. Then silence takes hold of you again. Leaning against your tree. As if you were closing yourself inside that tree, with all your foreign and mysterious ways . . . Bark is growing on your hands. A rough, gnarled bark. Beginning to cover your face, to reach your heart now. Turning you into a tree. I scream . . .

You look at me. To beg me to be quiet.

Your face emerges from the void, stands out from the shadows. Seems to be born again, a second time, clearer and more precise. The bridge of your nose, sharper somehow. A darker flashing in your eyes, set deeper under the ridges of your brow. Your pallor, brighter.

The summer day is streaming with light. You look at your hands, so thin. Examine them with care. Hold them out to me, open and defenseless.

"I don't have a murderer's hands, though, do I?"

Poor dear, you must expect me to reassure you. But all I can do is take your hands and kiss them, one at a time. Run them, warm and willing, over my face. Your dear, sweet, murderer's hands . . .

A kind of ritual between us. Each time we're together in the pine grove, when it's still not dark enough for us to . . . We make believe we're tombstone figures, lying flat. Playing at death. The tautness of death, stretched out to its final length. The stiffness of death, all feeling gone. Complete and utter emptiness. And anything not part of us has to be stripped away. Like mushrooms scraped off a rock with a knife. (An old school friend, an unfortunate husband . . .) Any link with the world outside must be destroyed . . . The body, frozen. The heart, drained hollow. Silence. Dizziness.

[147]

You touch my hand. The blood comes surging back through my veins. Untrammeled, purged of the great wide world, we have nothing inside us now but desire. Like a flame. And we let ourselves roll toward each other, ever so gently. When, all at once . . . Close by, the pine needles, crackling. Aurélie and the children . . .

And whispered in English: "Good-bye my love . . ."

The way you say that, darling. As if we were free, the two of us.

GREAT slapping sheets of rain are breaking against the window. The street is full of puddles. The rain's smell mingles with the musty stench of ink and paper. That sheet of paper, lying blank in front of me on the table. Over my shoulder, a burst of Aurélie's piping laughter.

"Look at that rain! You poor thing, Madame! Kept indoors like a naughty child! Just look at that rain!"

I sigh and chew on the tip of my pen. This dreadful assignment. And during vacation! May as well do it tonight, as long as it's raining. Besides, it's getting late. Better hurry . . . Now I want you to copy this over one hundred times: "My darling husband— your loving wife is writing—to announce a blessed event—a blessed event to take place . . . in the month of . . . (I count on my fingers, then count again) in the month of December, if my calculations are correct . . . My darling husband—your loving wife is writing . . . if my calculations are correct . . . your loving wife . . ."

Someone says it's time to go to bed. The rain is letting up. The countryside blows great sodden gusts in through the window. Little frogs, chirping, off in the distance. Their notes enclose the town in a kind of crystal circle, broken from time to time by the muffled croaking of the giant bullfrogs.

[149]

The rain holds me prisoner. And I think about that other prisoner of the rain. The one I can't be with. Out there, in his house. Out there, beyond . . . The sound of raindrops on the shingled roof. I see his face. I manage somehow to see it, but only through the window. Water, deep and impassable . . . Far from me now, but he's gesturing, speaking. Living. His every word, his every movement, there in that total solitude, meant just for me. If even one wave of his hand escapes me, my life could begin to slip away. Seep out through my very pores . . .

That gutter on the house on Rue du Parloir will have to be fixed. How can I live in Sorel, out here in the country, with all this rain, and that waterspout clanging in my ears? And Florida, lumbering between the bed and the table. She shouldn't make so much noise. Well, at least we don't have to listen to Jérôme Rolland and his breathless gasps . . .

"My darling husband—your loving wife is writing . . ."

The doctor's kitchen, filled with the smell of oil and smoke. The wick in the lamp is too short. It's smoking. He trims the wick. Wipes the soot from the globe. His deft hands show their dazzling skill. Such perfect control of the body. While the heart goes wandering off its course, lost in the summer night.

You have to go to sleep, Doctor Nelson. Stretch out on that bench. Don't even take off your clothes. Just your jacket and shoes, that's enough. Now roll up your jacket in a ball, under your head. Like a soldier, ready to leap to his feet at the least little signal. Rifle by his side. You're a doctor, don't forget. They can call you any hour of the day or night. For a child being born, or someone about to die, or . . .

I'm lying awake, joined to that man who sleeps through the rain. Far apart in time and space. Yet bound to him all the same. Bound to George Nelson. Now, at this very moment, while all the countryside around Sorel is foundering in a sea of rain. And all the while, in Quebec, my husband's every gasp wafts death itself through the house on Rue du Parloir.

HAT wonderful black horse of yours, Doctor Nelson. His legs, so long and slender. From far away they look like matchsticks holding up some strange, fantastic creature with a flowing mane. Hurtling across the landscape through the storm. Deep ruts all over. But you can't bear the thought of people suffering, people in pain. (That whimpering child at school. Or that young wife so mistreated by her husband. Or most of all that Protestant lad. Singled out, standing alone, over on the left, in the chapel of Monseigneur de Laval.) Now, riding your horse, you scour the countryside from end to end. Even the tiniest roads, rutted like the gullies of torrential streams. Not a single house where you fail to make your rounds. And usually through the kitchen door. And you ask: "Is there anyone here who's sick, or crippled, or distressed, or afflicted?" Looking for ills that can be cured, woes that can be confessed. To reassure yourself. But what about the others? Those monstrous, hopeless cases? Wouldn't it be better to destroy them all, at once, and the root of their ills along with them? Your specialty, if only you were willing. To wipe out all those living creatures marked with the look of death . . . You don't trust yourself, Doctor Nelson. You pretend you believe in pity. You cling to pity as if it were a sign of your own salvation. At least you can do your best. Tending the sick, healing them, day and night. Until your strength gives out. Sometimes a weariness so deep you almost think you're at peace. Going to sleep like some dumb beast, without even stopping to take off your shoes. Forcing yourself to get up again. To snatch a child from death. To wrest a victory from death, eyes filled with tears. And your hands, covered with pus and blood. See how grateful the parents are, weeping their thanks. Yes, everyone loves you here beyond belief. Why not? You do your best to make them love you. You've treated and cured the whole Richelieu valley . . . You're sobbing with joy, Doctor Nelson. Peace is on its way at last. With muffled step. From the depths of the earth. Another moment and the decree will be proclaimed, here, in broad daylight. In French and English: "Hear ye, hear ye. Worthy citizens of the town of Sorel, called William Henry by the English . . . Doctor George Nelson, residing in said parish, is hereby formally accepted, approved, and acknowledged as belonging to said parish of Sorel, in the county of Richelieu . . . Not only as a parishioner in good standing, and entitled to all the rights of citizenship, but indeed as an honored member of said community . . ." The whole county is there, in front of the church, out in the sun. My revenge. My recognition, total and complete . . . But look, Doctor Nelson, you can't hold back your joy. See how you noise it about. So loud that Mélanie Hus, the patient you tended and cared for with such devotion, suddenly wakes from that sleep of death that closed over her yesterday. Utters a cry of horror. Points her arm at you. Her long, endless arm, all stiff and withered. Found out! Master Nelson, they've found you out! No good to play the doctor who heals the sick and comforts the afflicted. They've found you out. Impostor. Just an impostor . . . And the crowd now, turning against you. Shouting, jeering. Protestants can't get into Heaven . . . A witness steps forward. Then a second, and a third, and a fourth . . . And all of them, testifying under oath that "Doctor Nelson and Madame Tassy have had an adulterous affair." Then someone

[152]

complains that "children are unbearable, with their faces full of tears." And Madame Tassy says that the only thing to do is to "take that big fat boy, bent over the icy basin, and push his blond head under the water. Get a good firm hold and let death do the rest." Doctor Nelson explains to the people of Sorel that "this child should never have seen the light of day." Madame Tassy replies that "it would have been better to drown the pup the moment he was born, whereas now that he's grown so big and fat it's terribly hard." Then the crowd again, with its jeers and accusations. "Foreigners can't get into Heaven . . ." And Madame Tassy, with an outraged look, cupping her hands and screaming that she "was born and raised here," and that this is where she belongs . . .

The man gets up from his nightmare. The burden of all his life on his shoulders, weighing him down. His stomach still caught in the grip of the dream . . . The pump, with its rusty squeak. The tin cup, tinkling. George Nelson drinks. He splashes cold water over his face. Turns his frightened eyes, his harried features, toward my dreams now. My own. And I—although I could spend my life caressing his face, wiping it clean of evil and death, easing his pain—instead I haunt and torment this man. Just as he haunts and torments me.

Now is the moment I choose. In the middle of the night. For the first time. And in the rain . . . Quietly I take the key from Aunt Adélaïde's purse and steal out of the house on Rue Augusta. Straight into George Nelson's dream. Myself, in flesh and blood. Here, now, knocking at his door. Soaked with rain, covered with mud, shivering with fever. Knocking at his door. Calling to him softly, pressing my mouth against the jagged wood.

"Doctor Nelson! Doctor Nelson! It's me, Elisabeth . . ."

Y OU, Elisabeth? Here? So late? What kind of madness . . ."

I've never come here at night before. It was bound to happen. Utter, unthinking madness. The risk of eternal damnation. A soul in peril, held up for all to see. In a loud burst of laughter. Yes, I'll push you to the very limit . . .

Your eyes, clouded with sleep. And yet, your whole being, taut, more and more on edge.

"You, Elisabeth? Here?"

I tell you about my letter to Antoine. I admit that I slept with my husband the very day he left for Kamouraska.

Your anger frightens me, thrills me, all at once.

You say you're glad to give him reason to curse his life, dog's life that it is! But still, some of the tricks a woman plays infuriate and disgust you.

"You, Elisabeth? With him? You . . . you liar! You nasty little hypocrite!"

You swear you're going to kill Antoine. You say you'll never forgive me.

I hang my head. I don't know how to make you understand. My silly little tricks. To deceive Antoine. Allay his suspicions.

[154]

Let him think that the baby . . . Make a fool of my husband. . .

I seem to be crying. You're crying too. I beg your forgiveness. You beg mine. You tell me that I'm sweet and good, and that I only did such an awful thing because I'm so unhappy . . .

A man and a woman, standing face to face. In the middle of a big country kitchen. No curtains on the windows.

People can see us from the road. Any moment someone might come looking for you, to take you to see a sick patient. Yes, now's the time to compromise ourselves for good. To cause a scandal. Take our stand. Let them point their fingers and accuse us. Both of us bound together in a single fate. Against the world. Utter totality of love and death. Justice restored. The reign of blessed savagery. That's what will save us. The two of us, possessed.

The man looks down, stares at the floor. Seems to be measuring out the minuscule space on the knotty boards between the woman and himself. The invisible line between livable existence and unpardonable folly.

"You're mine, Elisabeth. And so is the baby, isn't it? Mine, no one else's . . . Say it. Over and over. Loud and clear . . ."

"Yours, no one else's. I swear . . ."

The sound of his breathing, quicker and quicker. Filling the silence. The woman is trembling. Bends over the table to blow out the lamp. Can't stand the light. And those bare windows too . . .

A voice is giving orders. Rough, unrecognizable, abrupt . . .

"Don't touch the lamp. Now take off your shawl. And your dress. Your skirts. Go on . . . Take everything off. Your corset too. Your drawers, your chemise. Faster . . . Your shoes . . . Your stockings . . ."

My hands are trembling. So badly that I have to try and try before all my buttons, buckles, and laces will come undone . . . I do as I'm told. As if I were dreaming. Obeying a voice I can't refuse. Standing there, naked. My pregnant belly already beginning to bulge. Clutching the table to keep from falling.

[155]

"Stand up straight. People can see us from the road. Isn't that what you want?"

In a moment his clothes join mine in a heap on the floor.

"Now blow out the lamp."

I fumble about, trying to turn the wick. I try to blow. It's as if no breath at all were left inside me. Finally a kind of sigh escapes from deep inside my bosom. More like a spasm, a throaty sob. Then George's voice, in a whisper.

"There! Now are you happy? Now that we have nothing left to lose . . ."

All the countryside around the house. Who's out there, watching, hiding in the darkness? Spying. Ready to send the news flying off tomorrow, at the crack of dawn. Like a flock of pigeons. Straight to Judge John Crebessa of Sorel. And beyond Sorel. Even beyond Quebec. All the way down the river . . . In no time at all, reaching the squire in his manor. The squire of Kamouraska. A man condemned.

At last a groan breaks free from my throat. Even before George pulls me down to the floor, on the pile of clothes. A man's weight on top of me. The hair on his body, black as a beast's. His sex, hard as a gun.

ICK up my skirts, my crumpled bodice. Pull myself out of George's arms. Back to Rue Augusta. Quickly, before the cook lights her fire.

The sun is coming up. This barren world. The worst thing that could happen to me now. To be doomed to live in this barren world. Where are you, love? In what strange land? Away so long . . . I live on Rue du Parloir, in Quebec. People even say that I'm Madame Rolland, wife of Jérôme Rolland, a notary there, in the city . . .

Aunt Adélaïde begs me to think of the family honor. Of my children's future. I kiss her and slip the key to the house on Rue Augusta back in her purse, where I got it the night before. I laugh.

"Come now, Aunt Adélaïde. You know that my honor means more to me than life itself. How can you even suspect me of such an awful thing?"

Aunt Adélaïde looks down. Embarrassed by my lie, as if she herself were caught in some dreadful act.

"But my dear child, you have to be more careful. Antoine's last letter is full of threats. He says he's coming to get you. You and the children . . ."

"A letter from Antoine? For me, Aunt Adélaïde? And you didn't give it to me? And you read it? . . . But you had no right . . . Let me have it! Give me that letter, this very minute! . . ."

"I can't, Elisabeth. I don't have it. I burned it. . . Some letters we have to burn. And some things we have to avoid if we don't want to burn in the next world ourselves!"

"You mean hell, Aunt Adélaïde? You're putting the fear of hell in me? You, so good, so kind? . . . How could you? . . ."

"Sometimes you seem to forget your soul, my child . . ."

I heave an exquisite sigh. Like throwing excess baggage out the carriage door, while the team of horses whisks me off.

"It's so easy to forget your soul, Aunt Adélaïde. To leave it behind. If you only knew how easy . . ."

My mother comes out of her lair. Casts a lifeless glance at her daughter. Complains about the heat. Goes rambling through her weary soliloquy.

"What a handsome man, that Doctor Nelson . . . Such an excellent background . . . Fine old American family . . . Loyalists . . . Too bad the child didn't meet him first . . ."

"But Mother, he is the first! The very first, Aunt Adélaïde! There's never been another, and there never will be, you hear?"

"That's sinful, child. Terribly sinful."

"Even more than you think, Auntie dear. If you only knew . . ."

My soul will have to take strange paths to catch me . . . All of a sudden I feel so tired. This need of mine to be rid of my husband. To hurl him over into the void. At all costs, keep him away from Sorel. Rub him out of my life forever. Like a drawing erased from a sheet of paper.

My mother is bored. She straightens the shawl on her shoulders and leaves the room.

[158]

OH, what a summer! The heat, the storms . . .
And when that relentless sun decides to shine, you seem to see
the landscape through a prism of water. The weather is strange.
It changes so quickly . . . The phlox! I can smell the phlox again!
August is over already. I look so foolish with this five-month belly,
and these sudden red patches all over my face. The light, the
color of sulfur . . . The phlox, blooming in the garden, behind
the house. Their fragrance reaches me, even up here. Goes to my
head, gets on my nerves . . .

Anne-Marie is standing in the doorway with a big bouquet of
flowers in her arms. I'm talking to my daughter through a fog.
Telling her that just a couple of fresh, white sprigs will be enough
for the ceremony. They smell so strong . . . And then, she
mustn't forget the white lace tablecloth and the silver candlesticks.
And a crucifix . . . I can hear my own voice, thick, explaining
that they'll need two deep little cut-glass dishes. One with holy
water, and a twig that's been blessed to sprinkle it with. The other
one with plain water, and a white towel, so the priest can wash
his hands . . . Anne-Marie's timid voice asks me for my keys. I
tell her to take them, from under my pillow . . . The door is
already closed. I can't call her back. Can't even open my mouth

and move my tongue. But I absolutely have to tell her . . . Cotton! A piece of cotton, for the Extreme Unction! . . . Someone with a loud voice, out in the corridor, says that they'll come and get me when it's time . . .

I'm living somewhere else. A very specific place. A certain time in the past. Something no marvel of memory could accomplish. My real life, that's what it is. My perfect escape from Rue du Parloir . . .

Both of us, lying in the stifling shadows of that bedroom with its wooden walls. Midafternoon. (The quilt, tacked over the window, like a curtain.) And we speak to each other, saying frightful things, with the thoughtless freedom of the dying. (The very way Jérôme Rolland . . .)

The peaceful calm that follows love. The weariness. Our eyes, still resolutely closed. In an alcove whisper we talk about Antoine's death. It seems so perfectly natural that we should. Our bodies, scarcely done with the frenzy of love. As if we were given this moment of peace only to launch into a madness more violent still. As if the killing of Antoine were merely the supreme extension of our love.

We should probably kill ourselves as well, both of us together. Be sure that neither one outlives the other. One bullet, one thrust of the knife, one single deadly blow. Before the ordinary life of everyday dulls our pure fervor for living and dying.

We decide to wait until the baby comes before we make our move. Still, we'd better hurry. Afraid our resolve might wither away with time, the more it comes in contact with our nerves, our blood. The body, weakening. While the monstrous soul holds fast.

George shows me his pistol. Loads it with powder and a bullet, before my eyes.

The need to overcome our tenderness with terror. We'll bring about justice by fire and sword. And we'll be happy.

AFTER trying so long to lead a model life, a life of utter selflessness, are you finally going to see your dream come true, Doctor Nelson? Exiled so young from the world of kindness, are you going to find your lost kingdom and make it your own again? I'll give all my strength to help you. I'll give you my life itself. To punish the wicked, reward the good. Deliver the suffering princess, slay the fierce dragon that holds her prisoner. Justice, justice, justice . . . Antoine Tassy deserves to die. He's asking to die. By his very silence. His inscrutable absence. He's challenging you the way he's challenging me. He wants to destroy himself, and us along with him. That death wish, deep in his bones, from the very beginning . . . Will you conjure up the image of a blond lad's misery, reflection of your own despair? Will you let Antoine go free? Turn the gun on yourself? The crime is the same. It's all so strange . . . If you don't watch out, ideas like that can make you go too far.

But I'm with you, here. I want you to live, and I want him to die! I've chosen you, George Nelson. I'm life and death, bound up together, for good and all. You see how bittersweet I am . . .

The doctor is busy examining an old woman's hand. Her fingers, tightly clenched. He tells her to lay her forearm flat on the table and open her fist. She says she can't. That's where she burned herself. Inside, right on the palm, down deep. Some lard she was holding. And all of a sudden it caught on fire. How could she do such a thing, poor soul? . . . The doctor smooths some ointment over the burn and puts on a bandage. The old woman groans a little. Finally mutters that "in love and pain, tears are vain . . ." Digs down into her pocket with her good hand. Pulls out a coin and clutches it in her fist.

"Keep your money, Grandma, and buy yourself some sweets."

The word "sweets" seems to offend the wizened creature. "Sweets," at my age? What do you take me for? . . . She puts the coin back in her pocket and goes grumbling out of the doctor's house.

Never has George Nelson paid more attention to his patients or given them better care. Never has he been more sympathetic. Like a spring of compassion, gushing in his heart. Sometimes a kind of mournful sadness comes over him all at once. A very special sadness that he knows so well, drawing him up to the brink of despair. Only then does he look at his pistol for consolation. Takes it out of its gray cloth cover. Sits gazing at it. Unloads it. Loads it again. Gets a dark delight from the sharp, clear click in the stillness of his house.

Like a man about to die, he's putting his things in order. Arranging his papers, his powders and salves, his forceps and scalpels. Dawn often finds him at the kitchen table, poring over figures and minute calculations. That is, when he's not engrossed in his instruments, and flasks, and beakers . . . A certain powder, heated up, flashing in a puff of metallic smoke. Insoluble. And a strange scent of garlic . . .

The poison is Elisabeth's idea. A pregnant woman's obsession. Send Aurélie to Kamouraska with poison, so she can . . . No use trying to reason with Elisabeth. It's easier to pretend you agree . . . Like a good chemist, go on with your experiment. While that lurking sadness, creeping through our soul, becomes too much to bear. Erupts into such a frenzied fury that, at last . . .

WHO let the doctor into the house? What is he doing here? It's five in the morning! . . . At least let me take off this silly nightcap! . . . Aurélie must have opened the door. See, Aunt Adélaïde. See how the doctor heads straight for the child's room. All those closed doors in the corridor don't confuse him a bit.

This man is drunk with the weariness of sleepless nights. Mad with jealousy. Imagining things. Sure that Antoine is hiding somewhere in the house. He says he'll have to be ferreted out, like a rat. When things quiet down a little . . . My love sees Aunt Adélaïde and says hello. Whispers in my ear. All out of breath. Insists that we'll have to get Antoine away from Kamouraska. Out in the open. Get it over with once and for all . . . I beg him not to go before the baby comes. I'm so afraid I might die in labor . . .

Antoine sits sulking in his manor in Kamouraska. Selling land and planning his return to Sorel. Or is he here already? Hiding with Horse Marine, or maybe someone else? We'd better go scour the countryside around Sorel. The woods, the bushes, the streets in Sorel. The bed of every whore in Sorel. The taverns in Sorel. Search every house, probe every wall. He could swoop down on us here at any moment. "Peekaboo! It's me, your darling husband. See? I'm back!" With that stinking drunkard's breath of his. And

[163]

he'll beat me all over, shame me in front of the help. "Here's my wife, nailed to a cross with her feet in the air. I'd like you to meet her . . ." His loud, idiotic laugh. Then he'll grab me, and hold me. Won't let me go till I'm lying there dead, in a pool of blood. Like a woman dying in childbirth, gasping her last. And my baby, ground between two stones . . . Oh, what a strange and agonizing cry will send me hurtling into hell! So unresisting, so resigned. Letting myself be caught and killed in Antoine's snares. Too terribly willing . . . No, I want to live. I'm innocent. I won't give in. Won't do what my husband wants of me. It's my death he's after. Lurking in the shadows . . . No, Antoine's the one who has to die. And I'll be saved. Loving and faithful. Sweet and pure. And George too, George will be saved. By Antoine's death. A holy sacrifice. No other way. Just go on living!

My love says I have a fever. He kisses me on the forehead. Pulls the covers up around my chin. Says he'll come see me again this evening. Tells them to let me sleep, all day if I want to. Tiptoes out of the room . . .

I plunge into darkness. Won't open my eyes. Not before night comes falling all around us. Everyone sleeping.

I jump down from by bed, run out of the house. Don't take the time to dress. Don't bother to throw off the vestiges of sleep . . .

Too late! It's too late! The street is full of people. Incredible, all these people, milling about so late at night . . . Someone is saying that my trial has begun. The witnesses look me over, up and down. Seem to know me. Take their oath on the Gospels.

"Yes, she's the one who killed her husband! She's a criminal, that woman. See how she dawdles about through the streets, and in the middle of the night. Must be breaking her back with so much love!"

"Alexis-Paul Hus, seaman by trade . . . I was coming home, between one and two in the morning. All of a sudden I catch sight of Doctor Nelson and Madame Tassy. They're in a little garden, near where Madame d'Aulnières and the Lanouette sisters live. They seem to be getting up off the ground, both of them. Anyhow, I'm sure they weren't standing up a minute before, because the wall is real low over there, and I would have noticed them right away. And Madame Tassy has on a kind of dressing gown, a white one I think. And as soon as they see me, they separate. Madame Tassy walks across the courtyard into Madame d'Aulnière's house. And the doctor goes off in the other direction . . ."

Everything drowned out by the sound of hoofbeats. A horse, galloping along the horizon. The other direction! My love, running off. Far, far away. Over the border. He'll never be returned to face this country's justice. There won't be a trial. And the witnesses can all go home . . .

A familiar voice, muffled ever so slightly. Saying that nothing has really happened yet. That everything is still to come. Doctor Nelson has only gone to Quebec. To be with his sister, the Ursuline nun, who's terribly sick.

THIS horse is even more wonderful than you can imagine. Every innkeeper down the river sings his praises. From Sorel to Kamouraska. For some, it's his strength. For some, his endurance. For others, his dark, demonic beauty, like the devil himself. But only George Nelson can make you feel how really sensitive this beast can be. How perfectly his powerful stride echoes the frenzied rhythm of his master's heart.

The trip to Quebec, through rain and mud. There and back. Just time enough for this man to enter the convent walls and stand by the bed of the poor little nun about to pass away. To say good-bye. Receive her dying words. Carry them off forever. Not even stop to rest, or to rest his horse. Start back again, in the dark and the rain . . . The need to be happy. Not wait any longer. Now that death has come and gone. Get back to Elisabeth as fast as he can. Just one thing matters now: to live! Whatever the price. But live!

Cathy's dying words. Impossible to shake them off along the way. Even with the wind and rain. Feeling them etch themselves deeper and deeper. With each passing moment. Despite the noise of galloping hooves. Despite the terrible scraping of wheels . . .

My love is coming back. Go light the fire, Aurélie. It's autumn,

Aurélie. Don't make a fuss. My love is on his way, he's coming back. I want to soothe and comfort him. That awful look on his face, already . . .

Sister Catherine of the Angels has offered up her life and death to God. From her very first moment in the Ursulines' cloister. Gave up her long black hair. And that inkling of human warmth in her childish heart. Now, with all her tender passion stifled at its source, with her three vows faithfully kept each day, our little sister Cathy is about to die. Both her brothers by her side. Here, within these walls, by permission of the bishop. Because one is a doctor and one is a priest . . . Sister Catherine stops them in the midst of their prayers. The prayer of the dying. Calls out in a loud, clear voice. Calls to her brother the doctor. Holds out her departing soul to George. George, the impenitent thief, the brother lost beyond recall.

"It's too late now to pray. Doctor, save me!"

The other brother—the fiery preacher, the penitent thief by trade—crosses himself with trembling hand. Catherine of the Angels dies with that cry on her lips. In her loud, clear voice:

"Doctor, save me!"

George leaves the convent. Runs out like a madman. His horse, dashing headlong. Back to Sorel . . . I can hear him coming toward me now. With that tormenting cry ringing in his ears and mine: "Doctor, save me!"

I'll use Cathy's voice if I have to. The selfsame voice of every threatened life that wants to live. Save me, Doctor Nelson! And save yourself! No, not with prayers. Not with some righteous, abstract alchemy. But with all your body, with all my body. Living flesh of man and of woman. With your name, Doctor Nelson. A name to give your wife. Instead of a name she loathes. With your heart, your soul, your all . . . There's a man to be killed. There's no other way. I'm love and I'm life. And my need is as imperious and absolute as death itself . . .

[167]

WHERE you're concerned I move so near the edge it makes me dizzy. May as well ponder your family problems with you (and more than just your family problems . . .). All the way back from Quebec to Sorel. In the muck and mud of autumn. The wallow and rot of autumn. The heady smell, the lashing rains, the groaning gusts of wind.

"Poor Cathy. So grim, so serious, yet such a child. 'My calling . . .' That's what she used to tell me. In that strange and mystical way. Oh, what a farce . . ."

Now Aurélie looms up before you, ghostlike, over the muddy road. Her face, so white. Her woollen kerchief, black, twisted about her narrow shoulders. Tossing her kinky little head, like an actress. With a black girl's grace. You can't imagine how much shame and scorn will cling to this love of ours because of her. Fixed forever in a grimacing mask . . .

You breathe the decay of autumn until it makes you sick. Catherine of the Angels' death sticks in your throat . . . See, I won't leave you alone. Despite your grief, my love, I'll prod you on. Remind you over and over that you have your calling too. The real one. Just like your family . . . (The perfect alibi: to each his own!) A murderer! Yes, you're a murderer! And I'm your accomplice, your wife. Waiting for you here in Sorel. With Aurélie by my side, thrashing about, caught in the trap.

I make her sit down on the floor, beside me. Facing the fire. First, blow out all the candles. Solemnly, one by one. Only the glow of the fire lighting the room. Our shadows on the wall. And we hold out our hands toward the fire. Aurélie's, so tiny. Fingers spread, like rays. She asks if she can light her pipe. Wraps herself in a cloud of smoke. Sits musing. Eyes half closed. A dream of happiness, clear and simple. Surging waves of passion over her face, pink in the firelight.

"Your affair, Madame . . . You and the doctor . . . I'm dying to see what happens!"

Aurélie doesn't run around with bad boys anymore. Doesn't make her predictions over newborn babies. Never goes anywhere. Just follows me about, wherever I go. Comes to life when I give her a message to take to George. And only then. Bursts into bloom, atwitter and atremble, as soon as I tell her my pleasures or pains. I read a boundless admiration on her face. An infinite awe. A kind of enchantment. As if this hectic life of mine were quite enough for Aurélie now. Enough to spare her the need to live herself. But sometimes it seems to make her angry. And her old hostility toward the doctor comes back again.

"That dear little doctor of yours has hexed us for sure, no doubt about it . . ."

I put my arms around her. Stroke her hair. It's so essential now to soothe and calm her. Make her drop her defenses. Pamper her into that utterly passive state where docile submission will seem the most natural thing in the world . . . I offer Aurélie a glass of port. She drinks it down in little swallows.

"I need your help, Aurélie. You know what a wicked man I married. Well, I want you to go to Kamouraska and poison my husband . . ."

"That's a pretty big crime, Madame . . ."

"No one will ever know. And afterward you'll come stay here with me. Like a sister. For the rest of your life if you want . . ."

"I'm so afraid I'll burn in hell! . . ."

Between Montreal and Sorel. The ruts run deep. The earth, dug up. And the heart as well, by the same devastation. Impossible to tell just where it began. With the earth, more than likely. The countryside, eaten away from within. At first, an infinitesimal shifting of ground, somewhere in a rain-soaked landscape. Then masses of crumbling rock, great floods and rushing torrents. And a corner of the known world gives way and falls to pieces. (You mean you didn't know such villainy was in you, Doctor Nelson?) Now here you are, involved completely, bound up in the fate of this land. The collapse of this land. (Before you return there yourself, in the flesh, to rot.) All the good topsoil, ripped away. (Pride, self-respect, compassion, charity, courage . . .) The heart, stripped bare. So painfully naked. (Fatigue, despair, disgust . . .) "My God, why hast thou forsaken me?" Now just one thing to do. Be rid of Catherine of the Angels' death as fast as possible. And every other death as well. Those past and yet to come. Tonight, George Nelson, this very evening, you'll give way to Elisabeth's pleas. You'll speak to Aurélie and send her off to Kamouraska in your place . . . Weary. So awfully weary . . .

Poor dear, I'm sure I can never make you understand that beyond all saintliness the wily innocence of beasts and madmen reigns supreme.

A dozen miles or so before you reach Sorel. It's no use forcing your horse. Besides, Aurélie and I have so much to say to each other. Here by the fire, cozy and warm. And these sudden cravings of mine. Like every pregnant woman. Send Aurélie to Kamouraska. We must send Aurélie to Kamouraska . . . Put Antoine's death way out beyond our reach, yours and mine. Keep plenty of distance between ourselves and Antoine's death. Enough to restore our innocence. So difficult a peace to win. Dispel the agony. Heart

[170]

pounding, bulging out between the ribs. The terrible urge to kill, held at bay. Try frantically to reach the calm in the hurricane's eye. You'll see, it's all going to happen in another world. Aurélie is taking care of everything. We'll hear about Antoine's death as if we had nothing to do with it at all. His mother will write us a letter, I suppose. And no one will ever be able to say just what my husband died of. It was bound to happen, sooner or later. One party too many, and that's the end of the squire of Kamouraska. Nobody will really be surprised . . .

On a frightful night like this I hear someone whisper that the Marsh King is coming to get me. That he'll grab me by the hair and drag me off. Roll me about in a great morass of muck and slime until I drown . . . It's so hard to keep the fire alive. The logs don't seem to burn. Just fill the room with smoke . . . Maybe I've had too much port to drink.

Now I'm giving Aurélie some cakes. And ribbons too. Red ones and green ones. In an instant her sullen face lights up. Like a child, in tears one moment and laughing the next.

I speak to her softly, afraid of jostling her out of her sudden joy.

"What are you thinking, Aurélie?"

She sighs, tries to find her thoughts in the fire. Pokes through the crumbling embers. Snatches at tiny cinders with the tongs. All at once she utters a cry. Jumps up. Drops the tongs on the hearth. With an infernal clatter.

Someone has just come in. Someone we didn't expect so soon, comes bursting in. All out of breath. After a long, long ride . . .

H E'S been standing in the bedroom with us now
for several minutes. His muddy boots have left a black trail on
the floor. A three-day growth of beard covers his cheeks with dark
blue shadows. He's staring at us without a word. Long and hard.
As if he were blaming me and Aurélie for something . . . Now
he's saying that it's all a farce, that sooner or later you've got to
make up your mind. And his voice, by nature so gentle and pleasant, shatters the air.

"Someone could walk off with this house, the way you watch
it! I've been out there knocking for half an hour! . . . What on
earth is in that fire, Aurélie? What are you looking at?"

George Nelson throws his coat on the floor. His silk hat, his
cane. It's Aurélie he's after with his jibes. He doesn't seem to see
me at all. I'm beginning to find her hateful . . .

"You don't look like much of a witch to me, Aurélie!"

"When it comes to devils, Monsieur, no one is as good as you!
Now let me be, Monsieur. I want to go . . ."

"You're not going to leave me just like that, Aurélie. Not now,
when I need you. Oh, no! We're going to see whose power is
stronger, yours or mine. We'll see if you're as much of a witch
as you say you are!"

[172]

"I'd rather not, Monsieur. I want to go . . ."

"Look me in the eye, Aurélie."

"I never look anyone in the eye, Monsieur. And I'm not about to begin with you."

Aurélie looks down at the floor. Then at me. Seems to be waiting for help. I turn aside. We've reached a point where we have to let things run their course now without the slightest change.

"Come now, Aurélie. Whenever we go meddling in other people's business we have to go all the way. Like it or not. Put up with all their secrets, from start to finish. Their whole delightful tale of love and death . . ."

"Please, Monsieur, let me go. I'll mind my own business for the rest of my blessed days. I promise . . ."

A dry little laugh. That inflexible voice I know so well.

"Now don't start whimpering, Aurélie, for God's sake!"

Aurélie stares at the floor. Then at the dying fire. Begins to weep, but without a sound. Without even moving. As if the flood of tears streaming down her shawl weren't part of her anymore.

George comes over and sits by my side. Shuts out the world. The two of us, here in a corner. Kisses my hands. Calls me his "dearest." Lays his head in my lap and tells me about his sister. Tells me that she's dead. That she died at three o'clock, this morning. Like a sinner. And that we have to mourn her for two reasons now.

In a single bound he's back to Aurélie. Ranting and raving.

"Tell me, Aurélie . . . While you're sitting there looking for treasures in the fire . . . Do you hear people's voices there too? Do you hear their screams? . . . My sister's scream . . . Can you hear it somewhere in all those ashes? 'Save me! Doctor, save me!' . . ."

Aurélie stands transfixed. Weeping. Without moving a muscle. As if she were turned to stone.

The doctor looks at her and smiles. Sees how weak and defenseless she is, how easily hurt. He seems relieved, rid of a terrible burden weighing him down. He speaks to her now in the gentlest of tones.

"You see, Aurélie, the important thing is for you to know what's going on. For you to take care of everything. Even certain things your sweet little mind might not understand. That's how real witches work. We each have our calling. And you know what my calling is, Aurélie? Would you believe it? One day I swore I was going to be a saint!"

"You, Monsieur? A saint? You must be joking!"

"Yes, I'm quite a joker, Aurélie. You'll never know how much of a joker I can be."

The doctor is laughing now. Aurélie too. Wiping her nose and her eyes on her sleeve. She's coming back to life. And so is he. Light as a bubble. His white teeth gleaming in his dark, whiskered face.

"Tassy, that worthless scum! Watch, Aurélie. I'll cut him down like the dog he is!"

Aurélie is doubled up, splitting her sides.

"Monsieur really is a joker. Believe you me."

I go over and join them at the hearth, by the fire's last dying embers. Anxious to claim my share in this burst of hilarity flashing between my maid and my lover. I break out into gales of laughter. I tell them: "I'll fix the fire." But I'm laughing so hard I can hardly breathe.

Who else would dare have such a hearty laugh over the crime we're planning? Who but the three of us . . .

ANOTHER glass of port, another fire in the hearth. And Aurélie, steeping in the gentle warmth of it all. Beginning to soften. But George won't let her sink all the way. Keeps her on the narrow brink between dreaming and waking. Pulling the strings of the dream himself. Holding them tight. Calls me to help him. Gives me a special part to play in Aurélie's submission . . . I'm speaking now with such astounding ease. As if my role were being whispered to me line by line. My movements are effortless. So light and airy.

"You mustn't fall asleep, Aurélie . . . You're too close to the fire. Move away a little or you'll burn your dress. Come, lean back here against me."

Aurélie obeys. Moves away. Leans back against me. Heaves a contented sigh. Lays her head in my lap. Looks up at me with languorous eyes.

"I feel so good like this, Madame. You can't imagine . . ."

A sign from George, and I start to undo her hair.

"Good God a'mighty, Madame. What are you doing?"

The doctor, again in his stern, sharp voice. A voice I recognize, with a twinge of pain.

"That's enough, Aurélie. Be quiet! Now close your mouth . . .

[175]

Your mouth! . . . And your eyes . . . Your eyes, Alouette! . . . There, 'gentille Alouette'! Now you're going to have a dream. We're going to give you the nicest dream you ever had. From now on you're working for me, George Nelson. For good, understand? Just like a nun when she takes her vows . . ."

I begin unfastening Aurélie's shawl, twisted around her waist and shoulders. She hardly moves. Lets me turn her this way and that. Limp as a little stuffed doll. Her pale lips fixed in a blissful smile. George has gone to my cupboard, brought out my red velvet gown. Together we roll her out of the black woollen shawl. Take off her bodice, her skirt. Pass Aurélie's frail body back and forth between us.

Her shabby chemise slips down around her legs. Her long black stocking are thrown on the bed . . . Aurélie opens one eye. Makes believe she's upset. Fairly swoons with delight.

"Good God a'mighty, what are you doing to me?"

George's voice, so painfully gentle, rips right through me.

"Now you mustn't open your eyes until I tell you, Aurélie."

My Irish linen petticoat, my openwork stockings, my velvet gown. Here and there, a pin to pull in the sagging waist, tuck up the trailing skirt. Aurélie's narrow shoulders. Aurélie's tiny breasts . . . My comb, run through that halo of ringlets framing a face so deathly pale . . .

Aurélie makes a show now of being awake. A curious glint in her beady yellow eyes. We hand her a mirror. She looks at her own reflection in amazement. Gives way to a kind of unspeakable rapture. Claps her hands. Begins to stir. To flutter. Struts about the room. Comes back to the mirror. Declares, in a shrill little drawl:

"I'm absolutely gorgeous! Just like a high-class lady!"

Still reeling a little, she walks around, glances over toward the bed. Forces a yawn. Turns to the doctor, all excited.

[176]

"I wouldn't mind having a go in bed. With a real gentleman, I mean . . ."

George grabs her sharply by the wrists. Pulls her back to the chair.

"You'll have your go in bed all right. And with a real gentleman, too. You know Monsieur Tassy, Aurélie? And you know how much he likes the ladies, don't you?"

Aurélie guffaws. Covers her face with her hands.

"Look at me, Aurélie. Take a good look. I'm your master now, and you're going to obey me. You're going to do whatever I tell you."

He doesn't take his eyes away from her. Each time she tries to break loose, he snares the child's fleeting glance and mercilessly pulls it back. Aurélie dreams that she's struggling hard. Dreams that she finally escapes, runs far away. While all the time, in fact, she scarcely moves at all. Pinned to the chair beneath the doctor's gaze. Only the rapid beating of her heart, pounding all over her trembling body.

"Let me go, Monsieur . . ."

"If only you put an end to Monsieur Tassy, you won't have to work again for the rest of your life, Aurélie. You'll live like a lady. Red velvet and all. And I'll give you a place of your own, with beautiful things. Or an allowance if you'd rather. And you'll live out your days in a lovely room, with a sofa to sit on . . . All dressed up in velvet, red or blue. Or in fancy silk. Whatever you want . . ."

Aurélie tosses her head from side to side against the chair. Back and forth. While through her greedy little body the wondrous words go coursing, pell-mell, all in a jumble. "Red velvet," "blue velvet," "fancy silk." "A place of your own," "beautiful things . . ." If only you put an end . . . If only, Aurélie . . .

My neck in the noose, dragged back to my room on Rue Augusta.

[177]

Next to the fire. While my mother and aunts are at vespers. I deny that a scene like that could ever take place between George Nelson and my maid, Aurélie Caron. Except in a dream, that is . . . The nightmare clings to me, sticks to my skin, won't let me go, poisons my existence. As soon as I close my eyes. And whenever I call her to come and help me, it's to have her deliver me from my evil, absolve me, cleanse me. Rid my love and me of this tale of madness. Aurélie, my friend, my sister. Think of your mistress. Your suffering mistress and her wicked husband. Think of her wonderful love for the doctor, warm and tender. Like nothing you've ever seen before, and never will, no matter how long you live. Nowhere, from Sorel to Kamouraska. Not even in Quebec or Montreal . . . No one will ever know, Aurélie. You only have to pour the poison in some brandy. You remember how much he likes his liquor and his women! . . . Aurélie, I can't go on without my love this way. I'll die, Aurélie . . .

Rue du Parloir. Someone is stirring beside my husband's bed. But I, Elisabeth d'Aulnières, evil Elisabeth, I only hear the sharp, clear voice of Aurélie Caron, off in another world. A world where . . .

"This love affair of yours will be the death of me, Madame! How long . . ."

A voice I adore replies.

"We only have to wait for the snow and the ice. As soon as the roads get hard enough, you'll leave for Kamouraska . . ."

"I'm Aurélie Caron, from the town of Sorel . . . That's who I am. Still a minor . . . The next morning, Doctor Nelson called me into his office. He gave me twenty dollars for the trip, and nine more to buy myself a bunch of clothes."

NOW Antoine's murder is in Aurélie's hands. Such a feeling of calm. A rare peace of mind.

Nothing to do now but wait. Be patient and wait for the snow. Learn to live within ourselves. With just enough room to exist. Careful not to look too far ahead. George, Aurélie, and I, trying to pull the four corners of space about us. Gather them round us. Reduce them to their simplest terms. Even less than the walls of a room. A kind of small, sealed box. A jar, closed tight. And we learn to breathe as little air as possible.

We mete out our every word, our every gesture. Choose them sparingly. Only the really essential ones. Stripped of all far-reaching implication. Gestures and words that have nothing to do with a certain plan that could ruin us all.

I have to take a careful look at Aurélie's new clothes. The ones she bought from Jean-Baptiste Denis, just for the trip. We're speaking to each other in a whisper.

"You're sure you won't be too cold, Aurélie?"

"Oh, no, Madame! . . . Look how pretty everything is! . . . Did you see the knitted shawl with the red tassels?"

Worst of all is Antoine's silence. Not knowing what he's doing, where he is. Couldn't he surprise us and come bursting in? Here in Sorel? Even at this very moment, while we're planning to go to him in Kamouraska? . . . Isn't there some uncomplicated way the whole thing could be done without disturbing Antoine's silence? Without piercing the mystery of anybody's silence, his or ours. Working invisibly, somehow. Leaving Antoine to stagnate, tucked away, buried in his manor in Kamouraska. Leaving him there forever, to sleep off his liquor and lick his wounded pride. Letting him calmly be swallowed up. Then vanishing, like merciful shadows, without a trace . . .

Aurélie has her new shawl on, over her head. Won't even take it off inside the house. Each time it slips down from that mass of unruly hair, piled high on her head in a tangle, back up it goes. She's sitting on the kitchen floor. Over and over, trying to read the future in the cards. And when it comes out badly she turns very pale and looks as if she's going to be sick. With one dramatic sweep she whisks the cards away. Comes looking for me all through the house. Whispers in my ear.

"We're in for a bad time, Madame! I can read it in the cards!"

Oh, how I wish she would leave! I can't bear having her here in the house! That deathly pallor . . . Yes, that's what sets my nerves on edge. I seem to see her wasting away before my eyes the closer we come to a certain day, the day she leaves . . . May as well ramble on like this about Aurélie and how bad she looks. It's better than thinking about the drunken, sickly squire of Kamouraska.

Besides, it's so easy to flush that moon-white face of hers. Just start to talk about velvet and fancy silk, mad love and consuming passion . . .

Soothed and comforted, imbued with a sense of her own importance, grasping and greedy beyond all decent bounds, Aurélie Caron swears that she'll carry out her mission. She packs her carpetbag. Carefully making sure that there's room between the piles of clothes to slip in the two little flasks the doctor has prepared.

[180]

SNOW. It's not the end of the world just yet. It's only snow. Snow, as far as the eye can reach. Like being lost at sea.

I'm here at my post, at my bedroom window, behind the blinds. Rue Augusta lies out at my feet, covered with white. Sleigh tracks gleam in the hardened snow. The shadows are very blue. Rue Philippe, close by, goes out into the country. The dry trees crackle in the wind . . . The gift. I have the gift of second sight. That's why they've put me here. Massive and motionless. (Almost ready to have my baby.) To learn what's going to happen. See it and hear it all. That's why they've torn me away from Rue du Parloir, in Quebec, at this very moment when my husband . . . As if the most pressing thing of all, the most urgent thing in my life, were to sit behind a window, here in Sorel, and wait for Jérôme Rolland's hoarse, throaty gasps to grow still forever.

Let them say and do what they please. I'm still the main witness in this drama of snow and passion. The others will come in, one by one, and refresh my memory. And even the places along the way, the scenes of the action—from Sorel to Kamouraska, Kamouraska to Sorel—will open themselves up before me. Free to come and go as I please, as the need arises. Never failing, never dying. Still so strangely fresh, this tale of mine . . .

I keep my watch. Lift a corner of the curtain. Scratch my nails against the frost. And my eyes go running up Rue Philippe, out toward the country. In no time at all I see the doctor's wooden house. The roof, sloping sharply, and snow piled high around the dormer. The stone chimney smoking against the hard blue sky.

Aurélie Caron goes tripping over the snow, her airy shadow dancing before her. A man in a raccoon coat is coming down the road to meet her, here in the bitter winter cold. Waving his arm above his head. Gesturing Aurélie on . . . Now they're side by side. Aurélie and this man whose figure, stoutly wrapped in fur, sets my heart beating, heavy and hollow. I can see them both very clearly. Thick clouds of frosty breath streaming from their lips. Aurélie stares at the ground.

"Well, Aurélie, winter's here at last. You leave tomorrow."

Little Aurélie Caron . . . Is she trying to resist? All ready to do his bidding, but not without a grumble. Is that a quiver I hear in her fretful voice as she declares:

"If I do a thing like this for you and Madame Tassy, I'll be disgraced forever. Me and my whole family . . ."

Behind the window I can only imagine what George Nelson and Aurélie Caron are saying. Only try to reproduce the sound of those voices I can't really hear, clashing together. In the bright winter morning.

"There's nothing to be afraid of. No one will ever know. Think of your poor mistress and how miserable she is. Think of your future, Aurélie . . ."

Her face, red with the cold. Knitting her brow and squinting in the brilliant sun. An instant, no more, and a monstrous idea works its way through her head. Then suddenly an end to all resistance. Under the dark and penetrating gaze that holds her fast.

Aurélie's voice, with a haughty little pout. Almost in a whisper.

"Besides, Monsieur, it's an awfully long trip . . ."

[182]

I wish I could urge her on. Encourage this child entrusted with such a frightful mission. Smile at her from behind my window. Promise her all the wonders that can transform her life.

"You won't have to work for the rest of your days, Aurélie. You'll have the prettiest dresses money can buy. You're my friend, my only friend. More than my friend, Aurélie. My sister . . ."

No use to go and shout myself hoarse. She can't hear me now. And neither can anyone else. My whole life has to run its course again, and there's nothing I can do about it. Not even make the slightest change. I won't be spared the least detail. May as well save my strength. Here in my glass cage, stop all my futile shouting. Opening, closing my mouth, like goldfish in a bowl.

Nothing to do but count the hours, the days. Wait until Aurélie Caron comes back. Pay careful attention to how much time goes by. Try to imagine exactly what she's doing at every moment. This child, traveling down the river . . .

Monday evening George gives Aurélie two little bottles. One with a half-pint of brandy in it. The other, a whitish liquid, just about a wineglass full. Next morning, bright and early, Aurélie climbs up into the mail coach. Dressed in her new clothes, from tip to toe, like a bride going off on her wedding trip. A coat of homespun cloth, a green serge dress, a pair of Indian boots, heavy knitted stockings. And the red woollen shawl, with the tassels.

Aurélie doesn't let her carpetbag out of her sight. Keeps it by her feet all the way. At Trois-Rivières she takes the stagecoach to Quebec. Then the boat across to Pointe-Lévis. She meets a man from Kamouraska at the dock, and he offers to take her to Kamouraska for a couple of dollars.

[183]

M̲Y third child is born. I can hear a young woman screaming with pain inside me. I can hear a man, all by himself, singing a lullaby in a closed house on the outskirts of Sorel. Perhaps in some secret way he's actually part of the winter cold. Blended and fused together as one. Just as he seemed to be part of the mud-soaked roads one autumn night . . . I can hear the tune he's humming: "My baby and my wife, in one bouquet of love . . ." His tenderness, soft as honey. Shine a light on his heart, examine it. You won't find even a trace of sin. Now the murder is all in Aurélie Caron's hands. And the poison. We're saved. Both of us, peaceful and calm, as if by some miracle. Only time will tell if this deceptive peace might not make us shriek with fright one day . . .

I wish Aurélie could try her skill on my newborn son. Lick him all over from head to toe, and tell me whether or not he tastes of salt and death.

Do things like that shock and disgust you, Doctor Nelson? Risk stirring up the worthy country doctor's righteous wrath? Don't you know how useful it can be, at times, for nice little witches to be born and die? To walk the earth just long enough to bear the burden of crime and death for us?

Whatever you do, my love, don't think too much about Aurélie. Don't give a thought to taking her place in Kamouraska. I don't want you to leave me. To overcome a certain loathing and let your handsome face take on the mask of death. No, no, I beg you. No, not you . . .

My three fairy godmothers—a little more stooped, a little more bony and brittle—are leaning over my new baby's cradle. Blessing him, in the depths of their apprehensive hearts. Bestowing upon him the seven traditional gifts of the Spirit. But without much faith left in the power of their love. And with tears welling up in their eyes . . .

The midwife washes her hands. Folds up her butcher apron. Laughs with every wrinkle in her face. Goes off to bring the happy news to Doctor Nelson, just as he asked.

"It's a boy, Doctor Nelson. Madame Tassy gave birth to a boy. About three this morning. She's doing fine. And the baby seems set to stay around a good long time! . . ."

You're bending over this bed where I bore my child. Saying that everything is just as it ought to be. That only people who are really alive, the way we are, deserve to live.

Someone is here in the bedroom with us. Someone surprised at how long Aurélie has been gone. Three weeks already since . . .

AGAIN the window, covered with frost. The command to keep an eye on the street, be sure to notice if anyone comes or goes. Watch for the slightest sign. I'm hardly over my labor, hardly on my feet, and still I have to take up my post again behind the glass. Scan the horizon as far as the eye can see. To the utmost limits of my concentration. As far as Kamouraska. I must, I have no choice . . . I've just found out that Aurélie is back, and already George is going to leave. Right away. It can't be helped. And I have to say good-bye to him through a windowpane. Forever and ever, this screen between us, this layer of glass and ice. Your image, distorted by frost and death, off to the end of the world. Good-bye my love. Adieu mon amour . . . When you come back nothing will be the same. You won't be, I won't be . . . I plead with you not to go. You tell me that Aurélie failed us, and that now you'll just have to go yourself.

"He won't get away from me, that swine!"

Torture her, hang her, cut off her head, rip it from her body . . . Aurélie won't take back a word of her story. She'll shout it loud and clear through all eternity.

"I put the poison in his brandy and gave it to him to drink. Then

I left him for dead in the sleigh. And he was, too. He was dead . . ."

"But look, you little fool! I'm telling you that Monsieur Tassy is still alive! We got a letter from his mother just this morning. She says he's fine, in spite of those little flings of his once in a while!"

"Little flings! Sweet Jesus! He drank half the poison in the tin cup I gave him! And I left him in his sleigh. And I'm sure he was good and . . . No, that man must have nine lives, that's all. Like a cat! . . ."

Rose Morin, servant in the manor at Kamouraska, says she can't sign her name. Makes a cross.

"Thursday night, at about eleven, Monsieur Tassy came home, and he was very sick. He kept throwing up. He told me he was at the inn. The Dionnes' inn. And that this girl he knew gave him something to drink. Yes, he was really sick. Straight through till Sunday. And then he began to get better. Little by little. For a long time his face was all pale, and he looked just awful . . ."

The sound of a whip cracks through the echoing air. It's five in the morning. At the other end of Sorel a man is putting up the collar of his peasant coat. Tightening his woollen belt around his waist. Climbing into an American sleigh perched high on its runners. Speaking softly to himself. Like someone who's all alone in the world. Saying that now he knows what he's good for. That this is something that has to be settled man to man. The days of witches are over. Their poisons, their charms, their iron cauldrons . . . Put away, laid aside with lullabies and swaddling clothes. Evil Elisabeth, all because of you . . .

Black on white. Beard, hair, eyes, heart . . . Oh, yes, especially your heart. Black, black, black . . . The horse and sleigh. And the white snow, blinding, under pounding hooves, all the way to the end of the road. Of every road. Where the horizon teeters on the edge of emptiness. To kill a man, out at the farthest reaches of all that emptiness. To keep from falling over, into the abyss. Just long enough to take aim and fire. A gallon of blood to shed. About a gallon, not much more. You're a doctor. You know about things like that. No one knows as much about birth and death as you. No one, except perhaps those backwoods crones. Eternal seamstresses of swaddling clothes and shrouds . . .

Five in the morning. You let the sleigh bells on your horse's collar go jingling gaily along. As if they were around your neck, ringing out their joy. Nobody else could bear to be as strangely lighthearted as you are this morning.

If someone turns over in his sleep, as your sleigh goes by . . . Jumps up in bed . . . Pricks up his ears . . . Falls back on his pillow, and says: "It's Doctor Nelson off to take care of the sick . . ." Well, let him think so. I won't contradict him.

Rue Augusta. A woman at the window, chilled to the bone. Not a wink of sleep all night . . . Follow the plan. Look up at her, nod to her way up there. Standing in your sleigh. Your arms held over your head. The whip raised up against the blackened sky.

Farewell, my love. Au revoir, mon amour. We won't be seeing each other again until what must be done is done. Out there, in Kamouraska.

Farewell, my love . . . Your horse and sleigh are taking you off, taking you far, far away, over the hardened snow . . . I can't see you now. I can't hear you now. Your scent is beginning to vanish from my skin. Just a piece of your clothing . . . Your jacket, your scarf . . . And I'd curl up on it and bury my head. Like a faithful dog . . . Maybe then, secure and calm, steeped in the scent I love, maybe then I would fall asleep.

When I close my eyes I see you there, prey to the strange mutations of man and beast. One image haunts me more than the rest. You remember that cock in the stable? The one that would climb up on your horse and spend all night on his back? . . . One morning his spurs get tangled in the horse's mane. Your horse rears up. Stands on his hind legs. The cock is stuck, spreads his wings out wide. Tries to get loose. Flutters and flaps in wild despair. To no avail. Cock and horse seem joined together in one incredible, monstrous whole. A single creature, thrashing about. A single flailing of wings and hooves. A single bedlam of snorts and cackles. Filling the stable with its awful din, beating against the walls of the stall. In one great shower of feathers and hair, one burst of shattered planks and twisted nails . . .

I scream. That frenzied fury, my love. It's you. That cock and that horse, fused into a single being. It's you. You, galloping blithely off. Off on your way to horror and murder. Over a perilous snow-covered road.

O begin with, Aurélie's predictions about the weather come true. It's clear and mild. No wind at all. Sainte-Anne-de-Sorel, Saint-François-du-Lac, Pierreville, Nicolet . . .

Be calm and pleasant. Mustn't forget to nurse my son. It's Sunday and I have to go to mass. Say my prayers. Ask God to let George be successful. Smile . . . Someone is talking to me. Has to ask the same question twice, it seems.

"One or two sugars in your tea?"

"Two, please."

Keep my voice firm. Make sure it's crisp and clear. Allow them to train me in the social graces and never bat an eye. Go through this most demanding pastime. In such proper company too. Under the noses of the dear old ladies of Sorel. Follow the path of a sleigh over the snow. Deep within myself, secure behind my sweet and gentle face . . . My ear to the ground, sharper than any trapper's, listening for the slightest noise. Hears the distant sound of hooves. The steady swish of a sleigh running over the frozen road along the river, from Sorel to Kamouraska. The road that follows the southern shore. Over its every twist and turn.

"A little milk in your tea?"

"Yes, please. A little milk . . ."

[190]

Someone is saying that Doctor Nelson has gone off to the United States, that his father is very sick.

Ever so softly I pick up the thread of George Nelson's actual journey. Names of villages clash in my head. Sainte-Anne-de-Laval, Bécancour, Gentilly, Saint-Pierre-les-Becquets . . . My love is on his way. Farther and farther. Beyond the region where Aurélie said the weather would be fine. Through wilderness. Out beyond the silence . . . The road, till now so flat, hardly higher than the river. And now, hill after hill. Up one side, down the other. Up again, down again. And all that snow piled high in the ravines! If only I were sure that the road was well marked! Are those scraggy little fir trees there, along the sides, stuck like fish bones into the snow?

"Aurélie! Aurélie! Do you think the weather up there is still all right? Do you think the road . . . Is it marked, Aurélie?"

Aurélie is smoking. Never stops. Seems anxious to hide in a cloud of smoke. An old blanket wrapped about her, from head to toe. She says she's awfully cold. Looks like certain nuns. Pulls the blanket round her face till only a bit of sallow, pale-lipped profile shows.

"The weather, the roads . . . I don't know anymore, Madame. It's all too far away. In a damnable country I wish I never knew."

"Yes, Aurélie, that damnable country . . . But you do remember, don't you? A sleigh ride with my husband?"

"I told him I wanted to go to Saint-Pascal. He said he'd take me there in his sleigh. At first I said no. A girl like me, after all, with a gentleman like him. But he insisted."

Antoine is drunk already. You know how Monsieur likes his liquor and his women! Oh, how I loathe him. I grit my teeth at the very thought. And you, Aurélie. I loathe you too. Carrying on like a slut with my husband. The long trip to Saint-Pascal, in his sleigh . . . None of it makes any sense, except as a prelude to death. But look! All of a sudden Antoine has risen from the grave.

With his insides on fire . . . You've failed us, Aurélie! Monsieur Tassy is still alive! His mother says so in her letter . . . There he is, leaving his manor. Riding along the highway. Enormous, massive, terrible. With his tremendous fists. Looking for my lover, to kill him. Looking for us both.

"Aurélie, I'm so afraid!"

"And what about me? If you don't think I'm good and afraid, Madame . . ."

Aurélie goes about the house picking up all the worn and washed-out clothing she can find. Begs to be allowed to keep it. Claims that nothing but faded colors suit her now. (The red shawl with the tassels and all her other nice new clothes are nowhere to be found.) She tells me she's sick. George has already said that he can't do anything for her. That she doesn't have any real disease, but that still she could die from it all the same.

Aurélie and I embrace each other. A strange and frightful tenderness binds us together. Sets us apart from the rest of the world.

We whisper senseless words. To take our minds off other things . . .

"Your Easter duty, Aurélie?"

"And yours, Madame?"

"Damn you, child!"

"And damn you too, Madame! You and your husband both! And as for that darling doctor of yours . . . Well, that one's the very devil himself!"

LOBINIERE, Sainte-Croix, Saint-Nicolas, Pointe-Lévis . . . For how many days and nights . . . And here I am, hearing the winter cold, the winter silence along with my love. Hurtling with him headlong over snow-covered roads, until the end of time. No other thought for you now, only this deadly cold that consumes you. Strikes me to the heart. Works its way under my nails. The endless, motionless nights by the window. An invisible someone, strong and unrelenting, holding me tight, flat against the glass. Crushing me with gigantic palms. Squeezed to a pulp. Gasping for air, pressed thin as a piece of seaweed . . . Soon I'll be nothing but a flowery swirl of frost traced out among the window's icy arabesques . . . No! I want to live! And you? Tell me you're still alive. Your strength. Your unshakable will. Let this scheme of ours weigh lightly on you, easy to bear. Let it change to a flame, burn bright and clear. Protect you, help you all along your way . . . One constant thought, rekindled over and over. Like a beacon in the storm. Our passion . . .

Don't play the doctor, whatever you do. Don't claim that the trouble is all in ourselves. A clot in our veins? A wart on our skin? The secret deep down in our bellies? Some tiny creature caught inside? Some minuscule tick lodged just below the surface . . .

Is it sin? Who can probe the depths of our bodies, our hearts? No trap is fine enough. And the English law of this captive land that says we're innocent until they prove us guilty . . .

My heart, leaping, rattling inside me. Smashing against my temple, my neck, my wrist . . . Does my newborn baby taste my madness? Does he taste its heady flavor in every gulp of milk that bubbles from my breast?

"How many places should we set?" "Justine forgot to iron the napkins." "Baby Louis is kicking and screaming at the least little thing . . ."

The time has come now to split in two. Accept this total, sharp division of my being . . . Deep as I can, I probe the pleasure I feel. This rare delight, pretending I'm really here. Learning to leave my words and gestures far behind me. With no one any the wiser, no one to know how utterly empty they are.

I'm quieting the baby, calming his temper. And even as I do, I'm losing myself in a string of names, repeated one by one. Names of villages all along the river. Repeated over and over, to my heart's content. Like someone saying a rosary, bead by bead, and pondering all the while this world and its savage mysteries.

LAUZON, Beaumont, Saint-Michel, Berthier . . .
Time! Time! Piling over me in heaps. Covering me with an icy
armor. Silence, spreading itself in snowy sheets . . . Swept along
in his sleigh, George has long since gone beyond the human pale.
Now he's plunging deep into a boundless waste. Like a sailor, alone,
setting his course for the open sea . . . It's pointless for me now
to ask about the snow out there, the cold. We don't depend on
the same rules anymore for snow and frost, the same conditions
for fatigue and fear. Too far away. Why worry about a storm, with
its great gusts blowing over the roads and hiding the trails? Is my
love battling gales of swirling snow, treacherous as the waters of
torrential streams? Is my love breathing frost instead of air? Is
my love spitting snow in puffs of icy smoke? Are his lungs on
fire? Does his blood begin to freeze? . . . Once out beyond a
certain point of horror, he changes into someone else. Escapes
from me forever . . .

Clinging to the curtain in my room. Pressed against the window,
like a leech. Sorel. Rue Augusta. This sanctuary, hardly safe. The
refuge of my youth, exposed. Ripped open like the stuffed little
belly of a doll. And all my memory's wiles and windings, twists
and turnings, lead me nowhere. Nowhere but emptiness. What

[195]

is Doctor Nelson doing down by the mouth of the river? Has he managed yet to . . . ? Nothing. I know nothing at all about him now. I live in an utter void. A desert of snow, chaste and sexless as hell itself. No use to scan the limitless white expanse, stripped of its villages and their people. The endless forests. The frozen river. No black horse now along the horizon.

Has George Nelson lost his way? Has he frozen to death in the snow?

Watch out for the snow. It can seem so soft and gentle. But the flakes close ranks and attack us, hem us in. Warn George. But how? Tell him not to be lulled by the dreamlike visions that rise up from the snow. By that serene delirium, that fatal fascination. (A twinge in the heart, no more. And little by little we begin to give way. Go musing, slipping from dream to dream, and off into a deep, deep sleep.) Not let him drop his guard. Keep all his love and hate alive and green . . . Far as the eye can reach, a motionless sea of snow, covering country, town and village, man and beast, as one. Erasing every joy and pain. Stifling every scheme the moment it comes to life. And all the while the cold connives its way in and offers the solace of its deathly calm. That man out there, on the road to Kamouraska. That one man among all others . . . If only he can cling to the reins. If only he doesn't let them go, even for a moment. It's not that his hand has gone numb. Not yet. Just so consumed by the uselessness of every move it makes. Such weariness too. Such a need to sleep. Such a strange, dull, comfortable feeling spreading all through that hand. A hand that won't (or can't) hold on anymore . . . Now two hands letting the horse run free. Two hands in the lap, lying helpless, blissful, heavy, so heavy, so wholly at peace. A vast, perfidious peace . . . Two hands, side by side. It seems they're a little more numb, a little more clumsy, perhaps, than they were. Less clearly shaped, less well defined inside the mittens. One after another, each finger,

[196]

outlined thicker and heavier than before. Each one so crucial, and yet so still, unable to move. Less and less feeling in them all the time. Dying. Just dying, one by one . . .

Pushed to the limits my mind can reach, I feel the numbing cold down by the river's mouth. And the burning flash of blood as it starts to flow again. (The man is rubbing his hands with snow.) Can it be that I'm really dreaming this pain that somebody else has to suffer? A dream too clear, too sharp to bear. Behind me I feel the resistless force that drives George Nelson on and on toward Kamouraska. That sends him in search of the next inn's shelter down the road.

If only the nice little ladies of Sorel could help me. Rather put up with their senseless chatter than have to go through . . .

Montmagny, Cap Saint-Ignace, Bonsecours, Saint-Jean-Port-Joli, Saint Roch des-Aulnaies . . . I think I must be moving my lips, like old women in church.

"The child is in simply a frightful state. She's feverish and just keeps mumbling her prayers. We'll have to find something to keep her busy, don't you think?"

"We haven't had a spell of cold like this in a long, long time . . ."

Some way to shut these women up. Like covering a parrot cage at night. To make it all quiet again . . . But not for long. There's something alive. Moving, spreading, filling the depths of the silence. Rising to the surface. Bursting like bubbles, muffled and dull, against my ear. A man's voice. Slow, expressionless, choosing his every word with care. Speaking to me. As if he hated to have to do it. Telling me, almost in a whisper, about a stranger who came to the inn at Saint-Vallier. (Oh, yes, I forgot all about Saint-Vallier, between Saint-Michel and Berthier.)

"Michel-Eustache Letellier. Tuesday, the 29th of January, at about nine at night, a young man came to the inn. Not from these parts. A nice-looking fellow, he was. Black hair. Whiskers, but not too long. He stayed overnight at the inn and left the next morning, bright and early."

I try to stop, get a foothold at the inn at Saint-Vallier. Try to see what the young stranger looks like. But already the innkeeper's voice goes running along, faster and faster now, hurtling me on through time. At the speed of his words. With no image to cling to. No face to recall . . .

Now Michel-Eustache Letellier is speaking again. About the young stranger, and how he returned. Sunday, the third of February, at night.

"I noticed that on his way back those black whiskers of his were much longer than before. Almost covered the whole of his face. And he really seemed awfully excited and upset. Why, he pulled off his woollen belt and threw it away. Right in the fire. You could smell it burning all through the hall."

I wish I could fill my lungs with the odor of smoldering wool. In the hall at the inn at Saint-Vallier. Walk up to that man bent over the fire. Creep up behind him. Take my time gazing at my lover's neck. The back of his neck. Sure as I've always been that that's where you'll find a man's vigor and power. Such fierce determination in George Nelson's neck. So graceful, yet so strong. And hiding the secret of his energy deep inside. It fills me with awe and despair, both at once. Oh, to possess my love. To make him my own, like my very own hand. Be with him at every deed of his wonderful manly strength. Knowing his every thought. Feeling his every pain. To be two with him. Double and fierce with him. Raise my arm with him when the time comes to do it. To kill my husband with him.

HE belt he burned, his homespun coat, his little black hood, his fur-trimmed cap, his black horse and American sleigh, the bisonskin blankets lined with red . . . Sorel to Kamouraska and back in ten days. Four hundred miles, in the dead of winter, without even a change of horse.

No use for the innkeepers down the river to go over the same description, hit or miss. There's no one but me who could really . . .

The stranger says he's off to do what has to be done. Where nobody else can take his place. Or understand, or feel the way he does. Let Elisabeth d'Aulnières look after the children and try to comfort Aurélie as best she can. This is a job for a man to take care of. Between this man and his solitude, that's all. And now, coming to meet him at dizzying speed, this act that will give that solitude its meaning. The strange conclusion to the frantic battle George Nelson has waged for so long against death. Perhaps forever? Almost since the day he was born. Or maybe even in his mother's womb . . . ? His dead mother, snatched away so soon. And the child, so dark and thin. Struggling against the image of death within himself. Or perhaps the thought of his father's death? Or the son's (his own reflection, that is, so distorted, so terribly weak)? Or Antoine's childish face, with his big, fat cheeks, bending over a basin of icy water?

Raw flesh, rotting corpse, blood, pus, urine, filth of every kind, gangrenous decay, noxious stench, crushed bones, drowned beauties with eyes agape and swollen bellies, baby born deformed, woman raped, galloping consumption, diphtheria, dysentery . . . Doctor Nelson has fought so hard against disease and death. He's given so much of his life to the saving of men and women. But this one won't escape.

"He won't get away from me, Aurélie."

This one deserves to die. He's much too fat, too soft and weak. His wife is too pretty and so unhappy. He's lost her, and now he'll lose his life. Better if the squire of Kamouraska had never been born at all.

What can Antoine Tassy be doing on that lonely cape of his out in the river? Under the piercing gaze of Madame Tassy, his mother? Does he keep rehearsing his fits of rage and wounded pride, over and over, in endless drunken revels? Is he ready to go after some simple, frightened young peasant girl and chase her from barn to barn, from shed to stable? Isn't the one task left for him now to wait for his murderer, making his way over miles and miles to reach him?

Antoine's strange complicity drives me to distraction. Yet all of this is taking place beyond me. In a far-off land full of blood and snow. Between two men, bound to each other by an awesome, otherworldly mystery. What if each of them, both at once, were to wear the same fraternal face? Two men, with faces racked and transfigured by something strange and dreadful sweeping over them. The taste of death. And what if, somehow, I could see it all happen? There in the cove at Kamouraska. A loaded pistol, aimed at a young man's temple. A young man, much too fat, and rotten to the core . . . No, I would die! I'm sure I would die! I'm just the opposite of death. I'm love. Living and loving. Living and dying . . . No, I want to live! And I want you to live! Antoine is the one who has to die. Well, let him die then, and that will be that!

Sainte-Anne-de-Pocatière! A name that rings like a bell. A single peal, long and deep, echoing in the winter cold. Once past Sainte-Anne the witnesses' stories will start to multiply, make leaps and bounds, burst into view, cut across one another, complete one another. Strike like arrows against my flesh.

George Nelson has come this way. He's been seen. Looked over. Followed. His description will be picked up from tavern to tavern. From inn to inn. From village to village.

If only I could conjure up once more the chatter of the gentle ladies of Sorel. I'd make it a bulwark against the innkeepers' menacing voices, swelling together in a deep, hoarse drawl, all down along the southern bank. Buzzing around my head. Like a swarm of angry bees . . . Safe with my aunts again. Their boundless love. Their tender pity.

"The child is sick. We'd better put her to bed. Take care of her. Fix her some compresses, nice and cool . . ."

That little round woman! Her blue apron. Face all pink. Features melting together like an old cake of soap! What right does she have to stand at the foot of my bed? Who's forcing her, here in the darkness, to raise her right hand and swear in a tearful voice?

"Victoire Dufour. Wife of Louis Clermont, owner of the inn in Sainte-Anne-de-la-Pocatière parish . . ."

How on earth could my aunts let someone come bursting into my sickroom like that? . . . Oh, no! They've left! And so has my mother! Left me alone with her. Her and her blue apron. I can smell her sour breath. And there's nothing I can do to make her go. Now she's bending over my bed. With her big eyes, cold and hard. Lifeless, unmoving. Staring right at me. How long have those pale eyes been looking at me like that? Those eyes that can't blink. That just gaze at me and fill with tears. Can it be that they don't even see me? Those glassy eyes, still as the hands of a clock stopped dead . . . I'm spellbound, transfixed. Chained to my bed. And the woman in the blue apron is talking and sniffling. If she'd just give her nose a good blow, once and for all, and come right out with what she has to say. That's what she's here for, isn't it? And I wouldn't miss a single word, I'm sure of that. Trussed up the way I am.

Oh, how I wish she'd stop that whimpering! It wouldn't be so hard to stand her scene . . .

"I was really frightened, Your Honor. We're poor people, me and my husband, and we run a little inn. There's not too much close by, not many neighbors, you know. And it's a good thirty miles to the church at Kamouraska. Besides, our children are all still small. The oldest one is going on nine. And our hired girl is deaf . . . Well, it was the 31st of January, at about two in the afternoon. I saw this man, this stranger, coming along the road, heading down the river. So I stood at the door to watch him go by. He was driving a different kind of sleigh, not like the ones we have around here. And his overcoat was made of some sort of grayish cloth. It looked to me like what they make way upriver, a lighter shade than ours. With a black hood. And he had on a dark cloth hat, with fur all around. It was good and cold, and his face was red. He seemed like a nice-looking fellow, maybe a little young. Well anyway, afterwards, I went back in. It wasn't until later on, that night, that . . . No, my husband will tell you the rest . . ."

No harm in seeing the round, blue woman clutch at the foot of my bed with both her hands. (The witness stand.) And no harm in hearing her describe the young stranger in such exact, minute detail. The danger would be if I recognized him and let him recognize me. For our own good, his and mine, I really can't be too careful. Just play dead. Stay out of it altogether. And if they question me, shake my head on the pillow from side to side. Tell them, "No, no, I don't know who he is." Not lift a finger to put

[202]

George on his guard. Powerless to warn him about the innkeepers
. . . See! They've thrown us to the witnesses already, even before
. . . I speak to you softly, so softly . . . Without my lips, or my
eyes, or by hands. Even without my heart, held tight in the grip
. . . Make believe I'm asleep. Perfect imitation of a flat, hard stone.
And I urge you on, so softly that my voice becomes a kind of
heavy, muffled whisper, from the depths of my being. My love,
I'm here. I'll wait my whole life through until you're done, there
in the cove at Kamouraska. Until you wash your blood-soaked
hands and make your way back to me. Your handsome face,
triumphant over death, flashing with a wild delight. The way I
love you, yearn to make you mine. But first you'll have to push
yourself beyond the limits of your strength. That absolute, gnaw-
ing away inside you. Turn it to crime, to a deed of blood. You're
so much like Catherine of the Angels, you know. One day, in the
little chapel of Monseigneur de Laval, you swore that you too
would become a saint. No answer from above. Only your wild,
unfathomable passion. What dark god must have heard your vow?
But now your prayer is answered, granted beyond your wildest
dreams. Take care not to faint and fall!

I'm surprised I can stand the snow in this brilliant sun. The
blinding glare of the bright blue sky. Sainte-Anne-de-la-Pocatière.
January 31, 1839. That day of days. I can see it all. Everything,
so clear. The little clumps of snow kicked up by the horse's hooves.
That kind of white smoke following the sleigh. The highroad,
straight, packed down by all the sleighs gone by . . . Then a
man's face, red with cold, turning in my direction. Is it me he's
looking at? His upper lip curled in a strange, corpselike smile. And
his teeth! I never knew they were so long and pointed! There on
the sides. Like some wild beast. And it's terror, suddenly, that
clouds my eyes. Destroys the image of my love . . .

Gaily the sleigh bells jingle in the sharp, brisk air. Begin to
fade, a little at a time. Off in the distance, toward Kamouraska.
Then finally die . . . Innkeeper Clermont's wife closes her door.

IVIERE-OUELLE, Rivière-Ouelle . . . To hear that name ringing in my ears and not have the strength to get up from my bed.

"Madame is sick. See how she's trembling in her sleep?"

My mother and my aunts have really left the room. I think it's Léontine Mélançon's voice I hear.

Rivière-Ouelle. Cling for dear life to the name of that village. Like a buoy. (The village just this side of Kamouraska.) Try to stretch time, make it last. (Five or six miles from Kamouraska.) Draw out the syllables "ri" and "vi" as far as they can go. Then let them open out on the "ère". Try hard to hold onto the "Ouelle." But no use. That liquid name, rippling and rolling, runs off like a brooklet through the mossy grass. Soon the green-tart, jagged sounds of "Kamouraska" will jangle against one another. That old Algonquin name. Rushes-beside-the-water . . .

I play with the syllables. Hit them hard against one another. To drown out all those human voices that could rise up against me in one great throng. To raise a great roar of syllables, loud and harsh. Turn them into a shield of stone. A sling to protect me, tough and resilient. "Kamouraska! Kamouraska!" Rushes-beside-the-water! . . . Good God, they're coming! Those voices from down the river, they're on the move! All of them talking at once! The bees! Again the bees! . . . The people from down the river, closing their ranks, on the young stranger's trail. Their voices, louder and louder, clearer and clearer. Describing him, accusing him. And his wonderful, strange black sleigh, and his black horse more wonderful still . . .

Outside my bedroom door the witnesses wait, begin to lose patience. They've taken the whole house over, the house on Rue Augusta. Laid it waste. Destroyed it from top to bottom. My mother and my aunts are buried in the ruins, gasping for air. If only the witnesses stay where they are. Not go sneaking off to Quebec and Rue du Parloir, where my husband is so sick! It's easy to seize on a dying man's wild delusions and mix in a share of calumny and terror.

Besides, soon I'll be off where Jérôme Rolland can't touch me. Way out beyond the reach of everything that still draws breath. I'll be pulled out of bed. Stood on my feet with all my clothes. Dragged from my house. Thrown in with the witnesses. (Tell us all you know.) Mixed and stirred up with them all, in one soft, doughy mass. Put out in the snow. The cold. One silent, unresisting watch. Taking turns with myself, changing places with myself, here and there, from inn to inn. And everyone whispering in my ear. Everyone. Innkeepers, husbands and wives, hired girls and servants and stable boys, peasants and fishermen. All of them swearing to drag me along. To throw me out on the frozen road On the trail of a traveler that no one but me can name.

"Bruno Boucher, from Rivière-Ouelle, hired hand . . . It was last January the 31st, on a Thursday, at about half-past two. I was coming back from the woods with my cart full of logs, and I met a stranger. He stopped me and asked if it was far to the manor house in Kamouraska. I figured he couldn't be one of us, because he made a lot of mistakes when he talked. And I got a good look at his horse and his sleigh. Never in all my days saw anything like either one of them . . ."

"Jean-Baptiste Saint-Onge, from Rivière-Ouelle, hired hand at Pierre Bouchard's . . . A stranger came to the inn at about half-past three in the afternoon. He asked me to water his horse. I stood for a long time just looking at it. That horse and that sleigh were really something to see. I'd know them anywhere. The harness straps were black and the collar had a lot of little bells. He went riding off about five o'clock, fast as you please. Toward Kamouraska. Next morning, the first of February, a Friday, I saw him again. Same man, same horse, same sleigh. I recognized what he was wearing. There he was, going by my place, somewhere between seven and eight . . . I live just off the main road, up toward the northeast, half a mile or so from the inn . . . Well, I pointed out to my boy that the stranger didn't have those little bells now, the ones he had the day before. And just to be funny I said I wished I knew he wanted to get rid of them. I'd have been happy to take them off his hands . . ."

"The stranger hid the sleigh bells under the seat before he left for Kamouraska . . ."

"A little black hood, an overcoat of that cloth they make up-river, a dark blue rough-weave jacket with double pockets at the hips. Thick knitted stockings, or they could have been leggings, with little black buttons up one side, and leather soles if I'm not mistaken . . ." "Seemed like a nice-looking young man to me. Average size, well built. Black whiskers and a ruddy, dark complexion. I'd say he was twenty-five or six . . ." "I could tell by the stranger's clothes, and the way he talked and acted, that he wasn't just some ordinary man . . ." "Did you see how white his teeth were? . . ." "He snapped back that he was in a hurry . . ."

"He seemed uneasy and nervous, even more on the way back from Kamouraska than on the way there . . ." "That man's not one of us. If you ask me he's got an English accent. Or even some foreign country maybe. And that sleigh of his with the covered front, and the poles attached in the middle of the dashboard. You couldn't miss it . . ."

I try to draw out this torpor that surrounds me. Out to its absolute limits. The witnesses chattering by my bed. Their endless, almost solemn pacing fills the room. But I'm still unhurt, unharmed. All these people, pressing about me, puffing in my face, looking me over with gluttonous glances. Secretly plotting relentless ways to force me out of bed. Tear me forever from my house on Rue du Parloir. Far from my poor, dear husband who's about to . . . Planning to take me bodily to Kamouraska. I know I can't escape. They'll banish me to Kamouraska, dead or alive. The most I can hope for is to put them off. Hold out a little longer. An inert mass. Blind, deaf, and dumb. They'll have to grab me by the wrists and drag me along . . . And this stranger you all describe with such insistence, such precision. No, I won't give him refuge. I won't give him papers to prove he has a name. Not now. There's no one but me that can bring him back to life. Save him from time and oblivion. Condemn him again, and myself along with him. That's one thing I'll never do, as long as I live. Tell them, "Look, that man is my lover. His name is George Nelson. He's murdered my husband. And we're guilty, the two of us. So hang us why don't you, and let's get it over with . . ." No, no. I won't say a word.

ME, Elisabeth d'Aulnières. Not here as a witness, but to watch and play a part. Here in Sainte-Anne-de-la-Pocatière, at Louis Clermont's inn. Not like just another traveler, taken in and given a bed and room. Not like any ordinary guest. Bags sitting on the braided rug beside the bed. Toilet things on the sink, next to the flowered basin and pitcher. But set down, still and silent, right in the middle of the house. To see and hear what happens. Nowhere in particular, and everywhere at once. The hall, the bedrooms . . .

First I have to get to know the place. Before a certain stranger comes knocking at the door. I won't disturb a soul. It seems that no one can see me. Or at least no one bothers to look. Not the innkeeper, not his wife, not the one they call Blanchet. Resigned to my being here. Not willing, just resigned. Something that can't be helped. Forced on them here in Sainte-Anne-de-la-Pocatière, at Louis Clermont's inn. By some unbending will. Dropped like a bundle. Thrust into the bosom of this house barred shut. In the middle of winter. Just off the road between Sainte-Anne and Kamouraska. On the night of January 31st.

The cracks in the windows, plugged up with wadding, or with newspaper moistened and rolled in a ball. The two-decked stove, a solid mass of black, standing for all to see in the room that they use as a hall and a kitchen. Blanchet, the drunken beggar, asleep on a wooden bench by the stove, wrapped in an old potato-colored blanket . . . Like any other winter night at this godforsaken inn.

Outside, the huge expanse of snow, far as the eye can see. That kind of thick, white mist, rising from the fields, the road, the river. Wherever the wind can blow up gusts of snow. Great blasts that hide the roads and trails. And the thought of the cove at Kamouraska, boring through my head. The echo of the thought, throbbing its way through my head. Hard against my bones.

The darkening hall, the dying fire. The glimmer of coals through the slits in the little stove door, shut up for the night. The beggar and his noisy breathing, lying on his back with his mouth open wide . . .

I'm waiting for a stranger who'll come knocking at the door. Rattling its timbers with pounding fists. Asking for a place to spend the night. To hear his voice. To be here at the inn, just waiting for that voice. Unlike any other. Maybe to find it more harsh now, more hoarse . . . To be turned inside out by the sound of that voice. To be shaken and sapped and ripped apart by the sound of that voice, as if . . . To wait for that wonderful voice my whole life through, in vain . . . His dark and handsome face. This man of mine. His body bundled up in winter clothes. Stripping them off and standing bare. And me, stripped just as bare, as he comes to my side. Making his way to reach me, through layers and layers of disaster . . . Time, time! Great sooty clouds. The past, leaped over in one prodigious bound. Murder and madness reduced to size. Cleansed of their demons. Their right weight restored. No longer bigger than life, no longer seen through a glass with many sides. (Deformed by panic and anguish.) Our weapons, shining clean and undefiled. For attack, for defense. Spotless and polished now, after the battle. Love and freedom, bought at their terrible price. Their blood-price paid in coins of gold, heavy and gleaming, piled on the chair by the bed. Along with our clothes, neatly folded. A fine, big bed for the two of us, all night long. Where we're sure to have cool, crisp sheets to ourselves. In a room to ourselves. And a house all our own . . . Once more, there you are, between my thighs. Deep, deep inside me. I scream and call your name, my love! . . .

Dragged back all at once toward the mouth of the river. That beggar's fault, lying on the bench, snorting out his drunken stupor. One recollection, sharp and clear, that haunts his feeble brain and keeps returning to torment his sleep.

"I was on my way here, over by the cove at Kamouraska, and I saw this stranger, plain as day. He didn't seem to know which way to turn. Well, he asks me where the shore is. Can't tell anymore if he's out on the ice or still on land. Him and his horse and sleigh. And the snow blowing all around us. So I start climbing into the sleigh. But he stops me. Won't let me get in. I'm surprised, because he's all alone and there's plenty of room. Just makes me walk in front of his horse and take him to the highway. Then I point out the road to Rivière-Ouelle, like he asked me, and he gives me a dollar. I didn't get a good look at his face on account of the dark . . ."

That vision of the cove, to the north and east of Kamouraska, up toward Rivière-Ouelle, slips its way out of the beggar Blanchet's heavy sleep and takes its place in Louis Clermont's inn . . . The pity I feel for that helpless traveler. The knowledge of what it must be like to lose your way in the dead of night, in the snow and cold. When you've just killed a man. Lord, who would dare to beg your mercy? The terror, the agony of it all . . .

Victoire Dufour says something that makes her laugh. A big laugh deep in her throat. Her head thrown back. That thick, white neck. While Louis Clermont, dried up skin and bones, bolts the door. Says that it's time to go to bed.

Victoire goes waddling off, rolling her enormous hips. Her wizened little husband follows behind. Carrying the lamp. Moaning to himself that he's really got himself the fattest wife . . .

[210]

ONCE again I stand my watch at the sleeping inn. Studying the knots in the kitchen floor with care, as if they had some great importance.

What bothers me most isn't being deprived of the solemn, somber atmosphere of court. It's finding myself in all those places that the witnesses describe. With no counsel to guide me. No help of any kind. Not only forced to hear them tell their stories, but even to watch the scenes unfold as they relate them. Reduced to my most wretched state. As close to utter nothingness as I can be and not be dead. Growing translucent. My body, stripped of all reality. Of all its shape and depth and thickness. My every act, my every gesture, doomed from the start. Held back at the source. Even now, if I try to lift my hand, I can't go on. If I begin to shout, no sound will leave my throat. If I have to endure the next scene —and I must—it will be at the utmost limits of my attention.

Victoire Dufour, wife of Louis Clermont. Says she doesn't know how to sign her name, and makes a cross.

Her pale blue eyes, still blurred with sleep. A long, smooth wisp of yellow hair across her face. Like the lash of a whip. She sits up in bed, fast as her bulk will let her.

"I said to my husband, 'Clermont, someone's knocking at the

door.' So he sat up in bed beside me. And both of us listened. We let them knock one more time. Then Clermont got up and lit a candle. Pulled on his pants. When the one who was out there came in, I could see him through the door to my room. It's just off the hall. I could tell by his coat and his hood that it must be the stranger who passed by on the road that day. I don't much remember what happened after that, until next morning . . ."

Louis Clermont, innkeeper in the town of Sainte-Anne, is proudly signing his name, in giant letters, to the statement he's made under oath. The little man, brittle and nervous, tries hard to keep still. Does his best to look calm. Has about as much success as a live eel stuck to a pole! Sharp, sudden tremors shake his body, stiff and erect, with no clear relation to the things he's saying. The candle lights his dark, dull, almost leaden face. From time to time a twitch runs through his sunken cheek.

"It could have been anywhere between eleven and twelve. I let them knock a couple of times. And each time I asked who-ever it was to tell me their name. But they wouldn't answer, just kept knocking louder. Finally they said 'a friend,' so I lifted the bolt . . ."

Dark mass in the doorway. Beard and eyebrows covered with frost. Breath, quick and throaty. Sweat dripping from head to toe, soaked up by the thick woollen clothes. Little by little turning to ice. The smell of a manly body and dank, wet wool. A hoarse voice, panting between clenched teeth.

"A place for the night for me and my horse . . . And hot water . . . Lots of hot water . . ."

Is it the candle's glimmer? I seem to see dark blotches caked on the coat, powdered with snow.

Keep telling myself I'm dead, beyond all harm. Not hurt, not dying, but really dead. And no one can see me. Not even the stranger who just came in, huffing and puffing like an animal long on the run from his pursuers. Invisible, I tell you. No feeling

[212]

in me either. Hidden away at this inn. Transparent as a drop of water. Practically nonexistent. Nameless and faceless. Destroyed. Rejected. Yet there's something inside me that won't be held back. And it leaps from my body, though I've ceased to exist. Not the power to suffer, not the power to love. But only . . . Not even the five senses of a living being. Only one sense still left free to function. The other four tied down, in shackles. (Except for sight, of course . . .) Such a fine, upstanding woman, she is. (See how she cares for her husband, Monsieur Rolland . . .) Like an arrow, my sense of smell flies straight for its prey. Finds it and knows it at once. Greets it with open arms. Delights in the murderer's smell. The sweat, the panic. The musty stench of blood. Your scent, my love, that smell of the beast . . . Inside of me, a dog, crouching. Whining softly. Baying its long and deathly cry.

Again the traveler says that he wants some hot water.

Slowly, his every movement dripping with sleep, Louis Clermont fires up the stove. (There are still a few embers left glowing in back.) He fills the coffeepot with water, puts it on the fire. The stranger snaps at him. Says that he doesn't want the water to drink, but to wash off his sleigh and his bisonskin blankets, and that he'll need a lot more than that. Louis Clermont fills the kettle, puts it on the fire.

"You didn't get all that filthy on our roads around here, did you? Not with this nice white snow!"

"The last place I stopped, I had to leave my sleigh in their slaughterhouse. That's why all the blood . . ."

"They sure weren't awfully clean at that inn, to mess up your sleigh like that and get your skins so dirty. At least they could have washed them off . . ."

"I was in a hurry . . ."

The traveler's voice, choked up in a muted whisper, but sharp-edged all the same. Telling Louis Clermont to put the horse in the stable, and to give him some lukewarm water and a gallon of oats.

[214]

"So I did what the stranger told me, and took a bowl and a feed bag out from under one of the seats. There was a horse collar stuck away down there, under the seat, with a lot of little bells. And there were drops of blood, like tears, hanging from the sleigh, all frozen hard. I scratched at them with my nails. And believe me, I was good and scared. But not like later on, after the stranger left and I stopped to think it over . . . Anyway, he came to the shed with me to wash off the sleigh. I could see with my lamp that there was plenty of blood inside the sleigh too, on the floor. And on the seats. Practically all over . . . Well, he took some hot water and threw it against the sides and the front. And both of us began to rub. Me, with one of my wife's old petticoats. Him, with a gray cloth sack that looked like something to keep a pistol in. It was cold, and the water kept freezing up on us. So he said I'd better wait till morning to wash the sleigh. And be sure not to forget to wake him up at five o'clock. Then he bundled up the skins and took them inside the house, along with his bag. As soon as he got inside, he took off his gray coat and rolled up his sleeves. And he started to wash out the skins in a tub that I gave him. With hot water that I heated up in the kettle, and that he kept mixing with cold. He asked me to warm him up a glass of wine, and he drank it about halfway down. Then he went to his room to go to sleep. But first he looked the bed over and made me give him some more covers. A little while later, maybe fifteen minutes, he asked me for one of the skins from the sleigh to put on the bed. Said he was so cold he just couldn't get warm . . ."

The man is shivering from head to toe. His teeth are chattering. His bed shakes back and forth as if the floor were trembling beneath him.

Me, Elisabeth d'Aulnières, shut away in Louis Clermont's inn. Pushed up the stairs. Forced through the doorway of the traveler's room. Crossing his threshold against my will. Left standing there in the darkness, all by myself. Racked by the terrible shudders that

[215]

shake his body. Sensing in the very fibers of my nerves, drawn taut, the utter anguish of his sleepless night. Imagining his agonizing day, relived in the shadows. The visions, sharp and clear, dancing before his bulging eyes, as he lies there on his bed. Feeling those visions, batlike, fluttering past my face.

I can hear his breathing, a rattling deep in his chest. The darkness, thick between us. The thought of that haggard face, so close. His weary body, shivering under piles of covers. And the sleigh blanket, stained with blood, smelling of blood. My heart, bent on its own damnation, praying that the darkness never ends. That the light will never shine on that man, lying there in the depths of darkness. My dying heart, praying that never again will he come before me, loom up before me, run to me, hold out his arms to me, take me in his arms. This man who just murdered another. In the cove at Kamouraska. His solitude, beyond belief . . . Calling the darkness down on his face. Like the pall pulled over the heads of the dead.

The pity I feel inside me wells up in fruitless struggle. Desperately looks for some way to escape. A gesture, a word. Anything to force it free, out of my stifling cover of stone. The statue I've turned to. Saint Veronica standing spellbound in the doorway, upstairs at Louis Clermont's inn. Asking in vain for a piece of soft cloth to wipe the face of the man I love. Walled up here in my solitude. Transfixed in my own dark dread. Unable to make the slightest sign, the slightest gesture. As if the very sources of my strength, thrown out of joint, could suddenly put forth nothing but still, unmoving silence. I can't take even one step closer to you now . . .

Burlington, Burlington. My love is calling to me from across the border, from across the world . . .

Victoire Dufour unfolds an apron that keeps getting bigger and bluer. As if she had stretched it out and dyed it all blue again. Ties it round her waist, fatter and fatter. Fills up the bedroom with her fat, blue body. Becomes a giant. Pretends she got up early just to go swear out her story to the justice of the peace. But really concerns herself with me, Elisabeth d'Aulnières. Tries to hold me here at Louis Clermont's inn as long as she can . . .

The traveler bursts out of his room. I can see him from behind as he goes into the hall. The look of determination in his neck, nervous but still erect. And yet, a weakness that wasn't there before. Anxious, turning from side to side, again and again, more often than it should. A glimpse of his profile, dark and fleeting.

On the other side of the wall, the sound of Victoire Dufour waking her husband.

"Hurry up, Clermont. The horses are fighting in the stable!"

"Quiet, woman. He told me to wake him at five, and it's already daylight."

The traveler says he didn't sleep all night. Goes straight to the stove. Opens the oven and takes out the kettle. Tells Louis Clermont to come with him into the shed.

"He poured hot water from the kettle while I stood and rubbed. We got rid of the biggest one. But there was so much blood, all dried up and mixed with snow and straw . . . Then the one we call Blanchet woke up from his bench. Blanchet, from down the river. The one who slept by the stove that night and seemed to be so afraid of the stranger. And he showed up in the shed."

"Damn! How did you ever pick up all that! They sure must have been a bunch of pigs, whoever messed up your skins that way!"

"The stranger told me to hitch up his horse right away. Meantime, he went inside to get his skins and his bag and his whip. Then he got into the sleigh, even before I took it out of the shed. And he spread the skins around, with the hair inside. I led his horse out of the shed and handed him the reins. He didn't even have breakfast. Just drank a glass of gin and left . . ."

Victoire Dufour, face pink as a cake of soap. Features blurring,

[217]

blending together. Eyes growing paler and paler, immense, spreading like puddles. Gazing at me . . .

"When I got up it was daylight. I saw blood on the floor, all over. And I said to my hired girl, 'There's no two ways about it, child. That man's killed someone!' She said so too. 'There's no two ways about it. That's the only thing it could be. Just go and look outside, under the porch, where they threw all the blood.' I went and looked. There was blood on the snow. I was frightened to death and I started to shake all over . . . He was up before I was. He even came and looked in at my room while I was getting dressed. As if he was after something. I thought it was a pretty dirty thing to do. But he just kept looking at me, real nervous. And the whole time he was in the house he tried to avoid me, and always looked the other way. I didn't much like looking at him either. But I saw enough of him to know him anywhere. When I saw all that mess and all that blood, I said to my husband, 'Clermont, it's pretty plain. That man's killed someone . . .' "

"Quiet, woman. Don't talk so much. He could be an English officer and have us arrested. Times are bad. Maybe there was some fighting up the river."

"I told him a couple of times that that man must have killed someone. Then I went into the stranger's room to get the basin he washed his hands in. The water was full of blood. And that morning, before he left, I saw him rubbing and scratching his stockings, with his hands. His eyes were real suspicious, real dark. I was good and frightened. We're poor people and our inn isn't very big, so we notice anyone that stands out and looks different. Well, when I was in his room to make the bed, I found blood all over the quilt, and drops of blood on the floor, around the bed. And near the stove, and over where he put his bag . . . He never seemed to look us in the eye the whole time he was in the house. And I saw those skins of his, trimmed around the edges, all red with blood . . ."

Victoire Dufour leans over my bed. Her face growing pinker and pinker. Shining, dripping with sweat. Now, through her clear, transparent cheeks and nose, you can see a great fire burning over the bones, melting away her face. Drop by drop. And all the while, as it turns to liquid, Victoire Dufour tries to catch my eye and draw it to the great big basin of snow that fills her arms. Tells me, in a whisper almost too soft to hear, to take a good look, with her, this one last time, at the blood spreading and freezing over the white, white snow.

THE wind has died down. That furious some-
thing in yesterday's wind has died down completely. Those gusts
of snow, all over the cove at Kamouraska yesterday, have stopped
their blowing.

A traveler wrapped in blood-soaked blankets speeds in a black
sleigh up along the river. Far, far from Kamouraska. Riding away
from Kamouraska. Finished with Kamouraska. Now that he has
wrung from Kamouraska all the importance and urgency it had
to give him. Little by little he feels a boundless calm. A curious
peace. All at once, rid of the burden that weighed so long on his
breast. The frightful drive that held him in its grasp through his
whole long journey—perhaps his whole life—lets go of him without
a word of warning. Drops him, like an empty suit of clothes.
Leaves him utterly weak and lost. So terribly tired. The powerful
urge to lie down in the snow and quietly die. Now that his job
is done.

He looks at the reins hanging loose across his horse's back, and
spotted with blood. (He'll have to get rid of all that blood, really,
once and for all.) So many things seem meaningless all of a sudden.
Stripped of that terrible importance they used to have, and probably still ought to have even now. Disarmed, defused, reduced to

their simplest terms. Stripped of all their authority, all their prestige. No weight, no substance left, almost unreal. Even that furious passion. So trivial now, so far away, freed from the spell it was under. A dagger stuck in the heart, pulled loose all at once. Leaving behind it only a nice, neat wound. A sadness, that is, impossible to measure. All yearning calmed. All thought of worldly wealth so utterly foolish now. To sleep, to sleep . . . And yet, deep in the heart, that gentle tremor, that muted ecstasy, down where the blood goes flowing through the veins. The victor's exultation, buried away beneath his weariness . . . Back over the road, without a care. To the red-blond lady, aflame on Rue Augusta, in Sorel. His joyous news that she's finally a widow, finally free. Hypocritical tears . . .

Why, who would dream of marrying this woman now, after the tragedy at Kamouraska? Dear little Jérôme Rolland, you're raising your hand. Asking to speak. For a long time now that formidable child, too beautiful to bear, has made you tremble in the shadows. It's now or never. Just offer her a spotless name, above reproach . . . But let me warn you, George Nelson won't stand for such humiliation . . .

Your head is spinning, love, in the pale light of dawn. Your horse can hardly make his way through the soft, new snow. Since yesterday (long before the cove at Kamouraska), you haven't had a thing to eat. I'm on your trail. You can hear my sleigh bells jingling behind you. I'm Madame Rolland. And I'm haunting you, just as you haunt me. We're out of our minds, the two of us. Cut off from each other already . . .

Worn out and dying. After so great a passion, so strong a passion lived and suffered. The illusion of happiness, rising up before us. Like a fogbank over the frozen road. To live together, the two of us. Lovingly, tenderly, with no ado. Like two blue shadows on the snow . . . "Elisabeth! Your body, opening, closing about me. Pulls me down, engulfs me forever. That brackish taste of sea-

[221]

weed and brine . . ." Ah! That blood all over the reins and inside the sleigh! . . .

The morning of February first, at about eleven, the traveler stopped at the inn at Saint-Roch-des-Aulnaies. He asked for lunch. But he hardly sat at the table for more than a minute. What he really wanted was to have the landlord clean the reins and carefully scratch the crusts of blood off the leather.

Anxiously, madly, I scour the frozen roads and the hours forever past. Stopping a traveler from time to time, asking at inns. In the wild hope of finding . . . From village to village I hear his description. His black horse, hind hooves white to the shanks. The man's black whiskers. His ruddy, dark complexion. The blood on the blankets. The blood . . .

But something is missing. A gap in the agenda of this man I'm trying to find. A gap I help create myself. Careful to avoid one certain hour, the most important one of all. These roundabout roads, just to keep away from Kamouraska. The cove at Kamouraska. About nine o'clock. The night of January 31st, 1839 . . .

Up at the manor, they're already beginning to wonder why the young squire has been gone so long.

LOWLY the backwoods tidings make their way to Kamouraska. North from Sainte-Anne-de-la Pocatière. Trotting along with a dapple-gray old mare. Elie Michaud, a farmer from Kamouraska, told Blanchet he could ride back with him, in his sleigh. Blanchet, the beggar who spent the night at Louis Clermont's inn.

Now, in the barren stretches of his mind, Blanchet turns over the curious things he saw back there. A black rig, covered with blood. A stranger who didn't seem like any ordinary traveler . . .

The numbing winter cold. Blanchet's mind, asleep somewhere under a soft, mossy rock. More mossy and soft all the time . . . Snowflakes, one by one, dancing ever so lightly before his half-closed eyes. Elie Michaud sits dozing too. The mare knows the road. Slowly she wends her way to the stable . . . It's not so much the cold. It's that dreaminess in the flakes as they graze our faces. And we don't even try to brush them off. As if we were trapped in a glass globe, swirling with soft and gentle snow. Behind us, Louis Clermont's inn, and that curious traveler who . . . Ahead of us, the cove at Kamouraska, and that other traveler who, only yesterday . . . But none of that bothers us yet. We're all wrapped up in our furs. Thinking how nice it would be to pull those thick, warm covers over our heads . . . Blood-stains at the inn. A stranger in the cove, who doesn't know which way to turn . . . Should we say something to Elie Michaud about it? . . . Now it doesn't even help to close our eyes. The red spots follow us in our sleep. Well, why go running after nightmares? Let's open our eyes good and wide. Let's take a long look at the comforting snow. In front, in back, all around us. The blinding, honest snow. And let's keep watching those dappled haunches of Elie Michaud's old mare, trotting along at her easy, familiar pace . . .

Wide-eyed, Blanchet gazes at the real world spread out around him. There, on his left, the cove at Kamouraska. With blood on the snow, all over the frozen path along the edge. Here and there on the highway too, not far from Monsieur Tassy's little house, up by Paincourt . . . He crosses himself. Wakes his companion, snoring softly, head slumped on his chest. Elie Michaud opens one eye, sees what Blanchet has seen, and shuts it again as fast as he can. Takes refuge with Blanchet, safe in the depths of sleep, where sometimes men are glad to mix together their dreams and the outrageous sights of life.

The next day, Saturday, the second of February, Elie Michaud is pulled from his nice warm house first thing in the morning. Drawn outside, for no apparent reason. The thought of those bloodstains, on the path by the edge of the cove, grows harder and harder for his mind to bear. Unnerves and torments him. Pushes him out of the house. (Toward the village, abuzz with rumors.) Wrenches him out of his solitude. Makes him yearn to be with his fellow creatures. Carefully, slowly unburden his soul . . . Elie Michaud walks into James Wood's tavern.

The tavern is full, despite the early hour. Everyone talking about Monsieur Tassy, who went riding off, Thursday night, in a sleigh with some young stranger. And no one has seen him since. The servants at the manor have been looking for him high and low. In the village, out in the country . . .

Little Robert is telling his story for the hundredth time. His voice, shriller and shriller, more and more frightened:

"Thursday night, about half-past six, I was driving Monsieur Tassy to the village. We took the road from the manor and were just getting onto the highway, when we met a sleigh with a man in it that Monsieur Tassy knew. Both of them shook hands. The man told Monsieur Tassy that he was on his way from Sorel, and that he had some news about Monsieur Tassy's wife and children. Then he asked Monsieur Tassy to get into his sleigh. Said it might be nice to go to Monsieur Tassy's little house at Paincourt, next to the church. Said they could talk better there. So Monsieur Tassy got out of the sleigh I was driving and got into the stranger's. Then they turned around and went back up the road toward the church. Monsieur Tassy yelled that I should tell his mother he was bringing a friend home to the manor for supper . . ."

"Thursday night, at about half-past seven, I was on my way back from my brother Pierre's. Me, Bertrand Lancoignard, the one they call Sansterre. He lives about three-quarters of a mile up from the church at Kamouraska. Well, I'm walking along with Jean Saint-Joire (the one we call Sargerie), and with Etienne Lancoignard (he's called Sansterre too), when all of a sudden this sleigh comes along, fast as anything, going off toward the cove. We're pretty frightened and we get over to the side of the road. The man who's driving is singing at the top of his lungs. He's got one leg inside the sleigh and the other one out. The one on the right. And he's got his fur blanket in back, spread out over something that looks just like another drunk. You could hear a voice, kind of soft, moaning in back of the sleigh. The horse looked pretty big and black, and it was really moving right along . . ."

"Nine o'clock, Thursday night! I swear it was nine o'clock! Thursday night at nine o'clock! . . ."

The one called Blanchet. From Saint-Denis (or maybe Saint-

Pascal). The one who goes tippling from village to village, begging for a place to sleep by the stove. Spent the night of January 31st at Louis Clermont's inn, at Sainte-Anne-de-la-Pocatière. Remembers, all at once, the very hour that he met a stranger lost in the cove at Kamouraska. From the depths of his memory muddled with drink and cloudy visions, he holds the precise hour up triumphantly, for all to see. Casts a defiant look at the whole of Kamouraska's population, assembled in James Wood's tavern.

"Nine o'clock! It was nine o'clock at night! The man asks me where the shore is. He makes me walk in front of his horse and take him to the highway. I point out the road to Rivière-Ouelle, like he asked me. I didn't get a good look at his face. But he was wearing a country coat, with a hood. Next morning, at the inn at Sainte-Anne, I see a stranger. In a hurry, and he looks real nervous. And his blankets are all covered with blood. It could be the same one I saw at the cove at Kamouraska. The one that didn't know which way to go. But I didn't get a good look at his face the first time, on account of the dark . . ."

James Wood, the owner of the tavern, says that on that same Thursday evening, between five and six, a stranger came to his place and ordered some supper. Afterwards he asked how to get to the manor in Kamouraska, then he left. He wanted to know too if Monsieur Tassy was likely to be at the manor about that time . . .

"I'd know him anywhere if I saw him again . . ." "His sleigh was really different, not like the ones we have around here . . ." "He was wearing a coat like the kind they make upriver, a lighter shade than ours . . ." "He's English. Or maybe he's from some other country, even though his French is good . . ." "He said he had news about Monsieur Tassy's wife . . . And no one has seen Monsieur Tassy since . . ." "News about his wife in Sorel . . ."

They're all there, in James Wood's tavern. Talking back and forth, almost in a whisper. Trying not to look at one another. Just

[226]

staring straight ahead, at the bare wooden wall, above the shelf with its row of bottles and glasses. As if, while they speak, they were watching a series of rapid portraits, sketched on the wall, rubbed out, and quickly sketched again. Over and over they study the images on the wall. A man, a horse, a sleigh. Always recurring, always distinct, each time like the last. As if, in fact, they were all the selfsame sleigh, the selfsame horse, the selfsame man, come from Sorel in order to . . .

Elie Michaud threads together in his head, in one big bundle, all the facts he has at hand. (His own story, Blanchet's, and everyone else's.) Then he hears himself declare straight out that it's perfectly possible Monsieur Tassy has been murdered, and that they should really be looking for him over by the edge of the cove, where he, Elie Michaud (and the beggar Blanchet too), saw a trail of blood on the snow, on the way back from Sainte-Anne, yesterday morning . . .

HE shrill little bells in the church at Kamouraska peal out their death knell over the cove's expanse. Spread with the wind, far and wide, through the blue and frosty air. Like a tide gone wild . . .

Antoine Tassy was there, with an arm sticking out of the snow. That's how they were able to find him, buried in a mound of snow and ice, piled high. They dug him out and laid him on a sleigh. Then took him to the home of Charles-Edouard Tassy, his uncle.

Elisabeth d'Aulnières, widow of Antoine Tassy, arrives at the manor. Goes in the kitchen door. Pushed and prodded from every side. Joins all the folk from Kamouraska. Tries to get lost in the crowd. To pass unnoticed. Not even suspected. Creature out of time and place. Obliged to appear in person at the manor in Kamouraska. Mere formality, nothing more. Over and over, the same unbending, timeless summons. At intervals more or less the same . . . Young and fresh, back once again to a certain Sunday morning, the third of February, 1839 . . .

Little Robert is telling how, when he showed up, Monsieur Tassy was already dug out. But they hadn't moved him yet. His head and his hair were full of blood and snow . . .

They found him buried in the snow and ice. At the edge of

the cove at Kamouraska. Next to a wicker fence. A half-mile or so from the town. Not far from Paincourt and that little house of his. About two o'clock this morning.

In the manor at Kamouraska people are on the move. Everywhere groups are forming. In the kitchen, outside on the steps, even in the courtyard. Elisabeth d'Aulnières—delirious, all her born days behind her, pulled out of real-life time—merges and blends with the rustlings of cloth, the muffled outcries, the muted groans. Melts into the cautious, catlike tread of this hectic procession up and down, back and forth . . .

Rose Morin is saying that when Antoine's mother, old Madame Tassy, heard he was dead, she just doubled up like a broken branch. Fell in a heap on the rug, in a clatter of crutches. No sooner came to, than she took off her bonnet. The white one, with ribbons. (There's no one can boast they ever saw her with her head uncovered!) For a moment that tiny head of hers is showing, with its few thin strands of hair pulled tight. Pathetic, like a little plucked bird. Then Madame calls for a bonnet. A black one, with long black strings. Plants it square on her head, sticks in a few long pins to keep it in place. She'll send to Quebec for the mourning veils soon as she can . . .

Little by little the bits of ice and snow clinging to Antoine's clothes, caught in his blond hair, begin to melt on the canopy bed where they've laid him out. At his uncle's, Charles-Edouard Tassy. Rose Morin has come with old Madame Tassy, her mistress. Crying and crossing herself. Saying that it sure is a shame for a man as young as Monsieur to be lying there thawing, nice as you please. Like one of those poor little fish that they catch through the ice.

Old Madame Tassy's face, all hard and shriveled—no bigger than your fist it seems—betrays a tear that looks as if it's been there for ages. Like those long-forgotten tears on dead men's cheeks.

Now, this very moment, Antoine Tassy's widow, Elisabeth

[229]

d'Aulnières, makes her entrance. Struck by the utter crassness of her action. Pushed to her nightmare's farthest edge. No refuge left within herself. Thrown out. Leaving Madame Rolland and all her dignity and pride behind. Never before this total separation from her being. This urge to say such monstrous things to old Madame Tassy. This need to look squarely at that burned-out face, just at the utmost point of its destruction.

I go inside and look at this woman. I tell her: "I want to see Antoine Tassy, the squire of Kamouraska, your son and my husband." Her steady gaze. That tear on her cheek, never moving. And she answers in a voice no louder than a whisper: "You know Antoine is dead. You know. You killed him . . ."

I can hear the medical examiner, Doctor Douglas, speaking his piece. Little by little his voice grows stronger, more and more precise. As if my presence here at the manor were meant to drag that dry, brittle voice up from the shadows of time where it lies at rest.

"One of the bullets from the pistol entered just above the victim's ear, below the brim of the cap, and lodged in the brain, one inch in depth. The second bullet entered through the back of the neck and lodged below the frontal bone. The posterior portion of the skull is shattered. Seven separate points can be determined where it received sharp blows of unusual force . . ."

Doctor Douglas's voice. Dispassionate, colder and colder (almost turning to stone as he speaks), reciting the official report line by line. Somewhere, off in a house shut tight, they've begun to intone the prayer for the dying. At the home of Charles-Edouard Tassy, perhaps? Or in the kitchen at the manor? I listen, hard as I can, to the muffled litany of the saints. Hoping to pull myself free from Doctor Douglas's icy voice.

"The first shot was fired from the side. Such that the murderer must have been seated quite close to the victim, in the sleigh. The second shot was fired after Antoine Tassy was already dead, or dying, and stretched out on the ground, face down. The killer then struck the victim repeated blows with the butt of his pistol . . ."

Sancta Lucia, Saint Agnes, and Saint Cecilia! How gentle, how soothing the litany sounds! . . . That voice . . . Thank God! I recognize it now! . . . It's Anne-Marie's! My daughter's innocent voice! And all of this is taking place at home. In my very own house on Rue du Parloir. I'll run to my husband's side. My husband, Jérôme Rolland. Comfort him right to the end. No one will say that I let my husband die alone and unconsoled. Haven't I been a faithful wife for eighteen years?

The most moving, most compelling voice of all (that trace of an American accent). Doing its best to hold me back, to keep me in the realm of fevered dreams. And with that voice of yours (changing, decaying, crumbling to dust in my ear), you beg me please to hear you out, to hear your story to the end.

"But listen to me, Elisabeth. I stood Antoine up on his feet, just to be sure he was really dead. And he was. He was dead. I swear!"

No need to swear. See how I'm shaking. I believe you, love. But you frighten me so. Please, let me by. I can't live this way, in the face of such terror. That dreadful deed before my eyes. Please, let me go. Let me be Madame Rolland again, forever. Let me be rid of this game of death between you and Antoine. Innocent! Innocent! I'm innocent, you hear! . . . Good God, your face, racked with cold, turning toward me. A sudden flashing glimpse of black. Your eye, lifting its heavy, weary lid. So tired, beyond belief. Your lips, cracking, taut against your teeth. That pathetic little sneer, trying so hard to smile. My love, you're trembling . . .

And yet you tell me over and over that your hand was never so steady. So swift and sure. You're not a surgeon for nothing, after all . . . Again I beg you. Please, don't make me hear the rest of your story. All this is a man's affair. Just two men with a score to settle. I don't mind waiting here by the side of the road. (Like a sweet little child, lost in the snow.) Waiting for Antoine to be put to death. But don't think you'll make me follow you all the way . . .

The black sleigh passes by, brushes against me. Carrying both men off. Full speed. Over the highway. Up toward Paincourt and the little house. Doctor Nelson, you don't have a minute to lose. Whichever one takes the trouble to open his mouth and swear at the other is sure to be done for. Checkmate, Tassy old boy. The fastest player wins. You shouldn't have wasted your time cursing your old school friend that way. Already the gun barrel, cold, against your temple. Fires. Pierces your brain. You slump your head on your murderer's shoulder. Drench him in blood. Crush him beneath your bulk. And a voice above your head, saying that there's all the news you'll get from your wife in Sorel . . .

The sound of the first shot over the highway, swallowed up in the thick swirling snow. In the whistling wind. I seem to be holding my hands to my ears. My pulse, pounding madly against my hands. Only my beating heart, I swear. No other sound at all, for hundreds of miles around. And yet, three men are standing with me. Here, by the side of the road. Almost trampled (to hear them tell it) by a black horse coming on at an infernal gallop, bearing down, heading straight for us . . . Bertrand and Etienne Lancoignard, the ones they call Sansterre. And Jean Saint-Joire, the one they call Sargerie. They'll swear to it, all three. But I'm deaf. I'm blind. I can't tell you a thing. Just someone standing up in a sleigh, driving a dying man over toward the cove. Singing as loud as he can. To cover a muffled groan, back in the sleigh, under the blankets.

The sound of the second shot, far, far away. Out in the cove. Hardly noticed at all. Like a ship in distress, fading off in the distance, over the river . . .

A man, striking a corpse with the butt of his gun. A corpse

stretched out in the snow, face down. Striking him over and over, as long as the superhuman strength let loose within him lasts. Lord of life and death . . . The conqueror stops for a moment and wipes his face on his sleeve. Searches his heart to find the woman for whom . . . Yearns to possess her body, here and now. In triumph. Before his power and madness wane. Before his drunken frenzy cools . . . But even now he seems to be hemmed in by a ring of tears. Consumed by such a weariness, welling up inside him. Like madmen after their fits, or women after their labor. Or lovers after their passion.

Now nothing is left but to climb into his sleigh. Get back to land as quickly as he can. Try to make out the line of snow between the frozen river and the shore.

THE stark austerity of the manor table comes to a sudden halt. Old Madame Tassy must observe the convention that opens the doors of a dead man's house to one and all for days on end. There she is now, in the kitchen, giving the staff her orders. Two capons, two ducks, a suckling pig, a half-dozen little pork pies and a pig's-knuckle stew . . .

At Madame's request the justice of the peace swears in two deputies. James Wood, owner of the inn at Kamouraska, and little Robert Dunham, who works at the manor. Both of them sure to recognize the young stranger who took Antoine Tassy into his sleigh. Off to find him, right on his trail. Just follow the road to Sorel, that's all . . .

Sorel! See how that clear, transparent, limpid name strikes you square in the heart, Dame Caroline des Rivières Tassy! Can it be because of that daughter-in-law of yours, holed up on Rue Augusta, trying to choke back her less than proper feelings of hope and impatience? What do you really know about her after all? See with what loving care she nurses her third little son . . .

I'm waiting for a certain traveler. Waiting for the news he'll bring of my deliverance. Your son is a beast, Madame. He tortures me, tries to kill me. Again and again. The last time he tried to slit my throat with his razor. It's only right that he should be . . . No, don't look at me with those relentless eyes. Your face, so much sand, could crumble to dust, and still those gaping eyes would bore right through me. With only that strange little quizzical look. I don't let anyone stare at me that way. You'll see, I'll escape. Besides, there's so much to keep you here in Kamouraska. The death of your son, the coroner's inquest, the young squire's burial in the little parish church . . . A family council, arranged already. Only the first. Between you and his uncle, Charles-Edouard Tassy. And if, by some chance, the mere thought of me grazes you ever so slightly, either one, you're sure to keep it quiet. While rumors go buzzing around inside your heads. Rumors about that woman who used to be Antoine Tassy's pathetic wife . . .

The aristocratic old family machine grinds into motion. Parleys and ponders. My fate is sealed. Decided even before a word is spoken. Keep everything quiet. Condemn Elisabeth d'Aulnières to wear the icy mask of innocence. For the rest of her days. Save her, and save ourselves along with her. Measure her virtue by that haughty way she has of denying the obvious truth.

My strange, deep, dark, conniving fellowship with them both. My awful terror . . .

The tracks are fresh. The innkeepers start to loosen their tongues. At Rivière-Ouelle he asked for a glass of brandy. Didn't want to go inside. Had it served through the window, then didn't even drink it. At Sainte-Anne he tells how his sleigh and his blankets got all splattered when a whole pack of animals had to be slaughtered at once. At Saint-Roch-des-Aulnaies he asks to have the blood cleaned off his reins. It's just about two when he comes to L'Islet. He washes up, changes his clothes. The water he uses is all red with blood. He hardly eats. Goes off again. It's ten at night when he asks for a room at the inn at Saint-Vallier. He doesn't take a bite. Pulls off his woollen belt and throws it in the fire. Next day,

[235]

Saturday, the second of February, he's on his way at the crack of dawn.

At Saint-Thomas the tracks disappear. No trace of the high-perched sleigh. James Wood and Robert Dunham are ready to think that the big black horse must have some kind of magic power. Carrying off its fiendish master inside the earth. Over perilous roads. Through a desert of trees and snow.

The news doesn't reach Quebec until Tuesday, the fifth of February. On the sixth the coroner's inquest opens in Kamouraska. There's talk of a girl, a stranger, who came to the Dionnes' inn. Just before Epiphany. And gave Monsieur Tassy a drink with poison in it . . . James Wood and Robert Dunham keep following the southern bank. Realize all at once, a good ten miles past Pointe-Lévis, that they don't have a warrant to arrest their man. Turn round and go back all the way to Quebec to get one from the powers that be. And all the while the slow wheels of justice are being set in motion.

The horse goes trudging through the melting snow. Pulls its hooves from the mire with every struggling step. Leaves little holes that fill with water. Like walking along a sandy beach, gnawed away by the tide. A traveler, sinking in the snow. When he ought to be flying, swift as an arrow whistling in the wind . . . No breeze at all. No dead man, murdered, moaning in the breeze. A calm so deep. Everything gently sinking, swallowed down into a strange and mournful silence.

I'm watching for you, Doctor Nelson. Waiting. The prayers for the dying are pounding in my ears. Ready to lure me out of my real life. To bring me back at any moment to my house on Rue du Parloir.

> *Miserere nobis* . . .
> *For behold I was conceived in iniquities*
> *And in sins did my mother conceive me.*

Twice now that high-pitched voice of Léontine Mélançon perches above my head. Begs me to get up, out of this bed, where I wallow in my none-too-virtuous adventure.

I try to fight off a great mass of fog. Choke on my words, one by one. Unable to say a thing, to utter a sound. My every gesture shriveling, shrinking. And yet, by some monstrous effort, I seem to be telling Léontine Mélançon that I need so terribly to sleep, to dream . . .

No sooner facing the wall again . . . A horse's galloping hoof-beats whisk through the air like those great gusts of snow in the cove at Kamouraska. Sweep everything along in their infernal path. Chasing me! Ready to cut me down! Kill me dead! My God, I'm possessed! . . . No, wait. Now the frenzy has stopped, and the gentle gait of an undertaker's horse takes up in its place. I'm opening my eyes . . . I see Florida, standing in the doorway, with her big face and those gray braids of hers. I seem to hear her saying that someone should bring some coffee, strong and black, to bring Madame round . . .

Oh, no! Whatever else, don't leave the darkness. Not now. Not just when my love is on his way back . . .

> *To my hearing thou shalt give joy and gladness*
> *And the bones that have been humbled shall rejoice.*

The awesome, superhuman things this man has done, he's done for me. And I have to be there, on Rue Augusta. Be there to welcome George Nelson home. With all the thanks and tenderness he deserves. Jump into his arms. Lay my head on his breast. Hear the beating of his heart. Feel his labored breath against my hair. Breathe deep that smell still clinging to his clothes, his skin. The smell of blood and death. Learn of my deliverance from his own parched, fevered lips.

"It's done, Elisabeth. My darling, my wife . . . Now you're free. We're free, the two of us . . ."

[237]

But it's Aurélie's piercing voice that first strikes my ear.

"Madame! Madame! It's Monsieur . . . It's the doctor . . . He's back from Kamouraska! . . ."

Aurélie shudders and runs away. Shouting, off in the distance, into the wings.

"Monsieur looks so different. I hardly even knew him! . . . Really, Madame, it's too awful. Just looking at him, thinking about what he must have . . ."

"But Aurélie, my husband's a brute. You know he is. A brute, a wicked brute . . . We had to kill him, we had to . . ."

"We're all of us wicked, Madame. Like the plague . . ."

Someone has just come into my room on Rue Augusta. He's pacing back and forth. Goes over to the window. Lifts the curtain. Looks outside. Peers into the street at his horse and sleigh, in front of my house. Asks in a broken whisper, muffled and harsh at once, if somebody might not be out in the corridor, listening. I hear myself answer, in my sweet, schoolgirl voice, that my mother is sleeping and my aunts are at church.

It's time for me now to walk up behind this man, as he stands at the window. To look him in the eye. To see who he is and let him see me.

His body's shadow, against the light. The massive outline of his shoulders, that chink in the back of his neck as his head bends low. And he mutters his story in precise detail, spitting out his words.

"I'm a doctor after all, and I swear it's just not human. All that blood in one man's body! I'm sure that damned Tassy must have done it to me on purpose! . . ."

Then all at once his shoulders begin to shake, torn by an imbecilic laugh.

He's turning toward me . . . My God, is this how I'm going to see him again? His beautiful face, ravaged and racked and sapped by a madman's laughter?

[238]

How much do I really know of what happened between Antoine and George in the cove at Kamouraska? Executioner and victim, in a subtle give-and-take. Two partners in the awful alchemy of murder. The somber business of death, dealt and received. Casting its inconceivable spell. What if, in some mysterious way, my husband's mask were to spread itself over the conqueror's features? No, no! Don't turn, don't look at me now! What if I found on your dear, sweet face the selfsame look of that vicious young man who was once my husband? Sneering and cruel. Raising his arm to strike me. Dreaming of how he can kill me in time . . .

"Elisabeth, look at me. Please, I beg you . . ."

And finally we look at each other. For a moment, without a word. Standing there face to face. Filling each other with the shadows of darkness. Touching each other with unfamiliar hands. Trying to pick up our scents, like animals new to each other . . . Your face, with its growth of beard. Your body, so thin. Your hands, burned raw by the cold. And me, in front of you. My hands, so white. My heart, like a frantic bird. See, here she is, this silly, vapid, befuddled little creature with the red-blond hair. The one who made you kill.

Which one of us first breaks out in gentle sobs? Head hanging down, like a man on the gallows.

Which one of us dares to utter those two words "love" and "freedom," there in the dark, and still not die of despair?

Sleep. We have to sleep till morning. Don't we have all our lives to be happy, spread out before us? And we cling in a long embrace, as if we were going to drown.

OO late! James Wood and Robert Dunham, the ones sent out from Kamouraska, meet with the authorities in the town of Sorel. Next morning, February seventh, two policemen appear at Doctor Nelson's house with a warrant for his arrest.

Too late! It's too late! My daughter, Anne-Marie, is trying to bring me to. Tugging at my wrist, hard as she can. And Léontine Mélançon is there, making me take a deep breath of ammonia. Her pince-nez falls loose from those colorless, deep-set eyes. Against her hollow chest. Dangles at the end of a long golden string.

I won't let all that life and death on Rue du Parloir come near me. I'm setting up dams of stubborn, dogged defiance. Clinging to the darkness. Delving through the darkness. Feeling my way, as if I were blind. Two arms outstretched in the shadows . . . And all at once, beneath my fingers, a certain wooden wall looms up. Then another. At a perfect right angle. I'm sure I could count every pinewood plank. Back in the doctor's waiting room. The stove marked with the name "Warm Morning," standing cold. The crumpled bed, the red and blue quilt, the sheets strewn over the floor. A cupboard with its two doors open. Empty. The curtain rod pulled loose. A cretonne curtain, faded white by the sun, hanging like a rag . . . It's too late! Too late! Why am I here? Doctor Nelson has escaped. Slipped off. They say he's been seen at Saint-Ours . . .

Just time enough to sell his black horse, his American sleigh. Quick, the American border. In a new one, drawn by a brand-new horse. The police, right on his trail . . .

Through my lips a peevish voice is saying that their coffee isn't strong enough to wake me up. A certain urge, like nothing in this world, makes me hold my pillow over my mouth, my eyes, my ears. I don't want anything to do with Rue du Parloir. Or with my husband, Jérôme Rolland.

I dream that I'm all dressed in white. Silly little girl again, going to be married. Someone I can't see fixes my fine silk veil, hanging to the ground. Plants a crown of orange blossoms on my head, heavy with the smell of musk. I have to pass under an archway of stone, with the devil himself on my arm. My fingers clutching a bouquet of bees. And all my children, escorting me along. The darkest one, the smallest, nestled in my right arm, sleeping. Pulls at my spotless bridal gown. Opens the bodice ever so slightly. A breast appears, bursting with milk. And the guests all swoon with pleasure and sing my praises. Oh, what a lovely wedding! They can hardly believe it. Then Aurélie Caron . . . Yes, she's the one, I'm sure . . . Begins to laugh, splits her sides. And somebody says it's high time I looked my love in the face. I lift my head. His face meets mine so fast, I close my eyes with delight . . . Dizzy. Too late. Should have run . . . Like the wind . . . My love is gone already . . .

I beg Aunt Adélaïde to come with me, over the border, far away. But first to Montreal, to the lawyer, Maître Lafontaine. Then retrace our steps. Run off . . . But where can we look? How can we find him? Somewhere deep in the vastness of the woods and forests? He's lost, this man. I'm lost. Aunt Adélaïde and I . . . We're being followed . . . God, the police!

Monday, the eleventh of February. The widow of Antoine Tassy is arrested and taken to prison in Montreal.

You're not my friend anymore, Aurélie. I told you to lie when they put you in the box. Anything, so long as you didn't betray us. Now look what you've done. Here you are in prison, just like your poor mistress. I'm so afraid this awful place is going to taint me, Aurélie. You know how I shrink from anything foul or shameful. (Even in hell I would try to avoid disgrace.) Oh, I can't stand that look of yours. That prison-look. Your profile, pale and wan . . . How can they think I'm guilty of such an awful thing? Your Honor, this girl is a liar, a shameless slut. All the best families for miles around will come to my defense . . .

You'll leave Canada, won't you? Just tell me you'll come, Elisabeth. You will. You will come, won't you? . . .

That letter. The one I never got. Worse than prison, the thought of being left behind, deserted. Your endless silence. Your written words, kept from me. The sound of your voice, intercepted. Your call, your plea, lost somewhere in justice's endless pile of papers. Good Lord, I'm finished! And my dear Aunt Adélaïde, with me in prison. I'll kill myself, that's what I'll do. Saltpeter, oozing from every wall. And all night long Aunt Adélaïde, writing the judge a letter. Signed with a pathetic little flourish.

The party in question, Elisabeth d'Aulnières, always treated her husband, the late Antoine Tassy, with nothing but kindness and respect. She didn't know a thing about his death, anymore than the rest of us. That is, her mother, her aunts, or myself. What I mean to say is that we heard a rumor about it first, and then we received word in letters from Kamouraska. My niece Elisabeth, the party in question, has three small children from her marriage with the same Antoine Tassy. One of them isn't even four months old. Elisabeth herself is hardly twenty. And in very delicate health. I've been with her in prison all this time. Myself, her aunt, Adélaïde Lanouette. And I can tell you that she's getting weaker and weaker every day. She's even spitting blood. If she has to

stay in prison much longer it's sure to put her life in danger.
Besides, I know all about that person Aurélie Caron, formerly of
Sorel, and I wouldn't believe a word she says, not even under oath.
Written from the municipal prison, Montreal,
February 22nd, 1839.

Doctor George Nelson arrives in Burlington on February eighth, and a few days later he's behind bars too. At the request of the Canadian authorities. Then those long-drawn-out negotiations between Montpelier and Washington. And on March 23rd the grand jury of the criminal court in Quebec indicts Doctor Nelson for murder. The case of Elisabeth d'Aulnières is held over for the September session . . .

I've watched the icicles so long, melting on the little window of my cell. I've tossed and turned so long on my narrow bed. I've cried so long . . . Aunt Adélaïde puts compresses on my forehead. Weeps along with me. A taste of iron wells up from my throat. I spit up blood. What wicked old witch is whispering in my ear that it's all just so much theatre? . . .

Aunt Adélaïde begs me to fix my hair, my clothes. To splash cold water on my face and step out in the light for all to see. With Antoine's mother by my side, come all the way from Kamouraska just for this.

Released on bail. A sallow-faced young woman (long mourning veils and all) outside the prison gate. Seems to be walking in her sleep. And the warden bows low, as if it had all been some dreadful mistake. Wrapped in her shawls and crape, she hazards a glance out into the street. Hurries into the carriage standing there against the sidewalk, waiting. A little woman, older than the first, hidden in black veils too. Picks up a woollen blanket and tucks it around the young woman's lap.

A second carriage follows the first. In it the young woman's mother and aunt.

[243]

And in the first, two women, side by side. So careful not to look each other in the eye. Their very first meeting since . . . Tossed and shaken as the carriage jogs along. Elisabeth d'Aulnières and Madame Tassy, sitting protected against each other, like walnuts knocking together inside a sack.

And the strange procession winds through Montreal in the noonday sun.

REALLY, we'll have to find me a different dress. This one is all wrinkled . . . Please, a little Cologne . . . The coffee's so thick. Like syrup. It leaves such a bitter taste in my mouth . . . That woman in the mirror . . . Her eyes are so tired. And that big, round face . . . Dark circles . . . Her neck, too fat for her collar. That crumpled linen collar . . .

My daughter, Anne-Marie. Still there. Still trying to pull me out of the darkness, all the way.

"The priest wants to tell you good-bye before he leaves. Papa is asleep . . ."

My clouded image in the mirror. After this endless night. Rub the mist clear with the back of my sleeve. Recapture my youth . . .

At Sorel my dear little aunts look after me, ply me with flowers and sweets. Shed torrents of tears.

I wait for a letter that never arrives.

"The child is sick. See, she can hardly stand on her feet."

I try to save my strength to wait for a letter. Try not to move. Pretend to be living. Learn little by little what it's like to die. Wait for a letter. With all the right gestures, the look on my face, the clothing inside and out, the hair on my head, the shoes on my feet . . . Like a real living creature. And yet I'm dead. Only hope in my veins. The hope for a certain letter, still beating.

I wait for a letter that's not going to get through, that will never arrive. Yes, I mean, it will. But later, so much later, after years and years lost in those piles of papers on the magistrates' desks. Too late, too late . . .

Time, time. Goes by, spreads out, enfolds me, drags me along. And silence, doubling time, drawing it out to its merciless length. I learn what emptiness is, day after day, night after night. In the bedroom on Rue Augusta, living the life of a prisoner again. With no one to venture near my bed. No one, that is, but my lawyer, my mother, and the three little creatures who have sworn to save me or go down with me in the attempt.

Maître Lafontaine bends over my bed. His face hovers over me, goatee and all. And he keeps repeating something about an involved exchange of letters between the judges in Canada and the United States. My husband's killer . . . Extradition still pending . . . My own case, continued from session to session . . .

I put my faith in the guardian angels that stand watch in the shadows about me. I straighten my clothes, black with mourning. Ask to have my children brought in. A nice little stroll with them through Sorel for all to see, and I know the perverse joy of throwing the whole town off my scent. Pale and pathetic, learning my widow's role . . .

Two years go by. See, Aurélie, now you're free. They'll never extradite Doctor Nelson. Charges withdrawn.

What can I hope for from a man who treats me as if I were dead? Dead and gone so long himself. Dying once, twice, over and over, again and again, until that one last time. That's what life is, after all . . .

Jérôme Rolland calls for his wife. Wants her there beside him. Anne-Marie says her father is better, completely cured, now that he's had the last rites from the priest . . .

The medical student has a head of thick, red, curly hair. Shaking like a banner flaring in the breeze. Between my clasped fingers, I watch the hostile glints of sun . . .

"Anne-Marie, my dear . . . Yes, I'll go right down. First, get me a handkerchief. There, in the drawer."

Anne-Marie disappears for a moment. The young student's head of hair flashes above my bed. He speaks in a whisper.

"Four months ago I began to study medicine with Doctor Nelson. On the sixth of February, late at night, he came to my room and woke me up. In Madame Léocadie Leprohon's house, where I live. And he made me go with him to his office. He told me he had to leave the province for good, that he could never come back. He just stood there, leaning against the wall. With his head in his hands. And he began to cry, and his body began to tremble and shake all over. In all my life I never saw a man in such a state. Then he said, in English: 'It's that damned woman. She's ruined me . . .'"

You're talking in a foreign tongue, Doctor Nelson. No, of course I don't know this man! I'm Elisabeth d'Aulnières. My first husband was Antoine Tassy, the squire of Kamouraska, the one who was murdered. And my second is Jérôme Rolland, notary in the city of Quebec. Like his father before him, and his father's father, for countless generations . . . I'm innocent! See how George Nelson accuses me? See? "That damned woman!" That's what he called me . . . If your love shocks you so, rip it out of your heart. Which one of us betrayed the other first? I'm innocent! Let him go home, back to the country he should never have come from . . . My love ran away. Deserted me, left me alone to face the whims of justice. Yes, let him go home. An outcast in his native land. Back after thirty years. Exiled forever in the land of his birth. A stranger wherever he goes, to the end of his days.

And me. A stranger, a soul possessed, pretending I still belong in the land of the living . . . Faithless Elisabeth. Turning your back, betraying your sacred trust. Too late now, you say. Too late

[247]

for a life of delirious passion. The fire is dying. No use to stir up the embers. Should have taken my stand before. Gone off with George. Been cast out together. To the innermost depths of the earth's damnation. No longer just a foreign land. One whole foreign world. An exile, utter and complete. A madman's solitude . . . See how they point their fingers at us. Yes, I'm the one. The one who pushed you to the ends of the earth. (I stood back, off by the side of the road, while you . . . There, in the cove at Kamouraska . . .) Through all that crime and death. Like a boundary to cross . . . And then you come back. And your face, your look against mine. Unknowable, now, for ever and ever. So frightful . . . No, I don't know this man! Found out, Doctor Nelson! You've been found out! Murderer. Stranger . . .

And what if he's there, in Burlington, waiting in his cell for a letter from me? Oh, let me be sure. I'd be so happy I would die! My God, just to run to his side. Beg them to hitch up the horses, take me to the border. Get out of the carriage. Find him alive. Fling myself into his arms. Say to him, "Look, it's me, Elisabeth." And hear him answer, "It's me. It's George . . ." Together for life, the two of us. That cry in my throat . . .

Can it really be he's still alive? Or married? No, no! That's more than I could bear. I'd sooner see him dead, lying at my feet. Rather than let some other woman . . .

Nothing to do now but act so nicely that no one can doubt me. Pull the mask of innocence over my face. Against the bones. Accept it like some kind of vengeance, some kind of punishment. Play the cruel game, the tedious comedy, day after day. Until the perfect resemblance sticks to my skin. No joy on the long, bitter road. Only my haughty pride, here and there . . .

"Jérôme Rolland wants to marry the child. What a nice young man! He says he's sure he can make her happy, make her forget . . ."

[248]

Adélaïde, Angélique, Luce-Gertrude, my mother . . . They couldn't be more delighted . . .

Jérôme Rolland, his lordship meek and mild, lies propped up against a pile of nice cool pillows. The smell of candle wax floats through the bedroom. Darkened, shutters half closed. Florida, standing about like a vestry nun. Folds a white tablecloth. Madame Rolland's eyes, all puffed and swollen.

"Where were you, Elisabeth? I kept asking them to call you."

"It's that powder the doctor gave me. It made me sleep and sleep . . ."

A faint smile flickers over Jérôme Rolland's lips. Madame Rolland moves by his bed. And he whispers, still smiling. Tells her how happy he feels now, how much at peace.

"I've had the last rites, Elisabeth. The Good Lord has cleansed me of all my sins."

Madame Rolland looks down. Wipes a tear from her cheek . . .

Then all at once the nightmare breaks again. Dashes its winds against Elisabeth d'Aulnières. While on the surface everything seems so calm. The model wife, clasping her husband's hand in hers, poised on the sheet. And yet . . . Off in a parched field, under the rocks, they've dug up a woman, all black but still alive, buried there long ago, in some far-off, savage time. Strangely preserved. Then they've gone and let her loose on the town. And all the people have locked themselves in. So deathly afraid of this woman. And everyone thinks that she must have an utterly awesome lust for life, buried alive so long. A hunger growing and growing inside the earth for centuries on end! Unlike any other that's ever been known. And whenever she runs through the town, begging and weeping, they sound the alarm. Nothing before her but doors shut tight, and the empty, unpaved streets. Nothing to do now but let herself die. Alone and hungry . . .

Wicked Elisabeth! Damnable woman!

"You'll never know how frightened I was, Jérôme."

"Don't worry, Elisabeth. I'm here . . ."

Madame Rolland clutches her husband's pallid hand. A fragile thread that still holds her to life and might break any moment. Her eyes fill with tears.

And Léontine Mélançon whispers (unless, perhaps, it's Agathe or Florida):

"Just look how Madame loves Monsieur! You see, she's crying . . ."